Jo worked for many years as a writer and producer on soaps ranging from Radio 4's *The Archers* to TV's *Doctors* and *EastEnders*. She wrote several spin-off books and novelisations before inventing her own fictional world in six previous sagas: her World War Two 'Shop Girls' and 'Victory Girls' titles. She lives in the countryside near Bath – perfect for walking and plotting!

JOANNA TOYE

PENGUIN BOOKS

PENGUIN BOOKS

UK | USA | Canada | Ireland | Australia
India | New Zealand | South Africa

Penguin Books is part of the Penguin Random House group
of companies whose addresses can be found at global.
penguinrandomhouse.com

Penguin
Random House
UK

Published in Penguin Books 2024
001

Set in 10.4/15 pt Palatino LT Pro
Typeset by Jouve (UK), Milton Keynes
Printed and bound in Great Britain by Clays Ltd, Elcograf S.p.A.

The authorised representative in the EEA is
Penguin Random House Ireland, Morrison Chambers,
32 Nassau Street, Dublin D02 YH68

A CIP catalogue record for this book is available from the British Library

ISBN: 978–1–804–94605–3

www.greenpenguin.co.uk

To booksellers everywhere – thank you for keeping the printed word alive.

Chapter One

August 1939

'It's beautiful, Uncle Charlie – but you shouldn't have!'

'Ha! But I did!'

Carrie Anderson lifted the silver bangle from the velvet bed in its leather box. She'd been named for her uncle – Caroline to his Charles – and he'd always had a soft spot for her, and for her twin, Johnnie.

Johnnie was watching now, along with her parents, as her uncle clasped the bangle around her wrist and fastened the safety chain. Thrilled, Carrie turned her hand this way and that so the ivy leaves engraved on it caught the light.

'You spoil 'em, Charlie, you really do.' Carrie's father, Norman, shook his head at his brother.

'Ah, well, it's not like I've got kids of my own, is it?' Charlie grinned, leaning back in the best armchair and pulling out his cigarettes.

Carrie's mother, Mary, immediately edged the Bakelite ashtray closer to him on the little oak side table. Last time Charlie had called, he'd dropped some glowing ash on the rug. He'd been in the middle of one of his stories, as usual, waving his arms about and keeping everyone in stitches. No one else had noticed and Mary hadn't liked to interrupt and make a fuss, but she could still see the tiny scorch mark.

'Yes, very nice, Carrie, but if you've quite finished showing off, is it my turn now?' Johnnie raised an ironic eyebrow.

'Oh, go on, then, you martyr!' Carrie teased, giving her brother an affectionate swipe. 'I'm five minutes older than you, though, don't forget, so it's only right I go first!'

'Hmm, so you are, and you'll be sorry about that when we're eighty!'

Carrie pulled a face at him. Privately, though, she admitted it was good of Johnnie to have waited. Uncle Charlie's gifts were always something special.

Johnnie unwrapped his own birthday present – another leather box, which he opened, gasped at, then turned around so that everyone could see the contents: a tiepin and cufflinks.

'Oh, wow! Thanks, Uncle Charlie!'

They weren't just any old cufflinks and tiepin. The links were in the shape of a plane, and there was another perched on the bar of the pin.

'Well, planes are your pigeon, so to speak, aren't they?' grinned Charlie. Having lit up, he snapped his lighter shut. 'I dare say you can tell me exactly what model they are, and what's wrong with the design!'

'I wouldn't dream of it,' Johnnie shot back. 'They're great, honestly.'

'It's really very generous of you, Charlie,' said Mary as Charlie waved her comment away – this time, fortunately, with no ash hanging from the tip of his Craven 'A'.

Trust Charlie, with his big ideas, she thought, to smoke a

brand named after Lord Craven and his special tobacco mixture.

Mary had meant what she said, but Charlie's generosity only pointed up that she and Norman could never have afforded such lavish gifts. Their presents to Carrie had been a pair of stockings, some scent (only Yardley's Lily of the Valley, but it was her favourite) and a handkerchief sachet Mary had embroidered from a pattern in *Woman's Weekly*. Johnnie had had some new collars, a pot of shaving soap and a hand-knitted sleeveless jersey. Mind you, that was more than some in their street would have got for their eighteenth birthday.

The Andersons' newsagent and stationery shop provided a fair income, but there wasn't much left over for luxuries. And goodness knew, they worked for what they had, what with Norman up at five to do the papers with Carrie's help and someone having to be behind the counter till the sign was finally turned from 'Open' to 'Closed' at six o'clock. They worked hard six days a week and half a day on Sundays – especially on Sundays, so that other folk could enjoy their day of rest with the help of the *News of the World*, the *Express*, the *Mail* or the *Sunday Pictorial*. Then there was the ordering, the stocktaking and the books to balance. Almost every evening, once tea had been cleared away, Norman sat at the table in his shirtsleeves, braces hanging down, toiling away till ten o'clock or later, with Carrie helping him.

But if Mary ever tried to remonstrate, she knew what answer she'd get, and it would be a dusty one. Anderson's Newsagent & Stationer had been established in 1877 by Norman's grandfather, and passed down to Norman and

Charlie by their own dad. By then, the railway had come to Brockington, turning it from a large village into a small town. But a corner shop in a not especially prosperous area hadn't been exciting enough for Charlie, of course. He'd gone off to do his own thing, which had only increased Norman's determination to keep the business going.

Mary gave an inward sigh – inaudible to anyone but her – and got up.

'So, who's for tea and cake?' she said brightly.

'Uncle Charlie's a card, isn't he?'

Family celebrations over, brother and sister were walking to their local pub, the Rose and Crown. Johnnie was counting on at least a couple of birthday drinks from the friends he'd promised to meet.

Having crossed the road, he swapped sides with Carrie to make sure he was still walking on the outside of the pavement – he was always a gentleman with things like that. Whoever finally bagged him as a husband would be a lucky girl, Carrie thought loyally, though there was no one special in Johnnie's life at the moment, nor in hers for that matter.

Six feet tall, with dark brown hair and grey eyes like their father's, Johnnie wasn't short of admirers – all the girls in the typing pool at the engineering factory where he was training as a draughtsman, for a start. Carrie had noticed the giggles and the saucy looks they gave him, and the rather less friendly looks they gave her when she linked arms with him as they walked away from the factory gates on the days she came to meet him, jealous even after they'd realised she was his sister.

With their mother's blue-eyed colouring, lighter hair and peachy complexion, Carrie had her own admirers – the dapper reps who called at the shop with their cases of samples, cheeky van drivers trying it on, and some of the customers too. But she'd given Cyril, who worked at the barber's on Harold Road, the gentle heave-ho at Easter and she wasn't in any hurry to replace him.

She replied to Johnnie's question with a shrug.

'I never know whether to believe his stories. That one about the motorist, the monkey and the bunch of grapes!'

Uncle Charlie had left the business five years ago to go into partnership with 'a pal'. He had lots of pals, did Uncle Charlie. This one ran a garage in Catford – used car sales and repairs, as well as petrol. They'd had a boom time. Everyone seemed to want a motor, or, if they couldn't afford one, there was what Charlie called a 'private hire business' on the side. People could hire a car for the day and take a run out to the countryside, stopping for lunch or a drink at one of the new mock-Tudor pub-restaurants – they called themselves 'roadhouses' – that had sprung up along the ribbon routes out of the capital.

'Quids in!' Uncle Charlie had crowed.

No wonder he could afford such expensive presents.

But Johnnie wasn't listening. His eye had been caught by a poster showing a skein of planes, one after the other, coming in to land like swans on the flight deck of an aircraft carrier.

'WHY NOT JOIN THE NEW FLEET AIR ARM?' shouted the poster. 'GOOD PROSPECTS OF EARLY ADVANCEMENT.'

Carrie stopped so Johnnie could read the small print. The

advertisement was calling for people with all sorts of skills, from jig and tool fitters to blacksmiths. At eighteen – just – Johnnie was the right age, but Carrie realised with relief that he didn't fit the bill. He wasn't that interested in building or maintaining planes – he wanted to be a pilot. Desperately.

Carrie had lost count of the Sunday afternoons she'd spent cycling over to Croydon Aerodrome to hang about while her brother drooled over an Armstrong Whitworth Atalanta or logged the arrival of a huge Handley Page biplane. On one occasion, he'd ambushed a pilot who'd just flown in from Africa as he strolled through the terminal. Johnnie had quizzed him relentlessly about wind speeds and turbulence until Carrie had felt quite sorry for the chap. He must have been dying simply for a wash, a shave and a drink! But the pilot hadn't seemed to mind – two enthusiasts together – and his autograph was Johnnie's most treasured possession. Well, until today's tiepin and cufflinks, perhaps.

But learning to fly was only for the very wealthy – public schoolboys in the OTC, or people whose fathers had their own private planes. So when he'd finished school, Johnnie had done the next best thing: he'd started as an office boy at a nearby aircraft factory and by hard work and aptitude, and a bit of night school, had managed to get himself taken on as a trainee draughtsman. And as soon as he could, he'd joined the new Air Defence Cadet Corps, which had given him the chance to actually go up in a plane.

Carrie knew that if the war that had been narrowly averted last year came to anything, and things were not looking that hopeful, Johnnie would be among the first to

6

sign up to fly. With horrible irony, war would give him the chance that life so far had denied him.

She didn't even want to think about it. She tugged on his arm.

'Come on, there's a pint on the bar with your name on it, remember?'

Back at home, Charlie was getting ready to leave, shrugging on his jacket with its, to Mary's eyes, rather loud check – but that was Charlie all over. She pressed a large piece of cake on him. As a bachelor, doing for himself in digs, he missed out on home cooking.

'You're a good 'un, Mary,' he said, kissing her as he placed the cake in its greaseproof paper on the passenger seat of the Rover. 'Our Norm's a lucky man.'

'Don't I know it!' Norman beamed and slapped his brother on the back. 'Drive safely,' he warned. 'No more than thirty miles an hour now, remember.'

'Tch! It's a sin with this little beauty, but there you are. That won't be the only restriction we're under soon.'

Norman frowned and gave a warning tip of his head towards Mary, but it was too late.

'I think I'll go in,' she said abruptly, crossing her cardigan over her chest. 'It's getting chilly.'

'Sorry, sorry.' Charlie looked contritely after her. 'I know she doesn't like to think of another war, but it's coming. So much for poor old Chamberlain's "peace for our time" and "peace with honour", eh?'

Norman nodded as Charlie went on.

'Hitler's already broken the agreement, marching into

Czechoslovakia – he's never going to let things rest till all of Europe's under the jackboot.'

Norman knew his brother was right. While the others were clearing up tea, they'd gone out the back for a look at the Anderson shelter that Norman and Johnnie had built the year before. They'd lifted the yard bricks to half submerge it, Carrie helping them to pile the earth they'd dug out back over the roof. With her mum, she'd sown carrots, cabbages and beetroot, which her dad tended to in his limited free time. The shelters in backyards and gardens weren't the only things that were different. All over London, workmen had dug trenches in any bit of open ground. They'd carted off the sandy soil up Hampstead way for sandbags, and the parks were decorated – if you could call it that – with barrage balloons like tethered silver whales. However much the government might still be hoping for peace, all the preparations were for war.

The Rose and Crown was the usual fug of beer, smoke and bodies, despite the doors and windows being open to the summer evening.

'Hiding in the garden,' Johnnie concluded, having scanned the bar for his friends. 'Trying to duck their responsibilities! I'll get us a drink anyway and we'll go and dig them out. Shandy?'

Carrie nodded a thank you. She wasn't really a pub person: when she met her friends, it was usually at The Ginger Cat café or the cinema, or to go to a dance at the Mecca Ballroom. Her work at the family shop didn't pay a vast amount, though she didn't mind that. What she minded more was having to give up her hopes of a more exciting career.

All her life, she'd been a reader, haunting the local library and picking up tattered copies of anything and everything at jumble sales. While Johnnie's bicycle basket on planespotting trips contained a notebook and binoculars, hers always carried a novel. She'd wanted to be a librarian herself, but there wasn't the money to stay on at school to take her School Certificate. Not to be deterred, in what she hoped would be a cunning move, Carrie had taken a job at Boots the Chemists, hoping to progress from selling shampoo and suppositories to a position in their own lending library.

But before that could happen, her mother had fallen badly on an icy pavement and broken her hip. Carrie had had to leave her job, and with it her ambitions. Mary couldn't stand for long now, and Norman couldn't run the shop on his own. So for the last two years Carrie had been working alongside him.

' "Many a flower is born to blush unseen and waste its sweetness on the desert air," ' one of the more persistent reps had flannelled, trying to wheedle her into a night at the flicks. Carrie had refused – he looked the 'handsy' type – but a bit of her couldn't help agreeing, much as she loved her mum and dad and knew they couldn't really afford to employ anyone else.

Her dad knew how she felt. He'd cleared a space for her in the shop to start selling a few books alongside the Basildon Bond and bottles of ink.

'There you go, love,' he'd said. 'You choose a few books, I'll get 'em on sale or return, and you can have a little book corner here. We'll see how we fare.'

Carrie had been thrilled. She'd chosen a range of titles, including a lot of the classics she loved, but there weren't many takers. Everyone in their neighbourhood, men and women, worked hard. They hadn't the time or the energy – or, often, the money – for indulging in books. Those who did buy preferred Ethel M. Dell to Dickens. Not that there was anything wrong with that – Dickens did go on, and Carrie loved a nice romance as much as anyone. But she was disappointed she hadn't been able to persuade local readers to stretch themselves a bit. Books had meant so much to her. Through them she'd travelled back and forth in time, visited places she knew she'd never see for herself and experienced things she hadn't yet experienced. Love, for one . . .

Johnnie was paying for their drinks, and Carrie dragged her thoughts back to the bar. The radio that always burbled in the background blurted out the pips for the news and she sensed Johnnie straining to listen.

'Turn it up, Fred, will you?' he asked.

The barman obliged and Carrie wished he hadn't. Hitler, the BBC reported, had ordered mobilisation against Poland. The bar fell silent.

'That's it, then,' someone said. 'We've guaranteed Poland's independence, haven't we? This means war.'

Carrie looked at her glass. Condensation was running down the side, like tears.

She turned to Johnnie, her twin, her blood brother, the person she felt closest to in the world.

'You're going to volunteer, aren't you?' she asked. 'Before they even call you up. For the RAF.'

Johnnie opened his mouth, but before he could reply, Carrie went on.

'Well, you're not going on your own! I'll volunteer too. For the WAAF!'

Chapter Two

'Now, Mary, don't fret. It'll be over by Christmas!'

'Oh, Norm, honestly! You really believe that?'

'A short, sharp kick up the jacksie, that's what that nut-case Hitler needs. We've got France on our side, and Canada and Australia, of course. Plus all the colonial troops, maybe even America, with luck—'

'Over by Christmas!' Mary stabbed viciously at the carrots jostling about in the pan. 'That's what they said last time, don't forget! And I wouldn't hold your breath about America – they've got more sense. They didn't hurry to pitch in in the last war, if I recall.'

Outside, the sun was shining, next door's pigeons were burbling in their coop, and in the yard, next door's tabby cat, Topsy, was stretched out on the bricks, half in sun, half in shade. From the back kitchens of every house along Harold Road, which led off down one side of the Andersons' shop, and along Ethel Street on the other, came the smell of Sunday dinners cooking. It was the one time when every household tried to stretch to a bit of meat, even if it was only a small bacon joint or a stew of scrag-end.

Usually, Sunday dinnertime was Mary's favourite time of the week, when Norman actually had a few hours off. But this was not a normal Sunday. At eleven that morning, the third of September, Mr Chamberlain had been on the wireless. Sounding as though uttering the words was causing him physical pain, and no wonder after all his attempts at peace, the Prime Minister had told the nation that 'this country is at war with Germany'.

Minutes later, the air raid sirens had sounded. Johnnie was out, but the rest of the Anderson family were too shocked, too panicked, too paralysed to run out to the shelter that ironically bore their name. They'd hunkered under the stairs, barricaded by cushions and covering their ears. It was a false alarm, but no one could doubt that this war was a reality. The terror was certainly real.

Now, two hours later, Norman took the knife from his wife's hand and gathered her into his arms. Mary had seen her fiancé and her adored brother go off to the Great War. Her fiancé had never come back and her brother had come back gassed and broken: Mary had nursed him until he died two years later. Those early losses had stayed with her, wounds that never healed, making her anxious, tentative, always expecting the worst.

When they'd first met in the queue for the fried-fish shop, Norman had seen the vulnerability in her china-blue eyes, and his protective instincts had been aroused. It was only because he wouldn't take no for an answer that she'd finally taken another chance at happiness with him.

'Try to look on the bright side, love,' he said now. 'They won't be calling me up at the grand old age of forty-two.'

It was cold comfort, and he knew it. Mary had been one of the thousands of women who'd written to Mr Chamberlain in 1938, thanking him for averting another war when he'd come back from Munich with his supposed peace deal. But Hitler had simply ignored it. There'd been talk in the papers for months about the Air Cadets being drafted in to work at RAF stations in the event of war. When the bombing campaign that everyone was expecting began, Johnnie would be right in the line of fire. And that was if he wasn't in the air himself.

In the yard, Johnnie was buffing up his one good pair of shoes, Carrie watching him. He polished them every Sunday for the working week, but today was different.

As an Air Cadet, he knew he'd be called on to fill sandbags, carry messages and maybe even get to move aircraft on the ground. But that wasn't enough. He was polishing his shoes for the RAF recruiting office.

'When are you going to break it to Mum and Dad?' Carrie asked.

Johnnie concentrated on working the polishing rag round the eyelets of the laces.

'Well, today, of course. I hardly want the first they know of it to be when I come back kitted out in air force blue.'

He held his shoe at arm's length for inspection.

'Anyway, it's not me you need to worry about,' he went on. 'It's hardly going to come as a surprise. How and when are *you* going to tell them? I'm still recovering myself!'

'Why?' demanded Carrie. 'Why shouldn't I join the WAAF? Just because I haven't memorised every – what-do-you-call-it? – tail-fin identifier of every plane flying in and out of Croydon for the last ten years.'

Johnnie lined up his shoes – they wouldn't have much to

teach him about military discipline! – and answered her gently.

'Carrie . . . Because you don't have to. They won't call up women for ages, if at all.'

'That's not the point – I can volunteer, can't I? Can't you see? I thought you'd understand!'

'I can understand you see it as a chance to get away from' – he waved his hand in the direction of the back of the house – 'all this. Selling single Woodbines and quarters of pear drops.' He touched her elbow. 'I know it's not the future you saw for yourself, and I'm sorry, I really am.'

Carrie sighed. He was right, in a way, but it wasn't just about getting away from something, it was about staying close to something . . . close to him.

'The thing is, Johnnie, I want to . . . I want to know what you're getting into. I want to know your world. Really know it. We've grown up together, we've always done stuff together. I can't let this be the thing that drives us apart.'

She could feel her voice rising as she tried to explain, but still felt it had come out all wrong, making her sound jealous and petulant. It wasn't about the fact that boys had more opportunities than girls, much as that rankled. It was deeper than that. They were twins. If Johnnie went, part of her would go too.

They'd shared so much. The sugar-paper pages of the family photograph album showed them toddling along, side by side, holding hands, or their heads bent over a bucket of tadpoles they'd fished from the local pond. Carrie remembered the excitement of Christmas morning, creeping downstairs together in the dark to try to work out the contents of the presents under the tree. More recently, there'd been the late-night chats as they'd become aware of the like-lihood of war.

Johnnie looked at her with the tenderness he'd always felt for his sister. She might be five minutes older, she might say that mattered and try to pull rank from time to time, but he'd always looked out for her, punching the bully in their class who'd chucked her copy of *Heidi* in the canal, waiting for her outside the cinema to walk her home after a night out with her girlfriends.

'I'm not going to find it that easy leaving you, either,' he admitted truthfully, meeting her eyes, before adding: 'Who's going to darn my socks?'

'Oh you!'

But their dad was calling from the doorway.

'Oy! Table needs laying, please, Johnnie, and your mum needs you to do the gravy, Carrie.'

'Coming!'

Johnnie bent to gather up his things. Carrie retrieved the lid of the Cherry Blossom boot polish and handed it to him.

'Don't you dare tell them over lunch, that's all,' she warned him. 'It's blackberry and apple crumble for afters and that's my favourite!'

But it didn't take as long as pudding. Norman had carved the beef brisket and handed it round and they were helping themselves to veg when Mary came to the table, carrying the gravy boat. Putting it down carefully, she sat down, took her seersucker napkin from its ring and asked Johnnie directly.

'Well? When are you going?'

'Sorry?'

'Is the RAF recruiting place open today? Or have you got to wait till tomorrow?'

'Oh, Mum.' Johnnie covered his mother's hand with his own. 'I was going to tell you.'

'No need now, is there?'

Carrie said nothing. She was watching her mother. A vein was standing out on Mary's right temple and there was a tremor in her throat. Carrie could see what Mary's apparent self-control was costing – and how she'd under-estimated her.

It was easy to do that: quiet and unassuming, Mary naturally kept herself in the background, but it didn't mean she didn't know what was going on. As well as a quiet intelligence, she had a kind of sixth sense about her children.

Carrie realised that her father was passing her the gravy. She took the jug and poured, seeing all her hopes of getting away smothered like the food on her plate.

How could she go? How had she ever thought she could, when Mary would already be sick with worry about Johnnie, expecting a repeat of the losses she'd suffered in the Great War? How could Carrie expect her mother to bear the anxiety of two children away at war?

'Hey, Carrie! Leave a bit for the rest of us, can you?' Johnnie was tapping her gently on the arm and Carrie realised her plate was swimming in gravy.

'Sorry,' she said distractedly, passing him the gravy boat.

Johnnie took it with a regretful twist to his mouth. Carrie knew that he'd appreciated from the start what she'd taken till now to realise. In her desire to stay close to him, she hadn't really thought about what her going away would do to their mother.

But the fact remained. If she didn't join up, was she really going to sit out a war in Europe, a war that might come to their very doorstep, in a backstreet newsagent's shop?

They got through the meal somehow, though Carrie's favourite crumble was like cinders in her mouth. Then they had to get through the afternoon. Carrie helped her mother change all the curtains for the funereal ones they'd made out of blackout material at the start of the summer when it was only two shillings and sixpence a yard.

'Three and eleven now, Mrs Medlicott told me,' said Mary, shocked. 'If that's how prices are going to go up, Lord help us!'

Johnnie and Norman took down the grilles that went over the windows whenever the shop was shut and covered the panes in the criss-cross tape bought in readiness. Then they got out the leaflets the government had been sending about air raids and gas attacks and had another, closer, read of them.

'Alf Warburton's asked me if I'd sign on as an air raid warden,' Norman confided. 'His front room's going to be the local warden's post. But not a word to your mother. I haven't broken it to her yet, and she's had enough to take in for one day.'

Johnnie nodded. He was waiting for his chance to get Carrie on her own, to tell her properly how sorry he was that her dreams had taken another denting. But after tea, a couple of his friends called for him, the same cheerful, fun-loving friends he and Carrie had met in the pub just a couple of weeks ago, playing darts and slapping each other on the back, spilling their pints, when someone got a double top. They were serious now, all set to join up too, and carried Johnnie off to the pub with them to talk it through.

Carrie didn't know what to do with herself.

Her friends would be getting together at someone's house, but she didn't feel like seeing anybody. So she put on her cardigan over her old stripy sundress, stuck her feet in some canvas shoes and went for a walk.

The streets around the shop were typical of this part of Brockington – late Victorian terraces. There were gaggles of people on street corners, heads together, chewing over the news, but apart from that, everything looked eerily normal. There were children playing hopscotch on the pavement, others examining a wheel that had come off a makeshift go-kart. No one was shoring up their front door with sandbags or going about in a tin hat. In the golden sunshine of a September evening it all seemed unreal.

Carrie drifted on. Brockington was nowhere special – it hadn't produced a distinguished statesman, author or even a footballer. It wasn't known for cakes like Banbury, pies like Melton Mowbray or cheese like Cheddar. It had all the usual things – shops, banks, a Post Office, a railway station and, on the outskirts, a cottage hospital and a few small factories. Most of its inhabitants worked in its shops or offices or commuted up to London. In other words, it was a perfectly ordinary town, like hundreds of others up and down the country. But it was the only place Carrie had ever known. It was home, and for that reason she loved it.

Now she wanted to see all the familiar things she loved – the shops on the High Street, the comforting bulk of the parish church, the smart art deco façade of the Rialto Cinema. But when she reached the bigger roads leading to the centre, things started to change.

'Excuse me, miss.'

A policeman riding by on a bicycle had pulled up beside her.

'Yes?'

'War regulations say you must carry your gas mask at all times. You do have a gas mask?'

Carrie nodded dumbly.

They'd been fitted for the horrible things ages ago and had had to practise putting them on at speed. Hers was in its box under her bed. She hated even looking at it.

'You must have heard the sirens this morning?'

Carrie nodded again. 'Yes, yes, I did.'

He looked at her kindly.

'I'll let you off this time, but in future . . . I know it's hard to take in, love, but next time it might not be just a warning.'

'No, Officer. Thank you. I'll go back and get it.'

'Good girl. Mind how you go.'

He wobbled off again. Carrie leaned against the sill of a shop window and pressed her hand to her mouth. Her legs felt weak. Like someone in a book, she thought, a Victorian heroine who's had a shock. But she had had a shock. It was real. They were at war.

She about-turned, fetched her mask from home and set off again. When she finally got to the town centre, things were very different. Like her dad, the shopkeepers had come to work, taking down their shutters and applying Splinter-net tape to their windows. Carrie walked on, past the sandbagged town hall with its clock tower, and past the church, where, a further wireless announcement had told them, the bells would only ring to warn of an invasion.

An invasion . . . Carrie tried to imagine the regimented German troops she'd seen on newsreels strutting down their High Street, going house to house, perhaps, doing . . . what? Looting, taking people away? Worse? Would the shop be allowed to stay open? What would be left to sell? What if a German soldier came in? Would she have to serve them? Would she be brave enough to refuse?

The more the reality started to sink in, the more Carrie was convinced she couldn't just do nothing. She couldn't leave her mother, that much was certain. But she had to find something worthwhile to do that was close to home.

Carrie was on the railway bridge when Johnnie found her. He'd left his friends early and returned home, only to be told his sister had gone out. He'd searched for her in their old haunts: the old oak in the park, the tumbledown folly in the woods backing on to the big houses on Longfellow Road, and, finally, the railway.

It was here, before his obsession with planes, that Carrie had accompanied him just as loyally on his trainspotting trips. He'd expected her to be fed up, but when he tapped her on the shoulder, Carrie turned to him, eyes shining.

'I've got it!'

'Good!' he said, surprised. 'Er, what?'

Her words came out in a torrent.

'You know that saying "If the mountain won't come to Muhammad, Muhammad must go to the mountain"? Well, it's the other way round! The mountain has come to me! Or rather . . .'

She gestured to the platforms below. The evacuation of London's children, along with their mothers or chaperones, had started as soon as Hitler had invaded Poland the previous Friday. Now the trains were full of troops, a seething mass of blue and khaki, heaving kitbags on and off – army, navy and air force regulars and volunteer reserves.

'Well, Brockington Junction's the connection, isn't it,' reasoned Johnnie. 'For the army base at Caterham. And the air force bods must be on their way to Biggin Hill and Kenley by lorry.'

'Exactly,' said Carrie. 'And look at them, poor things!'

A few were peering hopelessly through the windows of the station's refreshment room, with its advertisements for PG Tips and Fuller's walnut cake. It was closed on Sundays.

'I see what you mean,' mused Johnnie. 'But there'll be a mobile canteen once the WVS get organised. Are you thinking of helping out? That'd be a great thing to do.'

'I'm not talking about feeding their stomachs,' cried Carrie. 'I'm talking about feeding their minds. Look!'

She pointed to where the station's former newsstand and bookstall sat shuttered and empty.

'They've been looking for someone to take it over since old Mr Staples died. But no one'd risk it with everything being so uncertain, or so Dad told me. Well, now's our chance!'

'Is it?'

'Yes! Don't you see? Anderson's can take over the bookstall – and I can run it! I may not be going to the front line, but those troops are. And the least they deserve is something to read!'

Johnnie looked at her admiringly.

'You could be on to something there,' he said.

'Of course I am.' Carrie's conviction blazed from her. 'That'll be my contribution to the war effort. I don't know why I didn't think of it before!'

Chapter Three

It wasn't quite that simple, of course. There was the little matter of money. Carrie knew there was no question of her dad being able to pay for the lease on the station bookstall or to stock it – he was worried enough about keeping their own shop going during a war.

In any case, something in Carrie – some streak of independence, of defiance, of needing to prove herself, even – made her shy away from asking her mum and dad, even if it had been an option. She wanted to present them with her plan fully formed – battle-ready, if you like.

Just thinking about it made her smile. In her mind's eye, she could see the looks on their faces change from astonishment to admiration – and pride. That was part of it. She wanted them to be as proud of her and what she was doing in this war as they would be, in a different way, of Johnnie. Oh, she loved her twin to distraction. But though neither would have admitted it – or maybe they didn't even realise it – they would always be affectionate rivals.

However, as Carrie had precisely two pounds, two and six in her Post Office book, this determined independence was something of a headache. Johnnie had offered her his savings (an impressive five pounds and threepence), but Carrie had declined. This was going to need serious investment: she needed to think big. And who did she know who thought big . . . ?

'This is a pleasant surprise, I must say!' Uncle Charlie ushered her into his office, a small back room behind the car showroom. Des, his business partner, was out on the fore-court, extolling the virtues of a Riley to a prospective customer.

Heaving a pile of papers onto the floor, Charlie dusted the seat of the visitor's chair with his handkerchief and waved her to it.

'We're most honoured. I'll break out the custard creams!'

'I should hope so!' Carrie smiled to hide her nervousness.

Uncle Charlie disappeared and began clattering about in the small kitchenette. While he was away, Carrie took off the plum-coloured jacket she'd worn for the occasion – her only jacket – and laid out her calculations on his desk. She could be pretty accurate about her outgoings, based on the whole-sale costs she knew from the shop and her own small wage, though she'd had to make assumptions about the cost of the lease and insurance. When it came to income, though, she could only cross her fingers and pray.

'Righty-ho!' Uncle Charlie bustled back in, carrying a tin tray holding a teapot, milk jug, sugar bowl, two cups and, as promised, a plate of biscuits. He put the tray down on the desk and squinted at the paperwork. 'Will you be mother? Hang on, what's all this?'

'Just something I'd like you to look at.' Carrie tried to keep the tremor out of her voice.

Now the moment had come, she was terrified that Uncle Charlie would take one look at her paperwork and laugh.

He'd always had a soft spot for her as his niece, but she was about to ask him to commit serious money, and to believe in her as a businesswoman. And that was a quite different matter.

'A station bookstall, eh?' Uncle Charlie said, sitting down and adjusting his tie, a jazzy number in emerald and peacock squares. 'All right. I'll pour the tea while you tell me about it.'

So Carrie did. She explained how since that first Sunday she'd spent all her free time at the station, watching the trains, counting the number of carriages, working out the number of passengers. She'd scrutinised everyone who was waiting. The locals knew to bring a book or magazine, but anyone passing through who wasn't a regular, and there were plenty of those – evacuee teachers and chaperones, European refugee families and troops – would turn away from the closed bookstall in frustration.

'It's the troops especially,' Carrie ended up. 'The thought of them going away, even in this country, to some cold billet in the middle of nowhere, with nothing to read . . . They're having to learn how to clean a gun and prime a bomb, they're learning how to kill, and have nothing to take their minds off it? It's – it's not human!'

Uncle Charlie listened with interest. He didn't call himself much of a reader – though he liked a decent western or spy story – but he'd read a recent interview with the bloke who published the newish Penguin books. His name was Allen Lane, and he seemed to have his finger right on the pulse. At just sixpence, his Penguins were the same price as a packet of cigarettes – and what's more, they were exactly the right size to fit in a battledress pocket. Alongside a few examples of the regular bookstall fodder – cheap hardback editions of the classics, romances, thrillers and the like – Carrie's stock would be almost entirely Penguins.

Charlie made a second pot of tea and quizzed her remorselessly about the figures. He knew the newspaper trade, after all. He knew that the family shop was in no position to help Carrie out. He also knew that the start of a war that might last nobody knew how long, was a risky time to begin any new venture, no matter how many troop trains might pass through Brockington Junction.

But he could see the desperate longing in Carrie and he understood that a young woman of eighteen – a girl in most people's eyes – with no proven business background of her own would have no chance of raising the start-up money she needed from a bank.

'I thought it was too good to be true,' he said when he finally shuffled the papers back together.

Carrie's heart stopped, and at the same time her stomach sank. It wasn't a pleasant feeling. He'd seen through the optimism of her profit projections. Maybe she should have scaled them back a bit. He'd found some flaw in her costings – what could she have missed out?

'I—' she began, but Uncle Charlie hadn't finished.

'You turning up here out of the blue, just out of family feeling, to see your devoted uncle, I mean!' he chuckled. 'I've been underestimating you, my girl! You've got a good business head there, inherited from me, no doubt! No offence to your dad, he does a sterling job in that shop, but you – you've got . . . you've got vision!'

'I have?'

'This is a copper-bottomed business opportunity, I reckon, and if you're here for what I think you are, which is to ask me to invest, or for a loan, then I won't keep you hanging about. The answer's yes!'

'No!' Carrie couldn't stop herself from jumping up in delight. 'Really? You mean it?'

'Come here!' Uncle Charlie came round the desk and gave her a hug. 'I'll need to look into my own finances, of course,' he said as he released her. 'And we'll have to have things done properly, to keep it on the straight and narrow. I'll talk to Des – I may need to take a bit out of the business . . . But yes, I'll happily be your fairy godfather!'

'Oh, thank you, thank you, thank you!' Then Carrie looked serious. 'There's just one thing, Uncle Charlie—'

'Just the one?'

'We need to be careful how we break this to Mum and Dad. That I've asked you, not them, to help me out.'

'They'll understand, surely?' Uncle Charlie's voice rose in disbelief. 'They're not in a position to put up the kind of money you need.'

'No, I know, but . . .' Carrie had been thinking about it on the bus to Catford. As with her realisation about her mother, she'd come to see that her initial vision of her parents' delighted surprise might be wrong; instead they might be upset that she'd fixed up everything behind their backs. 'But I wouldn't want their feelings hurt.'

'Do you know what,' Uncle Charlie smiled, 'that's what's going to make this idea of yours fly. It's not just about having your head screwed on right. You care about people. And in business, that's the most important quality you can have.'

In the event, Mary and Norman couldn't have been kinder. If there was a momentary hurt, it was only because they wished they could have funded Carrie's dream, not that they were jealous because she'd managed to do it some other way.

'I'm proud of you!' Norman declared when she told them, while her mother hugged her hard, with tears in her eyes. Yes, Carrie was doing something she'd always wanted to do, but Mary knew it was also her daughter's way of reassuring her there was no need now for her to join up, at least not in the immediate future.

After that, it all happened very quickly. Uncle Charlie came up with the money and came with her to negotiate the lease. Norman helped her register with the authorities, get insurance and establish wholesaler accounts in her own name.

Once Carrie had the keys, there was plenty to do when she wasn't in the family shop. She couldn't just abandon her dad, not when he was being so good, so most of the work had to be done in the evenings or on a Sunday.

Brockington Junction's bookstall stood on the up platform to London. It wasn't much more than a big wooden cabin with a roller shutter over the front counter and a little door on the side – and was adorned with rusting advertisements for the *Express* and the *Mirror*, with grilles below the counter to display the day's headlines on posters. Old Mr Staples had left the inside swept and tidy, but the minute cubbyhole office was dark and musty. Outside, the roller shutter needed the strength of Samson to lift it, and the weatherboarding needed a repaint. Mr Staples had had it a serviceable mud brown. Carrie chose a fresh forest green and, with Johnnie's help, stripped down and painted the stall herself. They whitewashed the office and oiled the roller shutter. Finally, in clean white lettering on green, a signwriter friend of Norman's painted: 'C. *Anderson: Books, Newspapers, Magazines'*. Her dad had insisted on the 'C' before the family name – 'This is all your doing, love!' – and Carrie had insisted that 'Books' came first in the line.

A few days before she officially opened, she was there to see the sign hoisted up above the counter. She was proudly thinking that this must be how shipbuilders on the Tyne felt when the Queen smashed the bottle of champagne and the great ship glided down the slipway, when someone spoke beside her.

'I thought a cup of tea might not go amiss.'

Carrie turned to find a woman of about fifty holding a cup and saucer. She had a round, pink-cheeked face and greying brown hair in an untidy cottage-loaf bun on top of her head. She was short and plump and sported a navy-blue dress with a white collar and a little fob watch pinned to the left breast, like a nurse. But Carrie knew she wasn't a nurse – she was the woman who ran the tearoom.

They'd hardly seen each other before. Carrie arrived in the evenings as the older woman was hurrying home, and on Sundays the tearoom was closed. If Carrie was there on a weekday, she'd had no call to use the tearoom. She brought a flask and sandwiches with her – there was nothing in her budget for refreshments.

'How funny!' she smiled now. 'I was just thinking about champagne!'

'Sorry, I'm sure!' said the other woman. 'Anyway, it's out of hours, duck. This is the best I can do.'

She placed the teacup on the bookstall's bare counter.

'Oh no, don't get me wrong,' said Carrie quickly. Ouch! She didn't want to get off on the wrong foot. 'I'd much rather have tea. Thank you – it's very kind.'

The older woman held out her hand and smiled. An olive branch. Thank goodness!

'I know what you meant, and I bet you do feel like celebrating. I can see how hard you've worked! Anyhow, I came to introduce myself. Bette Saunders.'

'You run the refreshment room,' Carrie smiled back, shaking her hand. 'I'm Caroline Anderson – Carrie.'

'Well, Carrie, welcome!' Bette surveyed the stall. 'Taken this on all by yourself, I hear from Mr Bayliss.'

Mr Bayliss was the stationmaster. He had a fob watch, too, a bigger one to signify his importance, which he wore on a chain across his waistcoat. With his bulbous nose and bowler hat, he was a regular presence on the platforms, chivvying the two porters with barked commands, all of which, he claimed, were urgent, although in Carrie's opinion none of them really were. The passengers didn't escape his gimlet gaze either, as he reprimanded anyone who dared drop a cigarette paper and gave a clip round the ear to any child banging the side of the chocolate machine to try their luck or caught probing the slot for forgotten change. The East End evacuees, now safe in the countryside, had been devils for that.

Carrie nodded circumspectly. Mr Bayliss's smile had faded when he'd realised it was Carrie, and not Uncle Charlie, who'd be running the stall day to day. He was clearly one of those who believed 'a woman's place is in the home'. Surely Bette, a working woman herself, couldn't agree?

'Well,' Bette declared. 'Good for you!'

Carrie breathed a sigh of relief. Bette was on her side. And, positions established, Bette was off and running.

'I'll tell you one thing and it isn't two, it'll be a relief to have another woman round here. Till now there's only been me and my junior.' Bette rolled her eyes. 'I had a really good girl till this bloomin' war started and she swanned off to join the ATS. I dunno how this Ruby'll make out. Spends most of the day patting her hair and pouting at her reflection in the tea urn, not that she's got the looks for it. But in times like these, what can you do . . . ?'

Clearly, once started, Bette didn't stop to draw breath. The flow might have carried on, an ever-rolling stream, but one of the two porters Carrie had seen around the station, the tall, lanky one, had joined them and was leaning on his broom.

'Now, now, Mum,' he reprimanded. 'Are you holding up the work?'

It was October now and the leaves were crisping and falling from the big horse chestnuts that overhung the furthest end of the up platform. He'd been sweeping them and collecting the conkers that might turn someone's ankle in the blackout – or at least the conkers the evacuee children hadn't snaffled.

Bette's face lit up.

'This is my boy,' she explained. 'Eric – meet Carrie!'

Eric executed a sweeping bow, so low that his porter's cap fell off and landed at Carrie's feet. She returned it with a smile. He beamed back, showing a mouthful of slightly goofy teeth. With his hat off, his mousy brown hair stood up in a comical tuft at the back of his head.

'Drat! Never happens to Fred Astaire, does it?' he tutted.

Carrie refrained from pointing out that the dapper dancer in the films always thought to take his hat off before he bowed.

'Ah, but can he play the spoons?' Bette turned proudly to Carrie. 'A dab hand with them, my Eric is. You can hear him for miles!'

'Honestly, Mum, they look so different!' Carrie told Mary when she got home.

It was half past six and they were in their little back kitchen, Mary scrubbing potatoes for tea. Johnnie was in the outhouse where he pursued his other hobby, woodwork – he'd made all the kitchen shelves, Carrie's bookends in the shape of elephants, and Norman's fretwork pipe rack. What he was working on now, though, was a closely guarded secret.

Their father was still in the shop, where he was training up the young assistant he'd taken on for a fraction of what he'd paid Carrie. This was because Terry was twelve. He lived down the street and had flatly refused to be evacuated with his younger brother and sister. But with all the schools closed, he had time on his hands, a mother who wanted him out of the way, and the sort of entrepreneurial spirit even Charlie would have admired. He'd come in asking about a paper round and had been rewarded with a proper part-time job for pocket money and a gobstopper a day. Compared to his peers, who, he chortled, were having lessons wherever they'd been sent, young Terry was in clover.

Johnnie came in, looking pleased with himself, as well he might. The RAF had accepted him like a shot, he'd told them, before apologising for the unfortunate turn of phrase. And just yesterday he'd had the official confirmation, along with his travel warrant to his initial training school. After ostentatiously checking the blackout and confirming that all the doors and windows were closed, he'd even revealed where it was – though he'd only say it was 'somewhere in Lancashire'.

'Walls have ears,' he said solemnly.

He'd be leaving next day, and the meal Mary was preparing was something of a last supper. She was pushing the boat out with lamb chops, a change from the sausages or meat pudding they'd usually have midweek. Johnnie had been to the off-licence and brought back beer for himself and his father. He mixed up a shandy for Carrie, while Mary permitted herself a glass of the Christmas sherry.

'A toast, I think!' Norman declared when the shop was finally shut and they were all standing around waiting for the potatoes to cook. 'This is a big moment for this family. A new start for us all. Johnnie's off tomorrow – and next week, Carrie's starting her own little business. All I can say is, we're so proud of you both!'

'We are!' Mary echoed bravely. 'We really are!'

Everyone chinked glasses and Carrie looked at her twin. He nodded. They'd talked about this moment.

'Well, we just want to say a big thank you,' she said, 'for being the kind of parents you are and for understanding and letting us do what we feel we want or have to do in this war. Thank you.'

Mary looked a bit teary but proud, too, of her children. Norman cleared his throat as Johnnie said:

'Agreed! But before we eat, I've got something to show you.'

He put down his glass and disappeared. They heard the back door open.

'Where's he off to?' fretted Mary. 'He hasn't closed the door. We'll have that Alf Warburton round here with his ARP armband and his attitude, saying we're showing a light!'

Norman coughed, recalling the awkward moment when he'd had to tell his wife that Alf had signed him up for air raid patrol duties. Mary hadn't been thrilled – 'Putting yourself in Lord knows what unnecessary danger!' – but Norman had astutely pointed out that if he didn't volunteer, Alf would very likely lean on Carrie to do it, and Mary didn't want that, did she?

'Thanks very much!' Mary had retorted. 'A right Hobson's choice you're giving me!'

'Sorry, love,' Norman had replied. 'But there is a war on. There's going to be difficult choices all round.'

So Mary had had to give way. Norman's training would start in the next couple of weeks – not that there had been any evidence of air raids, and not much of the war, in the weeks so far.

Before too long, the back door closed again and Johnnie

reappeared, wearing a big grin and concealing something behind his back.

'Close your eyes, everyone,' he commanded. They all obeyed, and when Johnnie agreed they could open them, he was holding the object out in front of him.

'UNDER NEW MANAGEMENT' it said in forest-green letters carved into a white background. There were two hooks to hang it over the counter.

'What . . . how?' Carrie spluttered.

'I had a word with that signwriter mate of Dad's and he siphoned me off a bit of paint. I just . . . wanted you to have a little something from me to say "well done".' The twins exchanged looks. 'I've been working on it whenever you were out of the way. Like it?'

'I love it! Oh, Johnnie, thank you!'

Carrie flung herself at her brother, who rapidly put down the sign and spun her round.

'Crikey Moses, sis! They talk about the g-force that pilots have to contend with – nobody mentioned the C-force! You're a human whirlwind!'

'Wait till you see the success I'm going to make of that bookstall!' Carrie warned him. 'You'd better brace yourself for a tornado!'

Chapter Four

Johnnie was leaving early the next morning, but as the whole family were early risers, no one had to set their alarm clock. Norman said his goodbyes first – he had to attend to the shop – but Mary bustled about in the kitchen. Carrie saw her brother's eyebrows move as their mother pressed a packet of sandwiches, two hunks of cake and an apple into his hands, as if he was going to Outer Mongolia, not Lancashire. He dutifully stuffed them into his bag and straightened to give her a hug.

'You look after yourself,' Mary instructed him, a wobble in her voice.

Carrie, seated at the table, looked down into her teacup. She hated goodbyes, and this was a more significant parting than most.

'I will,' Johnnie said gently. It was no good telling Mary that the first few months would be classroom-based and it would be ages before he was trusted with flying his own plane. He kissed his mother's forehead and disentangled himself. 'I'll be back on leave before you know it.'

'I know.' Mary stood back, knuckling the tears from her eyes. 'Anyway, I'm going through to the shop. You'll want to say goodbye to your sister.'

Carrie and Johnnie were left alone. There was so much

she wanted to say, and no words adequate to say it. But Johnnie had always been able to read her like the books she loved, and he did his best to lighten the mood.

'Can I go,' he said, 'if I promise not to come back wearing a signet ring and a gallon of Brylcreem and saying everything's "spiffing"?'

Carrie burst out laughing. The RAF was supposed to attract, or create, that type.

'If you dare, I'll bore you silly with my profit and loss account!'

'Deal,' grinned Johnnie. 'Come and see me off, then, waving a hankie like a proper sister.'

Carrie went with him to the back gate. He gave her a hug. 'Got that hankie?' he asked.

Carrie produced one from her sleeve.

'Right, then,' said Johnnie, hoisting his kitbag higher on his shoulder, and as if he was directing a film, he instructed: 'Action! Come on!'

Carrie obediently started waving her hankie, feeling pretty foolish: he was only about two feet away. Johnnie turned down the entry, looked back over his shoulder and gave her a wink.

'And cut!' he said.

He blew her a kiss. Carrie lowered the hankie. She stood there at the gate till she couldn't hear his footsteps any more.

Carrie spent the next few days deliberating about how to arrange her stock. Her newspapers would be on the wire racks hanging on the frontage, she decided, and also on the left of the counter. Then her stock would move through magazines and periodicals to books, on the right-hand side from the customer's point of view. The Penguins had a special carousel stand of their own. It had been another expense, but Uncle Charlie had insisted.

'Got to make a splash!' he said.

As she unpacked the pristine new books, Carrie breathed in the intoxicating smell of fresh print. She loved the Penguins especially – the clean lines, the clear typeface, the cheeky little penguin motif. The covers were colour-coded too – orange for fiction, green for crime, dark blue for biography . . .

On the shelves behind the counter, she arranged her 'Titles of the Month' along with oddments of stationery – luggage labels, correspondence cards, notebooks, writing pads, envelopes and ink. The trains were so unpredictable and crowded, though, that anyone who found a seat, let alone one with a table to write at, would feel their ship, not their train, had come in.

On Sunday night, Carrie laid out what she'd wear for her first day. She loved pretty things, but she'd never had much money and the week before opening she'd looked despondently at her washed-out blouses and out-at-the-seat skirts. They'd done fine for the shop, but now . . . ?

But Uncle Charlie also noticed these things. One day, he'd slipped her a couple of notes and told her to buy herself some 'business dress'. Carrie hadn't needed telling twice. She'd had a wonderful time in Etam, Dorothy Perkins and C & A, putting together a wardrobe of one black and one grey skirt, a clever grey-and-black houndstooth jacket that would go with either, and two blouses, one white and one cream. She'd felt extravagant buying jumpers – up till now, most of hers had been home-knitted – but she couldn't resist a cherry-red one with a sort of fan pattern, and a true sapphire blue with puffed sleeves.

On Monday (black skirt, jacket, white blouse with black piping on the collar and cuffs, Uncle Charlie's bracelet for luck), she was there at first light to take in the papers – her very own papers! – as they were chucked onto the platform from the mail train. All she needed now, she thought, as she lifted the pleasurably smooth-running shutter an hour later, were some sales.

She was rewarded when, shortly after seven, the first commuters trickled onto the platform for London.

Some had their newspapers; they obviously had them delivered. But more, who previously must have bought them on the way, were delighted to pick up their *Times* or *Telegraph*, their *Herald* or *Sketch*, *The Listener* or the *People's Friend* at the station. Carrie had to leave the cash drawer open, so fast was she funnelling coppers into it. High on excitement and a dream come true, she smiled her thanks at the compliments and congratulations on the opening of the stall. Someone jokingly asked if the refreshment room served champagne. Carrie knew it didn't, but didn't feel she needed it.

The first train to town was on time, but the second, the announcement told them, would be delayed by fifteen minutes, and several people returned to the bookstall to browse. Carrie held her breath. Who'd be the first to pick up a classic, or risk an author they hadn't tried before?

But then the train came in five minutes early after all and

they stampeded off to get a seat. Never mind, thought Carrie, she could do with a breather.

She unscrewed the top of her flask and took a bite of the bread and dripping that she'd packed up with shaking hands before leaving home. She'd barely finished chewing, though, when a train, unannounced, stopped on the down platform and out piled about thirty men, still in civvies, but from their ages, and their single suitcases or grips, obviously on their way to a training camp.

'Hey, look!' she heard one of them shout. 'The caff's open! And there's a bookstall!'

There was a tunnel between the platforms and the next thing Carrie heard was the thunder of boots echoing off its tiled walls. Hastily putting away her breakfast, she stood and waited, smiling. These were the very men she'd had most in mind!

In the end, though, the influx was something of a disappointment. For a start, most of them headed for the tearoom. Those that came to the stall fell on the *Daily Mirror* and the illustrated papers and she only sold two books, *The Thin Man* by Dashiell Hammett and a pulp western.

When the men scarpered back to the other platform for their connecting train, Carrie was left disappointed and not a little worried. She'd been so sure, but had she misjudged things? Yes, she had a reasonable stock of thrillers, murder mysteries and spy stories, but who was going to buy the Penguin reprints of the novels she loved – or the histories so well written that they read like novels? Was the bookstall going to be a repeat of her experience of trying to sell books in the shop – a dismal failure? Were her choices slanted too much towards the female reader? But then Carrie loved Dashiell Hammett too . . .

'How's it going, m'dear? Surviving?'

It was Bette. Carrie couldn't believe now that she'd been wary of the older woman's attitude to start with – they'd become friends.

'Fine, thanks!' The last thing she wanted was to admit to any doubts, but Bette was no fool and was looking at her shrewdly. 'Well, the papers are doing fine,' Carrie acknow-ledged, 'not so much the books.'

Bette broke out in a peal of wheezy laughter.

'You don't want much, do you? How many trains have been in? Six? Seven, if you count the express that doesn't stop. You can't expect everything at once! You wait till you've been on your feet for ten hours. I hope you've got a stool behind that counter – oh, hello!'

She broke off while the stationmaster ponderously announced that the nine-twenty would be the next train to arrive at Platform One – Carrie's platform.

'Now this,' Bette resumed triumphantly, 'is the train that takes all the wives with time on their hands up to town. Let's see how many of them want something to read in the hairdresser's or while they're waiting at the Ritz for their lover to turn up for lunch!'

As Carrie gaped, Bette conceded, 'Well, there's a couple of those, anyway. Oh yes, don't look so shocked, you'll soon spot 'em. Or smell them, by the amount of Chanel Number Five they've splashed on!'

The hitherto unsuspected secret lives of the housewives of Brockington came as a revelation to Carrie. The harassed womenfolk of Harold Road and Ethel Street barely had time to put a scarf over their rollers before hanging out the washing or trudging off to work, let alone take a lover and have him treat them to lunch.

'The rest,' Bette continued, 'are taking their children to the dentist or going up for a corset fitting.' That sounded more like the respectable wives and mothers of Brockington. 'But they're all readers, from what I've seen of them that wait in the tearoom. But I must go. I've left Ruby in charge – if you can call it that! A few sticks short of a fire, that one, if you ask me. Cheerio!'

Carrie waved goodbye, smiling to herself. Whatever the future of the stall, a whole world she'd never have experienced if she'd stayed in her parents' shop was opening up right in front of her.

Bette's prediction was right: the platform soon filled up with women taking a day trip to town. Carrie's first customers were a mother with a daughter of about fourteen in a school gymslip, her neatly shingled hair held back by two clips. A classic case of 'on their way to the dentist', Carrie surmised.

'You're open!' exclaimed the girl in delight, feasting her eyes on the books. 'I've been waiting for this!'

At last! thought Carrie. A book lover like herself. She saw the girl pick up almost every Penguin title in the carousel. She read the back blurb and the first paragraph before replacing the book carefully in its place. Carrie understood – it was just what she always did.

'Now come on, Miriam,' said the girl's mother, who was looking on. 'Are you going to buy one? Our train'll be here soon.'

'Only one?' said Miriam. By this time she'd put aside four novels and a biography. 'When I can get five for half a crown?'

She produced her purse and handed over the coin.

Carrie, who'd never expected to sell so many books at one time, was put on the spot.

'I'm afraid I don't have any wrapping,' she confessed.

'Oh, that's OK,' replied the girl. She produced a string bag from her pocket. 'I came prepared!'

Miriam's mother shook her head indulgently as her daughter stowed the books carefully in her bag.

'We've been giving her pocket money for odd jobs – I didn't realise how much she'd saved! But thank you. Those should keep her happy for ages.'

After that, another train arrived, and another ... Newspapers, magazines and stationery were selling almost faster than she could handle, and young Miriam seemed to have started something with the books. Carrie had to restock the Penguin carousel – twice! So it went on all day. In the late afternoon, before the commuters started arriving back on the other platform, there was something of a lull and Carrie was able to count her takings – which wildly exceeded what she'd imagined. Ecstatic, she shovelled coins and notes into little cloth bags and locked them away in the strongbox under the counter.

She couldn't wait to tell her mum and dad. She'd write to Johnnie, and she could phone Uncle Charlie – there was a telephone back home in the shop. He'd asked for what he called a 'progress report'.

The evening papers arrived and Carrie folded them into

the rack, removing the dailies to be returned next morning. By now her feet and back were aching and she longed for the stool Bette had suggested. Maybe Johnnie could make one, though it might be ages before he was home and had the time.

Just then, a train came in, this time on the up platform, with an announcement that it was terminating at Brockington: a replacement service would follow. Fed up, the passengers piled off, among them soldiers in uniform.

'Typical, ain't it,' Carrie heard one of them say. 'That's a good hour of me twenty-four-hour pass gone. My Elsie's gonna be thrilled about that.'

'Come on,' said his mate. 'Let's see if the tearoom keeps continental opening hours, eh?'

Cheered, they went off. They'd be lucky. Bette was very strict about her licence. But Carrie was soon too busy to think about Bette, as the soldiers and other passengers needed serving.

Eventually, they all drifted away to the refreshment room or the waiting room, or to lounge against the wall, smoking, leaving only one by her bookstall.

Carrie had noticed him from the start. He was tall, but not too tall, broad-shouldered but not burly, with a well-shaped face, a full mouth and dark hair under his cap. His eyes, she could see once he came closer, were grey-blue and crinkled at the corners as he joked with a couple of his men. Gosh, he was good-looking! But unlike some of the other officers she'd seen pass through, he didn't have that self-important swagger about him that meant he knew it. One button and one pip on his shoulder told her he was a second lieutenant. From her days setting up the stall and seeing the troops come through, she knew every rank in the British Army already.

He'd arrived with a bunch of flowers – lilies, which must have cost a bit – and now, with everyone else gone, he placed them carefully on the counter, leaving the stalks over the edge so as not to stain this week's *Radio Times*. Hmm . . . thoughtful, too.

Under the pretence of tidying the stall, Carrie watched him pick up one Penguin after another. He, too, read the back cover and the first paragraph. In fact, he read rather more than a paragraph – more like a page or two. Carrie coughed. He was being careful, but she couldn't afford broken spines or bent corners.

He hastily closed the book he'd been reading and replaced it in the carousel. An Ernest Hemingway.

'Don't say it – "This isn't a library, you know!"'

'I wasn't going to!'

'Really?' he grinned. The corners of his eyes crinkled again. 'Then you're the most understanding bookseller I've ever met! It's a dreadful habit, I know, but I've been starved of anything to read for the past fortnight. Apart from the dreadful bumf I have to din into the recruits.'

'Well, that's why I'm here,' smiled Carrie. And, surprising herself with a sudden burst of confidence, she added: 'I don't know what I'd do without a book to escape into. I couldn't help feeling that you – I mean, everyone in the forces – would need that more than most.'

She'd spoken with all her love of books and he smiled in agreement.

'There's nothing like losing yourself in a book, is there?' He glanced round her stock again. 'You're in the right job, I can tell. So, come on, who's your favourite author?'

Carrie blew out a breath. 'Oof! Ask me an easier one! Do you mean now, at this moment, or of all time?'

'Ha!' he grinned. 'Now I know you're a true book lover. Sometimes I think the last book I read is the best thing since shaving soap, but then I remember the ones I go back to time and time again.'

'Exactly!' Carrie echoed.

He smiled again. He smiled a lot.

'But where were you when I needed you?' he asked. 'When I came through last month?'

'Today's my first day,' said Carrie proudly.

'No! That's lucky! For me, I mean.' He stepped back and she couldn't help noticing how well his uniform jacket fitted his body. He took in the name painted above the stall, and Johnnie's sign. '"Under New Management",' he read. '"C. Anderson" – is that you?'

'Yes. Carrie Anderson.' And she added, not knowing where it had come from: 'Sole proprietor.'

Which wasn't strictly true, since Uncle Charlie was backing the whole thing, but somehow she felt she had to keep this conversation going.

He grinned again and held out his hand.

'Mike Hudson. How d'you do.'

He took her hand in a firm, warm grip and Carrie felt herself blush. His eyes caught hers and her heart and stomach did a forward roll in a way she had never experienced before. No wonder they called it falling for someone! But just then the bell rang and the voice of Mr Bayliss crackled over the ancient loudspeaker.

'The next train at Platform One will be a direct train for London Victoria. I repeat, this train does not stop. Will passengers kindly have all tickets and travel warrants ready for inspection as you board. The next train at Platform One is for London Victoria. London Victoria only, the next train at Platform One.'

Slowly Mike let go of her hand.

'There's my train.'

'Sounds like it.'

With a grimace, he glanced at the book he'd been reading.

'I wish I could buy it.'

'Why can't you?' asked Carrie. 'They're not rationed – yet!'

The air raids and invasion that everyone had been worrying about simply hadn't materialised. Poland had fallen, but so far there'd been no real fighting in Western Europe. British losses had all involved ships at sea. But as a result, people were already starting to worry about getting basic goods.

Mike shrugged, looking a bit sheepish.

'I know it sounds stupid, but I left my wallet back at camp. And I spent all my cash on these flowers. Sorry.'

Not as sorry as I am, thought Carrie – and not just for the loss of a sale. The flowers must be for a girlfriend. Lucky her.

'Oh, look,' she said impulsively. 'Have it – on me!'

'What? I couldn't possibly—'

'You must! You might be going off on leave now, but after that, who knows? Next week you could be – well . . .'

'Hanging out the washing on the Siegfried Line?'

It was a new song that was doing the rounds.

'You may joke about it, but, yes.'

She suddenly had a vision of him in combat, leading a platoon, throwing a hand grenade under fire. He'd be a good leader, she felt.

'Please take it.'

He turned as the train clanked in with a shower of smuts, a hiss of steam and a fearful grinding of brakes. Its windows were blacked out and it had a sombre look in the gathering dusk. That decided Carrie. What did they say? Seize the day! So, while he was distracted, she leaned across the counter, plucked the book he'd been reading – *A Farewell to Arms* – from the Penguin carousel and tucked it in his pocket.

'Wha—?' He turned back.

'There! It's done now!' smiled Carrie. 'You can enjoy it at your leisure!'

'Really? You're serious?'

'I'm serious.'

'I will. Enjoy it, that is.' He patted his pocket. 'And thank you. I'll pay you next time I'm through!'

'Don't be silly. It's a gift.'

'You'll never make a profit this way!'

'Sir!'

A sergeant was calling him.

'Drat,' he said, and called back, 'All right, Thompson!' Then he added to Carrie: 'Goodbye. Thank you again.'

'Goodbye,' she said. 'Don't mention it. Hey, don't forget your flowers!'

He tutted, picked them up and was gone, caught up in

the crowd pushing and shoving, everyone desperate to get on and find a seat. Carrie watched him help a mother with a small child climb up into the train, pat a couple of soldiers on the back and shepherd them on, and then finally swing up into the train himself. He looked back towards the stall and raised his hand in a wave. Carrie raised hers in reply.

'Miss! Excuse me! Is anyone serving here?'

Reluctantly, Carrie turned her attention to a stout man in a camel-hair coat who was waving a copy of *English Mechanics*.

'Sorry,' she stammered. 'Threepence, please.'

He gave her a shilling. While she was getting his change, Mike's train pulled out.

Chapter Five

That evening, Johnnie rang home for the first time. The telephone was in the tiny hall between the shop and the living room, quite a squeeze for Carrie, her mum and her dad, Norman holding the receiver away from his ear so everyone could hear.

Johnnie's first few days had been spent collecting his uniform and getting his inoculations. Now it was lectures.

'Mostly in boot and button polishing,' he told them. 'Marching in line and standing up smartly on parade. "No slouching at the back!"'

'You know all that from the cadets.' Carrie leaned in and spoke into the mouthpiece.

'Yeah, and the insults when you're not up to the mark!' Johnnie replied.

'Not quite flying yet, then?' joked Norman.

'Only down the stairs if I'm late for roll call!'

The laughter in his voice told them he was loving every minute.

Finally it was Carrie's turn to take the receiver for herself and Johnnie asked at once:

'So, how are you? How was Day One?'

Carrie babbled enthusiastically about Miriam and her mother and the man who'd joked about champagne. She told him how Bette had sent Eric over with an éclair mid-afternoon and how grateful she'd been, and how Mr Bayliss had waddled over to cast his eye over the stall and offer grudging congratulations. She didn't mention Mike Hudson, but that night, in bed, she started reading *A Farewell to Arms*.

A few years ago, one of the librarians had urged her to try Ernest Hemingway. Carrie had but, as she was only young, hadn't enjoyed reading about men drinking too much and having fist fights, and she certainly hadn't wanted to read about the bullfighting that featured – so cruel!

But over the next few days – she only read it at night, so she could savour it – she found that *A Farewell to Arms* was different. A young American lieutenant was serving in the ambulance corps of the Italian Army in the Great War. Yes, there was drinking and violence, but there was also a love story between him and an English nurse. The ending was one of the saddest and most powerful of any book Carrie had ever read.

She was fascinated, now, by Mike's choice. Over the next couple of weeks, she scanned every train that came in from London on the down platform, but there was no sign of him. Regretfully, she concluded that he must have come back through Brockington late at night or on a Sunday, when the stall was closed.

It was ridiculous to mind, she told herself, though his promise to pay 'next time' was lodged in her mind. It wasn't that she couldn't afford sixpence. The stall was doing well, and she'd genuinely intended it as a gift. But as he'd been equally insistent he'd pay her back, she'd thought he'd manage to get her the small sum somehow, as a matter of principle. If he couldn't in person, then with a friend perhaps, or even by post. She remembered the way his eyes had met hers for that brief moment. They'd been sincere. She'd felt instantly that she could trust him and that he'd be a man of his word.

Autumn crept on and Carrie had plenty to occupy her. Eric's leaf sweeping got more frequent, and if Mr Bayliss was out of the way, warming his boots by the fire in his office, Eric would stop by the stall for a chat.

'Look what I've had as a tip!' he said disgustedly one day, producing an orange from his pocket. 'I've met some tight so-and-so's before, but this takes the—'

'Biscuit?' suggested Carrie.

'I wouldn't have minded that!' Eric protested.

'That orange is worth more than you know, lad.' Uncle Charlie emerged from the tiny office. 'If Hitler gets control of the seas, we won't be seeing oranges in this country. You can kiss goodbye to bananas and lemons as well, anything like that. Anything we can't grow here, basically.'

Eric turned the orange over thoughtfully in his hands. 'Maybe I should hang on to it. Sell it on the black market.'

'It's not going to keep very well, is it?' Carrie pointed out.

'S'pose not.' With a sudden gesture, Eric thrust the fruit at her. 'Here, you have it.'

Carrie loved oranges. 'Ooh, Eric. Are you sure?'

Eric nodded happily. 'It's yours.'

He placed it reverently on a copy of *Woman's Own* and went on his way.

'That young feller's taken a shine to you!' Uncle Charlie teased.

Her uncle had taken to dropping by a couple of afternoons a week to 'keep an eye on his investment', he said, and Carrie found it a huge help. Whilst he minded the stall, she could sort her invoices and accounts in the cubbyhole office without having to take them home and do them at night. On a more practical level, it meant she could slip down to the refreshment room for a cup of tea in the warm, and, to put it bluntly, go and spend a penny, which previously she'd had to do between trains, leaving the stall either closed up or with Eric, if he was free, standing guard.

Carrie looked at her uncle wryly. She was well aware that Eric had a bit of a crush on her. She seemed to attract these devoted, puppy-dog types: Cyril from the barber's had been the same. Eric was very sweet, and she didn't want to upset him, or Bette, by turning him down. She was just hoping that he wouldn't actually ask her out.

Bette had become a firm friend, popping over for a chat in her quieter moments and filling Carrie in on the station gossip. Mr Bayliss had a shrewish wife, which, Carrie thought, explained why he threw his weight around at work, the only place he could, and why, possibly, he wasn't above smarming up to any pretty young thing travelling alone and handing her up into the train himself. The ticket collector, Jack, a thin, silent man, had a wooden leg from the Great War, which, Bette observed, hadn't stopped him fathering six children. No wonder, thought Carrie, he always looked exhausted, though his wife was probably even more so.

Bette had her own story to tell. She was a widow, Carrie learned.

'He worked the railways all his life, my Arthur,' Bette told her. 'He was a stoker on the engines, and filthy, hot, hard work it is too. I begged him to stop and find something else, but you know men, did he listen? It got him in the end. Dropped dead of a heart attack when Eric was three.'

Carrie winced. 'That must have been tough.'

'You have to get on with it, don't you?' Bette shrugged. 'At least I've got my Eric.'

Carrie looked at the older woman appraisingly. Bette had lovely features: a full mouth, and bright brown eyes. She was a wonderful cook and, in Carrie's experience, the kindest, most welcoming soul you could imagine. Yet she'd been on her own for almost twenty years.

She felt she knew Bette well enough to venture, 'And you've never thought of marrying again?'

'What? With a boy to bring up and working all hours to keep him?'

'Eric's grown-up now. There's still time—'

Bette snorted. 'For all that malarkey? You must be kidding! If I want romance, I can get it in a story, can't I? You should know that!'

Carrie smiled. Bette was an avid reader of the romances by Denise Robins and knee-tremblers by Ethel M. Dell that she stocked. She still thought it was a shame, though.

Carrie was really beginning to feel that she was a part of the station family. She still had the loving support of her family at home, and the people she knew in their neighbourhood, but she couldn't believe how much her life had changed since she'd opened the bookstall. She missed Johnnie, of course, and wrote to him at least once a week, but meeting so many new people had expanded her horizons in ways she'd never have imagined.

Word had spread that the bookstall was open and she got to know her regulars, folding their paper or holding out their magazine before they'd even produced their money. Her book-buying customers were even more gratifying. They smiled and stayed chatting when their trains were delayed, telling her in lowered voices about their factories having gone over to war work, and their pride – and sometimes fear – for their sons and daughters in the services. Younger women fretted about the children they'd sent to stay with relatives to be on the safe side. Soldiers, sailors and airmen, off the leash for five minutes before they boarded a lorry back to camp or caught a connecting train, winked and teased her. Their officers – none of them Mike Hudson, sadly – were courteous but often preoccupied.

The Penguin representative who dropped off Carrie's orders, Mr Parfitt, was a keen, fresh-faced chap with a bow tie. He had a full head of snowy-white hair and must have been touching sixty, but he had the vim and vigour of a man half his age. He was delighted with how Carrie was doing, bringing her fresh titles every fortnight – new novels and popular history, travel books, memoirs and, already, topical titles about the war.

'*Germany Puts the Clock Back* is selling like hot cakes,' he told her. 'And we're reprinting *Why Britain is at War* already – it's hardly been out five minutes!'

'I've sold plenty here, I know,' Carrie confirmed.

'The young whippersnappers in the Sales Department are looking towards shifting a hundred thousand copies,' Mr Parfitt confided. His bow tie was practically quivering at the prospect. 'See what you can do towards that!'

Carrie was happy to accept the challenge. In quieter moments, she sat on the rough stool that her dad had knocked up – 'Not up to Johnnie's standards, but it'll have to do!' – and read her way through her stock. Books were even more important to her now. They were her livelihood as well as her comfort and companions, and she felt she was being paid, or paying herself, to indulge her hobby. Perched on her stool, she read anything and everything – the range of Penguins was astonishing. She'd been transported to the other side of the world by *Out of Africa* by Karen Blixen and even read *Thinking to Some Purpose* – exactly what she'd done with the bookstall, she felt. She'd never been happier in her work: it didn't seem like work at all, and she soon felt as if she'd been there for ever.

And if she caught herself thinking about Mike Hudson, she told herself firmly that he was gone for good, and that anyway, he'd had that enormous bunch of flowers for his girlfriend. But she still couldn't help looking up hopefully every time she saw a khaki greatcoat and a slick of dark hair under a cap.

Chapter Six

'A penny for them? Or twopence, now I've got my RAF pay!'

Carrie almost dropped her novel – *Crewe Train* by Rose Macaulay. She'd selected it for the stall because of the title. It wasn't about trains at all, really, but she was enjoying it – it was about publishers and writers, and quite an eye-opener, at that!

'Johnnie!' she cried. 'What are you doing here? Your leave's not till next weekend!'

It had been ringed in red all month on the calendar that the Blue Bird Toffee rep presented to Norman each year. It would be the first time they'd seen Johnnie since he'd left.

'Time off for good behaviour, of course!' teased her twin. 'No, the bloke who was down for this now needs next weekend for some family knees-up, so I got permission to swap.'

'But there hasn't been a train for twenty minutes!'

'I hitched,' said Johnnie. 'Everyone stops for a uniform.' He eyed the stall appreciatively. 'So this is your little empire, is it?'

'Not so little!' said Carrie proudly. 'Do you know how much profit I made in the first week?'

Johnnie held up a warning hand.

'Uh-uh. I haven't had a bite since breakfast. You can tell

me about it over tea and buns. I came here first, to see you. It's not as if Mum and Dad are expecting me.'

Carrie hated shutting up shop, and there was a train due in, but this was special. She scribbled a sign saying 'Back in 20 Minutes', locked the cash drawer, pulled down the shutter, locked the door and walked along the platform in the company of her brother.

'You've grown!' she said when she was standing beside him. 'Up and sideways!'

'That's what daily PE does for you,' grinned Johnnie proudly. 'Now, shoulders back, chest out, quick march!'

The tearoom was its usual cosy haven, the windows steamy, the tea urn hissing, Sammy the cat in front of the stove, and the lights over the counter glinting off the domed glass covers on the cakes and pastries. Ingredients had already gone up in price and were harder to get hold of, but, for now at least, Bette was determined her tearoom customers wouldn't suffer.

Johnnie rubbed his hands.

'I could eat the lot!'

'We'll have to get some service first!'

Ruby, a big-boned, rather ungainly girl, her hair a dazzling peroxide frizz, was clearing a table – not very effectively. She was humming 'Cheek to Cheek', her eyes on a pair of Polish airmen playing chess at the next table. Bette was nowhere to be seen, so Carrie leaned across the counter and called her name. Bette came out from the back, where, from the crumbs on her dress, she'd been sampling her wares.

'Carrie!' she exclaimed. 'This is a—Oh, hello!' Then added archly: 'And who's this handsome young man?'

'I'm her brother, Johnnie, Mrs Saunders.' Johnnie took off his cap and held out his hand. 'I've heard a lot about you.' He'd always had good manners, but the RAF had polished them to a shine. 'I'm going to stand her a slap-up tea.'

'At last!' said Bette with a wide smile. 'I mean, I've heard a lot about you too, but it's lovely to meet you. I do try to get her to take a proper break every day, but she won't hear of it. Maybe she'll listen to some sense from her brother.'

'That'll be a first!' Johnnie knew his sister of old. 'But as she's here now, we'll have a pot of tea for two and a plate of cakes, please. And I could murder a sandwich – whatever you've got.'

'I've got a nice bit of ham, my love. You sit yourselves down— Oh, here we go again!'

There was an enormous crash as a teacup and its saucer fell to the floor. Other customers started, slopping their tea into their saucers.

'Sorry, Mrs Saunders,' cried Ruby, wide-eyed. 'It slipped clean out me 'ands!'

Bette lifted her eyebrows so high they almost met her hairline.

'Fetch the dustpan, Ruby,' she said, 'and in future, kindly keep your mind on your work!' Then she muttered, 'She did that deliberately, I'll be bound, all because of them two fellers. Man-mad, she is! I've warned my Eric to be careful. You watch out, Johnnie, she'll be hanging her hat up to you next!'

'Why do you keep her?' mouthed Johnnie as Ruby lumbered past with the grace of a tank.

'Hard to credit, I know, but when you can get her attention for five minutes, she's a dab hand with icing the fancy cakes.' Bette picked up her cake tongs. 'Gets enough practice with all that slap she puts on her face!'

Johnnie was slavering when, ten minutes later, Bette unloaded a tray that was almost bending in the middle. The Polish airmen were gallantly helping Ruby to pick up scattered pieces of china, to much simpering and cunning exposure of stocking tops and dimpled white thighs.

'You talk, I'll eat!' Johnnie declared.

So Carrie did, telling him all she hadn't been able to put fully in her letters: about Jack the silent ticket collector, about Mr Bayliss and his bullish ways, and, in a lower voice, about Bette and Eric's mother-and-son devotion. Then she moved on to her customers.

'I told you about Miriam and her mother, who go up to the dentist every few weeks – Miriam's reading *Cold Comfort Farm* at the moment – then there's Mrs Cattermole, who knits, so she buys all the women's magazines, and Professor Mason. He lectures in English literature, so we have great chats . . .'

On she went till Johnnie had demolished his sandwich and three cakes.

'Come on,' she pressed him, 'I've told you all about the bookstall.' She paused, framing the question to which she already knew, but dreaded, the answer. 'You're still determined to fly?'

'Has Hitler got a moustache? Of course I am!' Johnnie's eyes lit up. 'But it's going to be a fight to get accepted. I'll be swotting this weekend. There's a test when I go back.'

'Well, full marks for enthusiasm,' said Carrie, wishing she felt more enthusiastic about the risk. Everyone was saying this war would be the first to be fought in the air. But since she was doing what she'd always dreamed of, who was she to deny her brother his dearest wish, however dangerous?

'I sat in a Spitfire the other day,' said Johnnie in the same wondering tone he might use if he'd been in a spaceship. 'They landed a couple for us as a treat. What a plane! But not always easy to fly, apparently. Turn too tight and the engine can stall, and then . . .' He leaned in, sketching the design of a plane on the tabletop. 'The wing root stalls before the wing tips, you see, but there's this shuddering that warns you to ease up—' He saw her horrified face. 'Sorry, sis. Perhaps it's better for you not to know.'

'I don't mind you telling me if you have to, but for goodness' sake, as far as Mum's concerned, keep it to yourself. Just tell her it's like sitting in an armchair, and about as dangerous!'

Johnnie nodded. 'Message received.'

Carrie poured them each another cup of tea.

'Is everyone there as plane-crazy as you?' she asked, curious.

'At least. If not more so.'

Carrie rolled her eyes. 'And what else do you do with yourselves? Apart from drink yourselves silly.'

She'd seen plenty of evidence of that in the troops passing through the station.

'There's a dance next week.' Johnnie grinned. 'With the WAAFs.'

'Hmm,' said Carrie wryly. 'Well, if wing-tip problems are your idea of conversation, aren't they in for a grand time?'

*

Johnnie's twenty-four-hour leave passed all too quickly. He went back to camp and the house at once seemed emptier and quieter without him. The nights drew in further and Carrie's feet froze on the cold stone floor at the stall. But Alf Warburton gave her dad an old stair runner for her to stand on, and Mary found some fur-lined boots at the church rummage sale. They were a bit worn and a size too big, but with a couple of pairs of Johnnie's socks inside – the RAF had given him a whole new set of clothes, right down to socks and underpants – they kept Carrie's feet toasty warm.

All was going well, until, leaving the station one night, she was startled by a male voice from the shadows.

'Good evening.'

Approaches to lone women weren't uncommon in the blackout. Theft, robbery, assault – all sorts of crimes had already risen.

Carrie didn't even look in the voice's direction. She put back her shoulders and began walking briskly, following the white-painted kerb with the thin beam of her torch. Then she cried out as someone caught her arm.

'Let me go!'

He did at once, saying: 'It's all right, it's me! I'm sorry, Carrie, I'm an idiot, I should have thought. It's me, Mike. Mike Hudson!'

Carrie whirled around, her torch beam flailing wildly.

'What? What are you doing lurking there like a criminal?'

A car passed and in the light of its dipped and slitted headlights, Carrie could see it really was him.

'I came to the stall,' he explained, 'but you were busy

with the evening rush. I knew you wouldn't have time to talk. And I wanted to surprise you.'

'Congratulations! You have – you almost frightened me into fits!'

'I'm sorry, I really am. Am I forgiven?'

Carrie squinted up at him. Her heart was still doing funny things, but it wasn't thudding from fear now, it was something else. She didn't have to think very hard to identify it as excitement – and delight.

Mike touched her elbow.

'I tell you what. Come and have a restoring drink while you think about it, eh?'

There was nothing to think about, but she wasn't going to let him off that easily.

'Well . . .'

'Please?'

'Oh, very well,' said Carrie graciously.

'Great.' Mike steered her towards the portal of the Station Hotel. 'And if you need any further inducement, I'll give you that sixpence I owe you.'

Carrie rang home from the telephone booth at the hotel. Her mother answered; her dad would still be busy cashing up.

'Mum? It's me . . . Look, I won't be home just yet . . . No, nothing's wrong . . .'

Far from it! she thought. She bit her lip to keep the excitement out of her voice.

'I've met a friend from school, that's all . . . Evie, you remember her, and we're going to have a drink . . . Food?

Um, I'm not sure really . . . Well, yes, save me something if you like . . . Thanks . . . No, no, I won't be late.'

She replaced the receiver and took a deep breath. Through the glass door, across the lobby in the bar, Mike had his back to her, ordering their drinks. Carrie took in the long sweep of his spine, the broad shoulders and trim waist accentuated by his Sam Browne belt, the way his regulation haircut left the soft nape of his neck exposed. She had a strange, fizzy feeling inside, as if she'd eaten about a pound of sherbet lemons.

She tried to get things into proportion. He owed her six-pence; he'd found her to pay it back and the drink was interest on the debt, not interest in her. He was an officer, for goodness' sake, even if only a junior one. He was older – early twenties, she surmised – and just, well, so much more polished. And he was heart-stoppingly handsome. He was just being polite. He'd never bother with an ordinary girl like her. And anyway, he had a girlfriend. He'd had those flowers . . .

Even so, she scuttled off to the ladies' powder room. Thank goodness she'd washed her hair on Sunday! Carrie scrabbled in her bag for the little make-up she wore – a bit of powder and lipstick – and pulled the cherry-red jumper down over her neat figure. She could have wished she had her best shoes on, even with their thin soles, and not her clumpy furry boots, but there wasn't much she could do about it.

Carrie never fibbed to her parents – there'd never been any need. She'd tell her mum and dad the truth – but not yet. For now, Mike was her secret, one she wanted to keep to herself, just for a little longer.

And so, with her heart still somersaulting and her stomach positively vaulting – there was a whole gymnastic display going on inside – she walked back into the lounge bar of the Station Hotel.

Chapter Seven

'Oh, love, no!' Not far away, in their terraced cottage near the station, Bette and Eric were sitting down to their tea. Eric had a hangdog look.

'I'm sorry, Mum, but there it is.'

'Oh, Eric! Why didn't you tell me when you got the call-up letter?'

'I didn't want to worry you. And to be honest, I thought that dose of rheumatic fever I had as a kid might let me out anyway. You always said it gave me a weak heart.'

'It did!' Bette protested.

'Not weak enough. The army's still accepted me.'

'Oh, Eric!' Bette echoed.

She struggled to piece things together.

'So that morning you had off work the other week – the time Mr Bayliss owed you for staying to unload those boxes . . .'

'I went to the medical, yes.'

Bette shook her head.

'I do wish you'd talked to me about it! Why didn't you send your friend along, you know, the one that's got the bad asthma, to pretend to be you?'

'Mum! What? Where do you get these ideas? It's one thing hoping some ailment of my own might let me off, but how could you even think I'd do such a thing! Cheat the medical? It never occurred to me!'

'Well, it would have occurred to me,' said Bette stoutly. 'I don't stand there with cloth ears in that tearoom, you know. I hear what people are saying. Them that's done that very thing to get their sons out of the war, and them that's paid the committee to get their lad off as a conscientious objector.'

'You can't have wanted me to be a conchie!' Eric was truly shocked. 'Anyway, they don't just let you sit on your backside if you are. They still make you do something – drive ambulances or be a hospital orderly or something.'

'It's got to be better than being sent to the front line. Oh, love. I can't believe you didn't tell me.'

Eric sighed. His mother was starting to repeat herself, which meant the argument would be going round in circles and would only end one way. He loved her dearly and they were very close, but he knew what was coming next. It was Bette's weak spot, her Achilles heel.

Since his dad had died young, it had been Bette and Eric together against the world, and being kind and mild-mannered, he'd gone along with it. He wasn't particularly academic and when he left school he'd let her talk him into a job – initially as errand boy for the grocer who served the tearoom and then, when the job came up and he was old enough, porter at the station. Eric didn't mind; he had no particular ambitions of his own. What did it matter, if it kept his mother happy? But now there was a war on: it was time to be a man. It was time to grow up and stand on his own two feet.

His mother's eyes were shining with unshed tears.

'You know how it is, love. You're all I've got.'

Eric held up his hand.

'That's enough, Mum, please. It's done and that's all there is to it. I've got to report to the army next week, so I'll tell Mr Bayliss tomorrow. Now let's eat before it goes stone cold.'

Thank goodness, thought Carrie, as she approached the table Mike had chosen. He was again standing with his back to her, studying the prints of bygone Brockington on the walls. She was still conscious of the embarrassing boots as she walked over what seemed like a wilderness of scrolled carpet.

'Sorry about that,' Carrie said brightly. 'Here I am.'

Mike turned and smiled broadly, giving Carrie's heart and stomach another twist and turn. He pulled out her chair for her, then sat down himself and raised his glass.

'Cheers,' he said. 'And before I forget . . .' He reached into his pocket and pulled out a sixpence.

He pushed it across the table. Carrie pushed it back.

'I told you not to worry about it,' she scolded him, smiling. 'You must think me a pretty poor businesswoman if I can't afford sixpence! Anyway, it's accounted for as spoiled stock.'

She was presenting Uncle Charlie with weekly accounts. He'd said monthly, or even quarterly was enough, but Carrie had insisted.

'Well, I'm not taking it back!' Mike pushed the coin towards her again, as if they were two old-timers in a pub playing shove-ha'penny. This time, Carrie left it where it was.

'In that case, we'll leave it as a tip,' she replied.

She'd never been in the Station Hotel before, never had cause to, but it looked the sort of establishment where the barman might expect a tip for clearing the table, something poor Ruby rarely got. Maybe if she did, she'd try a bit harder, instead of fantasising about the day Errol Flynn was going to swagger into the tearoom, order egg on toast and whisk her off to Hollywood as his bride.

Mike grinned. 'You're a smart article, Carrie Anderson,' he said. 'You've got an answer for everything.'

Maybe she had. Carrie was surprising herself with how easy she felt with Mike now they were sitting down and talking. But alongside the answers, she had questions to ask him too. Uppermost in her mind was the one thing she needed to get straight from the outset.

'So,' she began brightly, 'did your girlfriend like the flowers?'

Mike frowned.

'Girlfriend?'

Oh Lord. He didn't look very pleased. Carrie cursed herself. Why hadn't she led into it a bit more gradually? Why hadn't she first asked where he'd been all this time? Had he, as she'd surmised, travelled back to camp late at night or on a Sunday, when she wasn't at the station? Why oh why hadn't she asked about an interest they both shared – books? She could have asked how he'd enjoyed *A Farewell to Arms* and kept the conversation on nice, safe ground.

Had she gone too far, too soon, getting personal? Or maybe – which was even worse – maybe he had more than one girlfriend and he couldn't remember which flowers they were and for which one? Maybe he was going to turn out to be a 'girl in every port' sort of man after all.

But she'd started now; there was no going back.

'You had a huge bunch of lilies,' she reminded him. 'You put them on the counter. That's why you didn't have the money for the book, you said.'

She had to repress an urge to say, 'Or so you said.'

Mike burst out laughing.

'Those! Fancy your remembering that. They weren't for a girlfriend. They were for my sister, for her birthday.'

And suddenly Carrie was laughing too, laughing from the absurdity of it all, her mistaken assumption, and from sheer delight. He wasn't attached! He wasn't two-timing, let alone three-timing, anyone.

'Crikey, if they gave out medals for conclusion-jumping, you'd be in the Olympics!' Mike shook his head in amusement. 'My sister's just turned fourteen. I thought the flowers would make her feel grown-up.'

'I'm sure they did,' said Carrie warmly. And couldn't help adding: 'What a nice brother you are. What's she like, your sister?'

'Jane? Hmm . . . well, if I tell you her favourite books as a child were *Peter Rabbit*, then *The Wind in the Willows* and then *Black Beauty*, does that give you a clue?'

'Animal-mad, then?'

'Potty about them.' Mike smiled. 'She used to go out into our garden and sing back to the birds. And she has a positive love affair with the milkman's horse – runs out every morning to give him a sugar lump. Don't laugh, she takes it very seriously! I expect she'll be a zookeeper when she grows up. Or a lion-tamer.'

And then they were talking about their families. Carrie told him about Johnnie, his obsession with planes and how he'd rushed to join the RAF. She told him about her parents' shop, and how it had been in the family for three generations.

'That's funny,' he said. 'Snap!'

'What?'

'My parents have a shop too. In Leamington Spa. Haberdashery, material, sewing-machine sales and repairs.'

'Gosh. I bet they've been busy, with all those blackout curtains everyone's had to make.'

Carrie's mind was whirring like a sewing machine itself. So he wasn't from a posh family, although he was an officer. How come?

'Quite similar backgrounds, really.' Mike grinned. He took a swig of his drink – a whisky and water, Carrie noted. Wanting to seem grown-up, she'd asked for a sherry. 'So I suppose your next question, Miss Curiosity-Killed-the-Cat, is going to be how, from there, I've reached the elevated status of second lieutenant.'

'No, I wouldn't dream of—'

'Yes, you would. And fair enough, because no, I'm not from the usual sort of background – upper class, public school and all that. The answer's simple. My great-aunt, that is, my well-off great aunt –'

All was becoming clear.

'– her husband was a career soldier, died at Passchendaele,' Mike went on. 'No children, so she's always rather doted on us, me in particular, the son she never had and all that. She paid for me to go to school, the sort of school that had an OTC.'

'Officer Training Corps,' Carrie said softly. How often had she heard Johnnie talk about it enviously. Some of the OTCs had access to planes.

'And, um, well, since I didn't fancy going into the business, and there was no real expectation that I would, and I rather enjoyed the scrambling through nets and log rolls down hills and even the ten-mile runs with a backpack, and I wasn't a complete slouch in exams, well, I thought in the end the army might not be a bad fit.'

He was being modest, Carrie was sure of it. She'd have put money on him being top of the class, probably teacher's pet, if the army allowed such a thing.

'Anyway, they seemed to like me, so I got accepted for army college, passed that and . . . well, here I am. All thanks to my fairy godmother.'

Carrie was sure he'd glossed over a lot of what had happened – the toughness of the army's officer-training course, the slogging for exams, the tough military regime of early-morning runs and cold showers. Still, he seemed to have come through it all right – and those exercises had certainly given him a good physique . . .

'How funny.' Coming back to herself, Carrie echoed what Mike himself had said. 'I've only got the bookstall thanks to my fairy godfather – my uncle. Not that he's well off exactly, not at all, really, but he doesn't have children either, so—'

'He was happy to help,' Mike supplied. 'And I suppose he knew you were a bit of a bookworm?'

'Oh, yes.' Carrie had explained about her attempts to sell books in the family shop.

'So,' said Mike, 'let's get down to business. You dodged the question last time. Books! Who do you like to read?'

'Oh,' exclaimed Carrie. 'Where shall I start?'

'Childhood,' said Mike firmly, and started firing out titles and authors. '*The Lion, the Witch and the Wardrobe*? *Peter Pan*? Did you like *Black Beauty*? *Children of the New Forest*! *Treasure Island*! Did you read Biggles because of your brother? I loved those, even though I was a bit old for them really . . .'

And after that, with Carrie on her pet subject, they didn't stop talking. Mike explained his mysterious absence too.

'They sent me on a training course directly after my leave ended,' he explained. 'I went off straight from home. Advanced Fieldcraft and Tactics.'

It didn't mean much to Carrie, but the way he said it made her nod appreciatively. What it did mean was that he had most likely returned to base at Caterham by army transport and not by train at all.

They chatted some more, about all sorts of things – their home lives, their childhoods, their loves and hates. Apart from sharing a passion for books, they both loved picnics and hated pomposity. Carrie admitted she was scared of spiders, and Mike that he didn't much like confined spaces. Carrie was horrified when she looked at her watch and found it was almost nine o'clock.

'Oh no, I must go!' she said, flurried.

'What? Already?' said Mike. 'We've only just started!' Then he checked himself. 'I'm sorry, you must be starving. Let's see if I can get us a table here.'

'No – no, really!'

She was starving, but Lyons and the Kardomah Café, the sorts of places she and her convenient friend Evie might conceivably have gone to for a bite to eat, would be closing, her mum would worry – and bang would go her excuse. And she mustn't be greedy. She'd had the best two hours of her life. She had quite enough already to relive in the privacy of her room.

'I'm sorry,' she said. 'But I have to get back. I promised I wouldn't be late.'

'It isn't late.'

'Maybe not for you, but we lead a very quiet life here, not like you soldiers roistering till all hours!'

'Roistering?' Mike hooted with laughter. 'Where did you get that from? I don't think I've roistered since, well . . .'

'The last regimental dinner?'

Carrie knew the state Johnnie had come home in when he'd been back and had met up in the evening with a couple of mates who also happened to be home on leave.

'OK, alcohol was taken,' Mike conceded. 'But if you must go, I'll walk you home. I insist.'

So he did – well, almost. Carrie made him stop before the turning from the main road. The last thing she wanted was to bump into Alf Warburton or her dad, or any of the local ARP wardens on their rounds. They and their wives had known her since she was a baby, seen her with her toddle truck and her doll's pram, bought their *Racing Post* and their Woodbines from her in the shop, and here she was in the company of a handsome young officer? The Ethel Street gossipmongers would be at it to beat the band.

'I'll be fine from here,' she said. 'It's two minutes away. I know every inch, and I've got my torch. And if you're going back to Caterham tonight, you'll have to run for it or you'll miss the last train.'

'I came in a car with a couple of others,' Mike explained. 'They'll be in the pub till closing time. I'll meet up with them.' He sighed. 'I can't believe you wouldn't let me buy you dinner.'

Nor me, Carrie thought to herself, because perversely, now it was nearly over, she didn't want her time with Mike to end.

'But next time . . .' He paused, and Carrie's heart skipped a beat.

'There will be a next time, won't there?' he asked. 'I'll see you again?'

There was only half a moon, but it was a cloudless night. Suddenly they were standing very close and Carrie could see, hear and feel that he meant it. If only he knew how she'd been willing him to say it – every step of the way from the Station Hotel. But she must be sensible. She'd had a wonderful evening, but – she went over the reasons again – Mike was that much older, more sophisticated, so good-looking . . . Tonight had been an interlude for him, that was all.

'Of course!' she said. 'Whenever you're next passing through.'

'No, not when I'm passing through,' said Mike, as if it was obvious. 'It's not that far from Caterham. As well as trains, one of the chaps has got a bike, a motorbike, I mean. There's this other fellow with a car. Or I can hitch.'

Carrie closed her eyes briefly. She could hardly believe it.

He wanted to see her again and he was going to come especially for it. Tall, dark, handsome junior officer Mike Hudson wanted to see her, Carrie Anderson, again! And he was so nice . . . and so handsome . . .

A tendril of Carrie's hair had escaped from the beret her mother had crocheted for her last Christmas. Mike reached forward and curled it round his finger.

'I'll come especially, Carrie,' he said. 'There's a bit of a flap on right now, trying to get new recruits up to speed, but I'll be back as soon as I can.'

Then he dipped his head and his lips brushed her cheek.

Her heart did that forward roll thing again. And Carrie knew for certain she had truly fallen for him – she had from the very beginning.

'I'll try not to surprise you again,' he smiled. 'I'll send you a note to the station or something. OK?'

Carrie nodded, so full of feelings she was unable to speak.

'OK. Goodnight, then.'

'Goodnight.'

Her voice came out as a whisper.

He gave a little regretful lift of his shoulders, raised his hand in a half wave and took a couple of steps off. Then he said, 'Oh, what the heck!'

He stepped back in, leaned down, and kissed her on the mouth.

Chapter Eight

Carrie got home somehow, relieved to find her dad was out on his rounds and her mum was switching off lights and damping down the fire, about to go to bed. Mary was helping more in the shop now, and it was tiring for her.

'You've had something to eat, I hope?' she said, gathering her knitting. The WI and the WVS had issued a call for socks, gloves and balaclavas for the troops.

'Um, yes, I have, thanks.'

It wasn't a complete lie. The barman had provided them with a dish of peanuts.

'Good, 'cos your dad had your bit of haddock. We decided it wouldn't keep. There's the usual bread, cheese and ham, if you're peckish,' smiled Mary. 'And ginger cake in the tin.'

'Thanks, Mum. I'll stay down here for a bit anyway. I'm not that tired. Night night.'

Mary disappeared upstairs and Carrie dropped into a chair. There was no point going to bed – she was far too excited to sleep. Her head and her body were full of Mike's face, his smile, his laugh, and most of all, the touch of his lips on hers.

Carrie had been kissed before, of course – Cyril from the barber's had tried to get fresh on several occasions. But she'd never experienced anything like the firm but gentle touch of Mike's mouth, or the warm, melting feeling it gave her. She closed her eyes and let the warm wave wash over her.

She was still in a dream the next day as she opened up the stall, unable to keep the idiotic smile off her face. Mike wanted to see her again! He was coming especially! He must like her!

The guard on the mail train saw the difference in her when he dropped off the papers.

'Blimey, can I have some of what you're taking? You look like you've lost a penny and found a pound.'

'Sixpence, actually,' Carrie smiled.

A sixpence that was worth a thousand guineas.

She hummed as she arranged the newspapers and set out the new editions of magazines. She tidied the books in the carousel and dusted the romances with a new reverence: could she be embarking on a romance of her own?

Her good humour only vanished when, once the early commuters had departed but the mid-morning rush in the tearoom hadn't begun, she saw Bette coming over. Carrie had been looking forward to sharing her good news with her friend, but the look on the other woman's face wiped the thought clean from her mind. Bette had aged ten years overnight.

'Bette! What on earth's the matter?'

Bette shook her head, her lips compressed.

'Oh, Carrie – he's been called up! My Eric!'

'Oh no!'

Carrie knew how Bette had been counting on Eric being

spared the call-up. Jack the ticket collector was excused on account of his gammy leg, and Brockington Junction's relief porter had signed up of his own volition, but jobs on the railway were supposed to be reserved occupations. Not all of them, it seemed.

Bette produced a hankie from her sleeve and dabbed her eyes.

'I haven't slept a wink!' she sniffed.

You and me both, thought Carrie, though for different reasons.

'And do you know what Mr High-and-Mighty Bayliss said to him just now when Eric told him?' Bette didn't wait for an answer. '"Well, I hope you'll be replaced!" That's the best he could do, after all Eric's done for this station, staying late, planting out Bayliss's precious pelargoniums in the summer, sweeping the leaves when he needn't bother, acting as ticket collector when idle Jack takes an extra ten minutes on his tea break, claiming his leg's giving him gyp . . .'

Carrie would have tutted in sympathy, but you couldn't put a wafer between the words.

'And now my Eric's going off to fight for King and country,' Bette went on, 'and that's all the thanks he gets!'

Carrie came out from behind the counter and put her arm around the older woman's shoulders. Bette sagged against her.

'I do understand, Bette. My mum felt – well, feels – just the same about Johnnie joining up.'

Though at least Johnnie's boss had patted him on the back and praised him, and said he'd keep his job open for him after the war, if it was humanly possible.

'I dunno,' sighed Bette. 'If this invasion they're talking about happens, and that Hitler feller dares show his face here, I'd stick it to him, I really would.'

The idea that the Führer might stop off in Brockington on his way to Buckingham Palace was a little fanciful, but Bette needed comforting, not contradiction.

'You and me both,' swore Carrie.

It was November now, but there'd still been surprisingly little action on the battlefront in Europe so far. People were sarcastically calling it the Bore War, and a lot of mothers had fetched their evacuated children back home. But Adolf Hitler had quite enough on the charge sheet already in Carrie's view, thinking of the land grabs, the senseless attacks on Jews and anyone else he didn't approve of, Kristallnacht and the burning of books.

'We could pelt him with rock buns, couldn't we?' she suggested.

'A waste of good food,' retorted Bette. 'Stuff from the pig bin, I say. And there's plenty of umbrellas in Lost Property to give him a good hiding.'

Just then, Ruby called from the door of the tearoom that the Lipton's tea rep was on the phone, and with a sigh, Bette hurried off. Carrie went back behind the counter just as Eric materialised like a genie from a magic lantern. He must have been listening from the cleaning cupboard.

'Sorry about that,' he said. 'Mum's taken it badly.'

'She'll get over it, Eric, don't worry,' Carrie soothed. 'She'll be proud of you in the end, you'll see. Once you're in uniform, she'll have your photo up in the tearoom next to the one of the King!'

'Blimey, I hope not.' Eric blushed. 'But Carrie, when I go . . . will you keep an eye on her? Buck her up if she needs it? I know it's a lot to ask . . .'

'It's not, Eric, it's nothing! Of course I will.'

'Thanks. You're a pal.'

Thankfully, Eric's seeming crush on Carrie hadn't developed into him asking her out, possibly because he was simply too shy to do anything about it. She was relieved: she hadn't wanted any awkwardness between the two of them, or between her and Bette. And now he was going away anyhow, he seemed quite content with her friendship.

He was a such a nice, quiet lad, a gentle giant really, thought Carrie as he wandered off. Mike had said last night that the army's mission was to turn boys into men and men into fighting men. Privately, Carrie wished them luck with Eric.

A whole fortnight went past and, in early December, Eric departed for his training camp near Northampton. Carrie besieged Mr Bayliss's office daily, but there was no note for her from Mike, only invoices from the wholesalers and the usual buff envelope containing government bumf that everyone was already complaining about. The Salvation Army band came to play carols for the evening commuters. Mr Parfitt delivered some special Christmas titles and checked Carrie had enough Penguins in stock to last her into the New Year – he was, he said, taking time off to visit his sister in Yorkshire. New posters arrived for the station, urging men to join up and women to volunteer for the ATS, the WAAF, the WRNS, air raid patrols or the Women's Voluntary Service.

Carrie felt a pang of guilt. She ought to be using her evenings more profitably than going over her meeting with Mike for the millionth time and wondering when – or if – she'd hear from him again. She'd felt a real connection with him that first evening, and he'd seemed so sincere about seeing her again, but now all her doubts resurfaced. Had she been kidding herself? Whatever he'd said about his parents' shop, it sounded a rather bigger concern than Anderson's Newsagent & Stationer. And whatever he'd said about the fluke of good fortune that had got him into his position in the army, he was an officer, for goodness' sake, mixing with other officers and equivalent ranks in the ATS, with brighter, smarter girls who'd had a good education or had even been to university. He was older than she was, and so good-looking, so confident – postively dashing. Could he really care about her in the way he'd seemed to – the way she thought and hoped? But still she couldn't stop thinking about him. She'd never felt like this about anyone before – surely he'd felt it too?

She felt guilty about another thing as well. She'd still not told her mum or dad the truth about her evening at the Station Hotel, but as the days passed without a word from Mike, she was glad. Her dad would have been giving her sidelong looks, and her mum would surely have asked outright if she'd heard anything from him. Carrie just prayed Mary didn't meet Evie's mum at the grocer's and say anything out of turn.

She pulled herself together. Uncle Charlie would be along in a bit – it was his afternoon for calling and she didn't want him to find her mooning about. He'd only tease her, and he'd be right – she was no better than Ruby and her fantasies about Hollywood film stars. And at the weekend there was something to look forward to – Johnnie's initial training was over and on Sunday he was coming home on a forty-eight-hour pass!

Even without today's excitement of her twin being home, Sunday had become Carrie's favourite day of the week. In her previous life she'd had to get up and help in the shop; now that her dad had Terry, she could luxuriate in bed till at least eight o'clock. After breakfast, and promising she'd be home in time to help with dinner – there was a joint, in honour of Johnnie's leave – Carrie decided to pass the time by cycling out towards Petts Wood, one of her favourite places locally.

It was one of those bright, crisp December days, and the thrum of the wheels on the lanes, the lungfuls of fresh air, and the dappled sunlight through the bare trees when she got there would be restful for her mind and body after the daily dose of dirt, grit and bustle at the station. The fresh air would do her good and blow away the cobwebs – maybe even what had clearly been her ridiculous fantasies about Lieutenant Mike Hudson.

Back at the shop, the early-morning rush was over. Norman was totting up how much he was owed in overdue paper bills, while Terry, a gobstopper bulging in his cheek, was counting off balls of string and gummed labels against a stock sheet. The shop doorbell jangled and a customer, young, in uniform, came in. Norman looked up.

'Good morning. Can I help you?'

'Blimey!' Terry dropped his clipboard with a clatter. 'Let's see – oh, no holster. You ain't got your revolver with yer!'

'I didn't think I'd need it,' smiled the customer.

'Terry!' Norman hissed. And then: 'I'm sorry, sir—'

'No, don't be. It's quite all right.'

But Terry had clamped himself to the visitor's side.

'What's that ribbon for? You got medals?'

'Terry! Let the gentleman get into the shop.'

Terry reluctantly stepped aside and the man took a couple of paces, which was all it took to reach the counter.

'I hope I'm in the right place,' he said. 'Are you Mr Anderson?' He held out his hand. 'Pleased to meet you, sir.'

'Er, likewise.'

Nonplussed, Norman held out his hand too. An officer, come to the shop, pleased to meet him? Him, Private Anderson, RASC S/068961 in the Great War? And calling him 'sir'?

'I'm Michael Hudson,' the officer said by way of explanation, sounding as if this shouldn't be a total surprise. 'Mike. I'm a friend of Carrie's.'

'Oh!'

Terry couldn't contain himself any longer.

'Are yer? Wow! Can I try your cap?'

Norman winced. Now there was no school, there was no nit nurse and Terry had been scratching like mad the last couple of days. He opened his mouth to intervene when there was a rush of air as someone clattered through the bead curtain that separated the shop from their living quarters.

'Norman! Norman! Guess who's here? He came in round the back – he's early!'

Norman turned to find Mary behind him, and behind her . . .

'Johnnie!' Terry, who had a severe case of hero-worship, flung himself round the counter, grabbed Johnnie's arm, then flung himself round again with a jabbing finger. 'This 'ere's Mike! He's Carrie's boyfriend!'

Mary gaped, Johnnie grinned, Mike laughed and Private Norman Anderson, feeling that despite the presence of a senior officer, this was after all his territory, said:

'I reckon I could close up a bit early. Shall we go through?'

It was after half past twelve when Carrie got back, flushed but happy, restored by her cycle ride and the beauties of nature. As she put her bike away in the outhouse, she could hear voices and laughter inside. Johnnie must be home already! But there was another male voice too, and it wasn't her dad's.

Johnnie must have brought someone with him. Drat! She'd been so looking forward to having him to herself. If she was going to tell anyone about her evening with Mike Hudson, it would have been him. Then she pushed down her disappointment. How selfish of her, and how typically generous of Johnnie. Maybe some RAF pal of his had no family and nowhere to go on his leave – there were lots of Polish airmen already in the country, for instance. Well, he'd come to the right place. They'd make him welcome!

Snatching off her beret, she hurried into the house. She was so keen to see her brother that although she could smell meat cooking and hear the potatoes sizzling in the oven, she didn't even think it odd that the carrots were on the draining board unscrubbed and the cabbage was still waiting to be shredded, let alone stop to check her appearance in the little mirror that hung on a nail by the back door. Instead, she opened the door to the back room to see three men clutching beer glasses, and her mother with a lemonade. A very merry party, including—

'Mike!'

He got to his feet with the smile she remembered so well, that she'd last seen as he'd waved her goodbye that evening, and which she'd tried to recreate so many times in her memory.

'Hello, Carrie.'

She should have been thrilled, and she was, but above all she was surprised, wrong-footed, and because of that she said the first thing that came into her head.

'Well, you're a fine one. You said you'd let me know! I wish you'd stop popping up like a jack-in-a-box!'

'Carrie!' It was Mary, shocked. But Mike laughed.

'She's got every right, Mrs Anderson. I've been very poor at keeping in touch.'

'You can say that again!'

'I can explain—'

'Oh, yes? What were they training you in this time? Not communications, obviously!'

Johnnie cleared his throat.

'Do you think you two had better take this outside? And I don't know about everyone else, but I could do with something to eat sometime today.'

Mary leapt up, all of a flurry.

'What am I thinking! I've got the Yorkshires to put in and everything!'

'You will stay, won't you, Mike?' Johnnie asked. 'I want to hear all about . . .' he lowered his voice '. . . what you were saying before, when Mum and Dad were getting the drinks.'

'Well . . .' Mike looked awkward, but only slightly. 'I'd love to, if it's not an imposition.' Then he added mischievously: 'And if that's all right with Carrie, of course.'

Chapter Nine

Lunch was over and Carrie and Mike had escaped for a walk. She was certainly getting her ration of fresh air today! He offered her his arm, and after a pretty feeble stab at feigning reluctance – wonderful as it was to see him, she still hadn't quite forgiven him for taking her by surprise – she took it. Mike smiled down at her. Carrie felt the now familiar tumbling of her insides, but she was still Carrie enough to say: 'I meant what I said, you know. You've got to stop doing this – turning up out of the blue!'

'I'm sorry and now we're on our own, I can explain.' His mouth twitched as if he was trying to suppress a smile. 'I might wish you'd thought enough of me to mention me to your folks, though!'

Cheeky thing! Carrie wasn't having that.

'What was there to mention? I'd only met you twice, and one of those was as a customer!'

And I'd only kissed you once, she thought – not that she hadn't relived it several times . . .

'Look . . .'

They were in the park – there was nowhere else to go. The benches had been taken away so that their iron arms and fixings could be melted down for armaments and the wooden seats used in construction. Half the grass had been turned over to allotments. The flower beds, usually bright with winter pansies, were bare. Mike stopped by a clump of laurel and turned to face her.

'I'll tell you what I told Johnnie on the quiet – he'd probably tell you anyway. He seems a great bloke, by the way.'

From the way Mike and her brother had talked over Sunday dinner, Carrie had seen for herself that they'd hit it off. She was pleased, of course. She didn't need Johnnie's approval, but she always hoped she'd get it, for anything from a new hat to a new . . . boyfriend? She certainly hoped so. Even so, she gave Mike a look that said: This had better be good.

'OK,' he began. 'After our evening, I went back to camp. If you must know, I was pretty chuffed. I couldn't wait to see you again. But the next day, no warning, I got packed off with my unit.'

Pretty chuffed! Couldn't wait! The afternoon was getting chillier, dampness rising from the ground now the sun was going down, but his words warmed Carrie from the inside out.

'No warning . . .' she echoed.

'None,' he shrugged. 'I'm sorry, Carrie, but we're at war and that's how it is. You wait around for ninety-nine per cent of the time, but when it's action stations, you jump to it. We had orders from HQ to deploy straight away, right up to the wilds. In Scotland.'

'Scotland!'

That was where Johnnie was going next, he'd revealed, to start his elementary flying training. He'd passed his initial training with a distinction – of course he had. But Mike was speaking again.

'I can't tell you where I was, what I was doing, or why,' he went on, 'but trust me, we were so far from civilisation there was no way of getting any post in or out. Anyway, the whole point of the exercise was being completely cut off without any communication.'

'I see.'

And she did – now. Carrie had appreciated from the first that the country was at war; you couldn't miss it: gas masks, sandbags, tin hats, notices in the shops already warning of shortages. But she realised now that she'd only appreciated it from a civilian's point of view. She hadn't really considered what it was like to be a soldier – or sailor or airman, come to that.

'We only got back yesterday,' Mike went on. 'Today's the very first chance I've had to see you. I couldn't faff about writing to try to fix a date, then waiting for the reply. I suppose I should have phoned, I could have found out the number, but . . .'

He looked so like a little boy pleading for forgiveness for kicking his football through a window that Carrie had to smile, and Mike seemed to take encouragement from it. He blurted out: 'I just . . . came. I wanted to see you so much and I wanted to make the most of it, the whole day.' He paused and his eyes held hers. 'You do believe me, don't you?'

She believed him; after that declaration, and that look, how could she not? He liked her that much! She put her hand on his arm. He'd been so open and honest, it was time for her to be the same.

'Oh, Mike. I'm sorry too. I should have thought of that, and I should have trusted you. But when time went by and

I didn't hear a word, I felt I was just making excuses for you, and I'm afraid I . . .' She tailed off. 'I thought I must have got things wrong, misread the signals, that you didn't like me after all. And I sort of gave up.'

'*Me* not like *you*? You mustn't think that! I was desperate to see you again. You mustn't do that, Carrie. You mustn't give up on me, ever!'

He spoke with an urgency she wasn't expecting.

'No. All right,' she stammered. 'I won't.'

'Good.'

Then suddenly she was in his arms and he was kissing her again. Her arms went up around his neck and she felt the buttons on his tunic pressing against her. From his perch in the laurel, a robin watched them with his bead-bright eyes. Then, with a chirrup and a rustle of leaves, he flew off to find his mate.

'Well, he seemed like a perfectly nice lad to me.'

Mike had offered to help, several times, but he and Carrie had been excused from the washing-up and shooed off for their walk. Instead, Norman was having to forego his usual Sunday-afternoon 'read of the paper' – in other words, a quick forty winks – to lend a hand in the kitchen.

'But an officer, Norm!'

Mary, wrist-deep in suds, half turned to her husband.

'He explained all that, love, didn't he?' Norman replied reasonably, wiping a plate. 'The rich auntie putting him through a posh school and everything. It's not like he was born with a silver spoon.'

'No, all right, but in that case, why didn't she tell us about him? You don't think Carrie's ashamed of us, do you?'

'Our Carrie? Come off it. Don't you know her better than that? And like she told us in here on the QT, she'd only met him a couple of times – she didn't know if it was going to come to anything.'

'Even so . . .'

'Even so what?' Johnnie, who'd been upstairs unpacking, came into the scullery.

'Nothing,' Norman shrugged. 'Your mother's quite happy – she's found something to worry about!'

'What? Oh, Mum, not my flying training?'

Norman gave a bark of laughter.

'No, she's past worrying about you – sorry, son. Just 'cos Carrie's new bloke's had one Sunday dinner with us, she's off in her head buying a new hat, Mike's made up to a five-star general and Carrie's turned into Lady Kiss-Me-Quick, too above herself to bother with us ever again!'

'Norman! I never said any such thing.'

'It's what you were thinking, though, isn't it?' Norman gave his wife an affectionate squeeze round the middle. 'When you should just be glad he called on a Sunday and you'd got your best frock on and the lace tablecloth laid!'

'Exactly.' Johnnie took the dried plate from his father and slotted it in the rack. 'Mum, you've got to realise, if this war does one thing, it's going to throw us all together with the kinds of people we might otherwise never have met. I'm mixing with all sorts now. And if you ask me, that's a very good thing.'

Mary scrubbed determinedly at the roasting tin with a scrap of wire wool.

'It's all right for you young people. You like change. When you get to my age, all you want is for things to stay the same.'

Johnnie glanced at his dad: both had picked up the tell-tale catch in Mary's voice. He softened his tone.

'Well, I'm sorry, but there's a certain person in Germany who doesn't seem to agree. If Carrie likes Mike, and you don't need night sights to see he's pretty struck on her, that's good enough for me. Can't it be for you?'

'I want her to be happy, of course – that's why I worry!'

'Well, don't,' chided Norman. 'Just let 'em take every day as it comes. That's all any of us can do right now.'

'Dad's right, Mum,' Johnnie added. 'Mike seemed a pretty decent bloke, not the sort to break her heart.'

'I never said he wasn't—'

'Then we all agree,' said Johnnie, as his mother propped the roasting tin on the draining board. 'And by the way, when I pass my pilot training – and sorry, but that's when, not if, as far as I'm concerned – I'll be an officer myself. Pilot Officer Anderson. So you'd better get used to saluting the pair of us!'

Carrie had always thought of herself as a happy person. She had a comfy home, a loving family, friends. She'd sailed through school, bright enough but never picked on as a swot. She'd never had the spots that plagued some girls like poor Ruby; instead, she had, golden-brown hair with a natural wave, long legs and a trim figure. She hadn't been unhappy working at Boots or in the family shop, and she loved the bookstall . . .

But now there was Mike, Carrie realised that she hadn't known what happiness was. Or if she had, it had been more the absence of unhappiness, whereas now ... Well, it sounded stupid and schmaltzy, but she felt as though she'd stepped from a black-and-white British B-film into a Hollywood picture in Technicolor.

Everything was heightened: the song of a blackbird in a leafless tree, the lacy patterns of frost on the pavements, the sugar crust on Bette's apple turnovers. She knew she was going around with a silly grin on her face and she didn't care a jot. Nor did she care that, in the winter weather, she'd had to abandon her idea of smart business dress for a vest, a cut-down flannel shirt of her dad's, two jumpers, and a coat. She'd also taken to wearing thick, worsted stockings under her skirt, plus fingerless gloves and the boots she'd cursed on that first evening with Mike.

'I can hardly get my arms round you!' he laughed when he met her at the end of the day – because now they had evening after evening together.

He was stationed at Caterham 'for the foreseeable', he said. Carrie didn't want to see too far ahead anyway. She missed Mike enough on the days they were apart – and he was only stationed down the road. She knew that one day she'd have to bear a longer and further-flung parting, but for now, she pushed the thought to the back of her mind. Why think about the future when the present was so good? Mike usually managed a pass out one or two evenings a week, and, when he could, a day pass on Sundays. The army appreciated that in him: most men needed a full twenty-four or forty-eight-hour pass to see their loved ones.

Was Carrie his 'loved one'? It certainly felt like it as they danced to 'It Had to Be You' at the Mecca Ballroom. Warm boots discarded, Carrie wore her sandals with the stretchy lurex straps, her best stockings – not a single ladder or darn – and the dress Mike liked best: midnight-blue sateen, with a diamanté buckle on the belt and a low, draped neckline.

'Let's go for a walk,' he murmured against her hair after they'd taken a couple of turns round the floor.

'I haven't got my walking shoes on,' Carrie pointed out.

Mike gave her a slow smile.

'I wasn't thinking of walking very far,' he said.

At Christmas itself he would be with his family in Leamington, but before he left, he and Carrie went for a drink at the Rose and Crown.

'I didn't know what to get you,' he said, 'so I played safe.'

He handed over a small box, and Carrie had a sudden memory of unwrapping Uncle Charlie's birthday present. Surely he must have noticed her silver bangle and hadn't bought her the same? That would be awkward!

'Shall I save it till the day?' she asked.

She'd already given him his present – a leather-bound copy of *A Christmas Carol* –which he'd opened and stowed away in his greatcoat pocket after giving her a kiss. He'd told her ages ago it was one of his favourites, but that he'd lent his copy to someone and had never got it back.

'No,' he said now. 'I want to see your face.'

So Carrie tore off the paper, lifted the lid and . . .

'Oh, Mike!'

It was a silver locket on a chain, heart-shaped and chased with the exact same ivy-leaf pattern as her bangle.

'How did you manage this – to get it exactly right?' she asked, amazed.

'Uh-uh.' He wagged his finger at her. 'Can't give away battlefield secrets.'

'Oh, go on!'

Mike grinned as he remembered the doubt, suspicion even, in Mary's voice on the phone. He'd rung in the middle of the day when he knew Carrie would be at the bookstall.

'I need your help, Mrs Anderson,' he said, explaining his plan to get Carrie a piece of jewellery for Christmas. 'I'm at a loss, to be honest. I know she has her silver bangle that she wears a lot . . . What else would she like best, do you think? Earrings? A necklace?'

Mary, touched by his appeal, melted like snow.

'That's very thoughtful of you to ask,' she said. 'Very. And I do know what she's always wanted, Mike, and that's a locket.'

Mike grabbed at the suggestion enthusiastically. 'Perfect! And hang on – do you think if I got a plain one, I could get it engraved in the same design as the bangle?'

'Oh! That would make it really special!'

Plotting together, they'd planned the gift. Mike bought the locket, then Mary sneaked him the bangle. He took it to a jeweller to copy the engraving, then hurried it back before Carrie got home and missed it. And through working together in secret, Mary had seen Mike not as an officer but for what he was – a kind, considerate young man, genuinely fond of her daughter.

'Well, OK, then, as it's you,' Mike conceded to Carrie now. He leaned in as if it really was a secret. 'I had help from a spy in the camp. Your mum gave me the bangle to get the design copied. I knew you didn't wear it to work as a rule, so we thought you wouldn't miss it provided I could get it back pronto. And you didn't!'

'And Mum never said! You sneaks!'

But Carrie was thrilled. She knew her mum had been wary around Mike, partly due to her own personality, partly because she was overawed by his rank, however much he played it down, and partly, of course, because he was a serviceman, a constant reminder of her own painful wartime experiences. Now, without even meaning to – or perhaps he had meant to, because Mike was smart enough to have noticed Mary's reserve – he had her mother well and truly onside.

She leaned forward and kissed him.

'Is that for the present?' he asked.

'Yes,' said Carrie. 'And it's also for your very impressive Fieldcraft and Tactics!'

Chapter Ten

Mike, it turned out, had been lucky to do his training in Scotland before the bad weather set in, because Johnnie was stuck up at Montrose surrounded by snowdrifts. He called them on a very bad line.

'I'm not so worried for me,' he explained on Christmas morning, 'but there are married men here who can't get home to their families.'

'What's the point of being in the RAF if you can't fly out!' Norman joked, knowing how disappointed Mary was.

'We've hardly been doing any flying, with the wind-shields iced up and the fuel freezing in the tanks.'

Johnnie sounded more fed up about that than missing Christmas with his family, and no wonder. It sounded as if they were making the best of things. The men had been given a double rum ration with breakfast, he told them, and in the background they could hear 'God Rest Ye Merry, Gentlemen' being belted out to a piano accompaniment. The men stuck up there were obviously keeping their voices well lubricated – and it was only eleven o'clock.

So Carrie spent the day with her mum and dad, opening presents, having her locket admired, peeling potatoes, pulling crackers, and in the afternoon, after listening to the King's broadcast to the Empire, popping round to see Bette and

Eric. She'd hardly ever seen Bette out of her work uniform of navy or black with comfortable lace-up shoes, but today she was resplendent in a dress of red panne velvet, sheer stockings and dainty black court shoes with a pom-pom on the front. Carrie could see that without her usual thick lisle stockings and sensible shoes, Bette actually had very dainty feet.

'Didn't he do well, bless him,' said Bette, who'd also been listening to the King. 'He got better, didn't he, after those great long pauses at the start, trying to get over that stammer of his, but, ooh, I did feel for him! Now, Carrie, will you have a mince pie, a slice of Yule log or a piece of my Christmas cake? I've been feeding it brandy for over a month!'

Carrie, still full from Christmas dinner, accepted a small piece of Yule log – Bette's Christmas cake sounded dangerously alcoholic and Carrie was on her bike. Eric, ensconced by the fire, was already wolfing down an enormous slice.

'Aren't they feeding you, Eric?' Carrie asked innocently. She could see that Eric, previously a strip of wind despite his mother's cooking, had filled out since joining the army.

'All muscle, this is,' Eric claimed, flexing his arms. 'Feel my biceps!'

'I can see them from here,' Carrie demurred, and it was true that Eric's formerly puny arms did seem a bit beefier.

'You should hear what they've put him through,' Bette fretted. 'Six-mile runs with a pack, scrambling through nets and over walls . . .'

'And I know all the best places to bayonet the enemy—' Eric began.

'Not while Carrie's eating, love,' Bette chided. 'But tell her your news, Eric!'

'What? Oh, yeah. I've got my posting!'

'He's going to be attached to the 46th Infantry Division!' Bette leapt in proudly.

'Oh. Er, good!' Carrie didn't know what response was expected. 'Is it good?'

'Yes!' cried Bette triumphantly. 'Because he won't be going anywhere! Twelve months' training and preparation they've got, apparently.'

'At most I'll likely be on guard duty somewhere,' Eric added. 'Fetching and carrying, manning a barrier, checking passes, supervising a queue—'

'Exactly what he's been doing at the station!' Bette chimed in. 'With better pay and a warmer uniform – and no sergeant major can be worse than old bossyboots Bayliss. Do you know, getting called up could be the best thing that ever happened to my Eric – the war could be over before he's even needed!'

Carrie smiled to herself. That was choice, coming from Bette, who'd been so distraught at Eric going in the first place. But she was glad about her friend's obvious relief.

Eric seemed pretty puffed up with his newly acquired knowledge too.

'Come on,' he said, stuffing the rest of his cake in his mouth and hauling Carrie to her feet. 'I'll show you where to aim for in hand-to-hand combat!'

'No, thanks – when am I going to need that?' Carrie protested.

'Shoplifters,' said Eric firmly. 'Anyway, it's heart, stomach, kidneys. You give 'em what for, Carrie!'

*

The snow that had marooned Johnnie in Scotland soon made its way south. Now that she was less worried about Eric, Bette transferred her motherly concern to Carrie, plying her with mugs of tea and Bovril at hourly intervals, while Uncle Charlie urged Carrie to take some time off.

'Make the most of your young man while he's still here,' he said with a wink. 'Gather ye rosebuds, and all that!'

'In winter?' teased Carrie.

'Hips and haws then,' Charlie conceded.

'Doesn't Des need you at the garage?' Carrie asked. 'I don't want to take you away from that.'

Uncle Charlie pursed his lips.

'It's pretty quiet,' he admitted. 'Who's going to buy a car when Ye Olde Pub's sandbagged and the beaches are covered in barbed wire? Plus, you can't exactly take a run down to Monte come summer, can you? And now your motorist's got to eke out every drop of petrol, well . . .'

'I should be paying you back,' Carrie fretted, but Charlie waved the suggestion away.

'Don't you worry about me,' he said airily, puffing on an imaginary cigar. 'I've got a few irons in the fire and I'm in this for the long haul. You're my pension, girl!'

At this point, Mr Bayliss bustled up and nodded to Charlie. He approved of his presence. Despite the station master's weakness for a pretty face when it came to the travelling public, it confirmed his long-held suspicion that a 'slip of a girl' could never manage the bookstall on her own. But then Mr Bayliss didn't know Carrie!

'I've received some good news,' he announced importantly.

'I won't get my full complement of portering staff back in the foreseeable future . . .'

'Full complement' thought Carrie, suppressing a smile – all two of them! Honestly, did the pompous old twit ever listen to himself?

'. . . but,' the stationmaster continued, 'they're finally sending me one replacement anyway. We're to expect a certain P. Edwards in the next couple of days.'

With that, he bustled off again to shoo away a pair of pigeons having a tug of war over a dropped chip.

Carrie wondered who P. Edwards might be, and why Mr Bayliss had sounded so pleased about it. If he thought about it for a moment, it could only be someone medically unfit or even a conscientious objector, if they weren't all on ambulance duty, waiting for the air raids that still hadn't happened.

But as Bette remarked when she heard the news: 'Like I used to say to my Eric when he asked about pudding: "It's wait and see"!'

A couple of days later, Carrie looked up from her midday tot-up of takings to find a pair of frank brown eyes surveying her and her stock.

'Hello – a bookstall! That's a bonus!'

Carrie put aside her calculations.

'Yes – can I help you? Are you looking for any title in particular?'

'I'm looking for a Mr Bayliss, actually,' came the reply. 'The stationmaster? I've been told to report to him.'

'Hang on . . .' Carrie's thoughts were tumbling like a tombola drum. 'You're not . . . you can't be – you're not the new porter?'

'I certainly am!' The girl on the other side of the counter smiled and held out her hand. 'Penny Edwards.'

'Well!' Carrie took in the girl's dark hair, tip-tilted nose and rather determined mouth. Then she shook the proffered hand and introduced herself, adding: 'Pleased to meet you.'

It's more than Mr Bayliss will be, she thought.

She leaned over the counter and pointed down the platform. 'His office is down there, just past the tearoom.'

'Thanks!' said Penny cheerily. 'I'm hoping he'll have a uniform for me. I've had to improvise. What d'you think?'

She was wearing thick corduroy trousers, a checked Viyella shirt, knitted tie, pullover and what looked like a man's tweed jacket.

'I'm sure he'll find you something,' hazarded Carrie, thinking that Eric's uniform would be about six inches too long in the leg and the jacket would hang off this rather slight girl like something you'd see on a scarecrow. 'Um, can I ask – you volunteered for this, did you?'

'Yup!' Penny nodded. 'Didn't fancy the Land Army, a factory or the services, but I wanted to be useful.'

'Right . . . Are you local?'

She didn't seem to have any kind of accent that Carrie could place.

'I'm from Norfolk originally,' offered Penny. 'But I've moved about a bit lately.'

'And you've landed here. Welcome to Brockington!'

'I'm looking forward to it,' Penny smiled. 'A fresh— Well, new faces, a new place, a new challenge and all that.'

It'll be that all right, Carrie thought, as she saw a familiar form strutting down the platform.

'Here's Mr Bayliss now,' she said, sneakily delighted to have a ringside seat for this encounter. Penny wheeled round. As Mr Bayliss approached, she confidently held out her hand.

'Penny Edwards, sir, your new porter, reporting for duty!'

Carrie had the blissful experience of seeing Mr Bayliss's face turn from red to purple, then back to mere magenta. He actually had to loosen his collar.

'A . . . You? You? They've sent me a girl?' he spluttered.

Penny squared her shoulders and her head went up.

'To quote someone rather grander than me, Mr Bayliss,' she began, 'I may have the body of a woman – I won't say a weak and feeble woman, because I don't believe women are either of those things . . .'

Mr Bayliss blinked. Carrie bit her lip to stop herself from laughing. Penny was quoting Queen Elizabeth I, she recalled from her history lessons. You tell him, she thought, the pompous old windbag.

'I may have the body of a woman,' Penny went on, 'but I have the heart and stomach of a man – and an appetite for work. If you find me lacking, you're welcome to ask to have me moved, but I don't plan to give you any cause to do that. Now, I was wondering, do you have a uniform for me?'

'Mr Bayliss still doesn't know what to make of her. She's really shaken things up around here!'

Reluctantly, and after several phone calls of protest to his superiors, Mr Bayliss had had to wave a white flag. He also handed over Eric's old uniform, telling Penny sternly she was not to alter it, as the minute his regular porter was released from the army, he'd be needing it back. Penny had had the good sense not to argue: she merely rolled the trouser bottoms up several inches and belted the jacket tight. She lined Eric's greasy old cap with a handkerchief and set it on her thatch of curly hair, so dark it was almost black.

Now, a couple of weeks later, Carrie and Bette were watching from the window of the tearoom as Penny spread grit on the down platform ahead of the evening commuters' return.

'It's a funny business, if you ask me, though,' Bette said. 'Why would any girl want to do a hard, dirty job like that? Lugging people's cases, manhandling drunks, doing all the manual work . . .'

Carrie found herself leaping to Penny's defence.

'I admire her for it,' she said. 'She's got a lot of grit, in more ways than one!'

'Don't make much of herself, does she?' Ruby, who was passing with a tray of salt and pepper pots, butted in, uninvited. 'Looks like she's cut her hair with a hacksaw. You wouldn't catch me going around looking like that.' She patted her own brassy hair, permed within an inch of its life and set off today with vivid blue eyeshadow. 'And she bites her nails.'

'It's not a crime, Ruby,' said Carrie mildly, but Ruby sniffed and went on her way.

Carrie went back to the bookstall. Uncle Charlie had a date and he wanted to get off in good time for a wash and brush-up. Carrie would have liked to know more about her uncle's private life, but it didn't seem appropriate to ask. Anyway, she had a date herself: Mike was coming to walk her home.

After tea, they were going to the Rialto to see *Honeymoon in Bali*. Mike had rolled his eyes at the prospect – 'If this gets out to the men, I'm done for!' – but it was Carrie's turn to choose.

'It's not a soppy romance, it's a romantic comedy,' she stressed. 'And I did sit through your choice last time.'

It had been a creepy horror called *The Face at the Window*, but Carrie strongly suspected Mike had only picked it so she'd spend the entire time with her head burrowed into his chest.

Penny had moved across and was gritting the up platform now. Passengers who planned to spend the evening in London were drifting in to wait for their train, despite the miserable weather and the fast-fading light. Mike arrived and began to help Carrie close up, carrying the carousel of Penguins round to lock it inside the stall for the night.

Suddenly, there was a squeal from further down the platform.

'My handbag! Stop, thief! Stop him, someone!'

Carrie hurried out round the counter. Mike dropped the carousel with a thud, but it was Penny who moved the fastest. Seeing the hysterical woman pointing shakily into the distance, she sprinted along the platform and past the bookstall. The bag-snatcher was obviously intending to vault the low fence into the matted shrubs that lay beyond and make his getaway.

'Oy, you!' Penny called. 'Stop!'

She was a nifty runner: she'd almost caught up when the thief, a scrawny creature obviously stronger than he looked, turned and gave her a vicious shove. Carrie gasped as Penny went down, her head hitting the wall of the Lost Property Office. But Mike, hot on Penny's heels, leapt nimbly over her and, reaching for the thief, brought him crashing down in a rugby tackle. Mr Bayliss panted up. He'd missed the action as usual, but was, also as usual, keen to be in on the act and, no doubt, claim the credit for himself.

The would-be thief was wriggling and cursing in Mike's grip, but Carrie wasn't bothered about him, or the woman passenger who was tearfully thanking Mike and collecting the scattered contents of her bag.

Carrie knelt by Penny and helped her to sit up. She looked dazed.

'Penny? Are you all right?'

Penny gulped.

'Yes . . . I think so. Feel a bit sick, that's all.'

'Of course you do. You shouldn't have gone after him like that—' Carrie checked herself. 'Anyway, it's all right. Mike got him.'

Penny closed her eyes. 'Did he?'

Then she blacked out.

Chapter Eleven

Honeymoon in Bali would have to wait for another night. Someone called the police and an ambulance, which took Penny, accompanied by Carrie, to the infirmary. Along with the thief and the woman whose handbag it was, Mike was whisked off to the police station to give a statement.

The doctor who examined Penny was old and looked tired; most of the young doctors had swiftly joined up or been called up to tend the expected battlefield casualties. But he knew his stuff and after various tests, he led Penny back to where Carrie was waiting.

'You're an extremely lucky young woman,' he scolded. 'You could have cracked your skull.'

'Well, I didn't,' Penny replied, rather curtly, Carrie thought. 'May I go now?'

'I can't keep you here against your will,' the doctor said mildly. 'Though I'd prefer it if you weren't alone tonight. Do you live with family?'

'No. I'm in lodgings.'

'Ah.'

He didn't even have to look at Carrie.

'She can come home with me,' she said quickly.

'There's no need—' Penny began.

'Yes, there is,' Carrie insisted. 'You might suddenly feel dizzy, or be sick – you need to be with people.'

'Your friend's talking sense.' The doctor sounded relieved. 'On that basis, I'm happy to discharge you, Miss Edwards.'

Penny was left with little choice as Carrie insisted on a taxi home. She'd phoned her parents while Penny was being examined, so Mary had already changed the sheets and put a hot bottle in Johnnie's bed. Penny didn't want anything to eat, which Mary said was probably wise, so Carrie led her upstairs.

Penny seemed to be feeling the after-effects now and sat down with some relief on the bed.

'I'm sorry about the decor.' Carrie indicated the model aeroplanes hanging from the ceiling. 'But I don't think you'll see much of it. You look done in.'

'I'm fine,' said Penny, but she wasn't even convincing herself.

'You are not,' said Carrie. 'I'll help you undress.'

Penny didn't raise any further objections, so Carrie untied the laces of Penny's brogues, easing off her thick socks. She took the clothes off her top half, then helped Penny to stand while she undid her trouser buttons and let them drop to the floor. Underneath her vest, which she also peeled off, Carrie was surprised to see that Penny was wearing beautiful peach camiknickers in what was obviously real silk.

It was the first time Carrie had seen Penny display any femininity. She was even more surprised to see that the underwear was embroidered over one breast with the initials 'P.E.' The letters looked to have been done by machine or perhaps by a professional hand, at a dressmaker's. They certainly hadn't been hand-embroidered amateurishly at home.

'I'll get in like this,' Penny said. 'I just want to go to sleep.'

'Of course.' Carrie peeled back the covers. And added: 'I'm not surprised you don't want to take off your camiknicks. They're lovely.'

'What? Oh, these.'

'And monogrammed too!'

Penny frowned.

'Your initials,' Carrie explained.

'Hmm?' Penny was lying down now, but her fingers went to the letters over her breast. 'Oh . . . yes. They're not my initials, though. I mean, they are, but . . . it's just from a rummage sale. Lucky find.'

'Really? Huh, take me with you next time, will you?' smiled Carrie. 'I only ever find moth-eaten pullovers and odd socks.'

Penny closed her eyes. The little bedside lamp on its barley-twist stand wasn't bright, but the light must have been paining her.

'I'll put it out,' Carrie said, reaching for the switch on its cord. 'And look, Penny, I'm only next door. If you want anything in the night, just knock on the wall.'

It was what she and Johnnie had done as children, developing a code all of their own – their own twin language. Two knocks for 'Are you awake?', three for 'Come in, I've got something to tell you!' and so on.

Penny put out a hand and grasped Carrie's wrist.

'Thanks, Carrie. Thank you.'

Carrie gave her a smile and went downstairs to give her mum and dad a fuller explanation of what had happened. Later, Mike rang from the police station to apologise for their ruined evening.

'No chance of getting away,' he lamented. 'There's been a knife fight in a pub and they've got half a dozen drunks to process before they get to a petty thief. How's the patient?'

'Asleep,' Carrie confirmed.

'Best thing for her,' Mike said. 'The police can talk to her in the morning.'

Her own evening wrecked, Carrie went to bed, but she couldn't sleep, listening for the slightest sound from next door. When she didn't hear any, she worried even more – what if Penny had slipped into unconsciousness? The elementary first-aid training that Mr Bayliss had insisted on in her first week at the station was still fresh in her mind. Maybe he had his uses after all.

At midnight, unable to stand the worry any longer, she slipped out of bed and crept in to Penny. She seemed in a deep sleep, so deep she might have been unconscious, but she stirred and muttered when the telltale floorboard by the bed creaked. Carrie, reassured, could finally get some rest.

The next morning, Penny said she felt OK, apart from a splitting headache.

'And "Two Lovely Black Eyes",' Norman couldn't help commenting as they assembled for breakfast, quoting the music hall song. 'Sorry.'

'Yes, bang goes my hope of being a poster girl for the railways,' said Penny wryly. 'But I think I'll live. Thank you so much for looking after me.'

Mary, refilling her visitor's tea cup, tutted.

'You're welcome to stay as long as you like, isn't she, Carrie?'

'Of course!'

'I wouldn't dream of it. I can't expect you to use up your rations on me!'

Rationing had begun at the turn of the year: a measly four ounces a week of ham, bacon and butter per person, and twelve of sugar, which had to cover everything – sugaring drinks, sprinkling on your porridge and baking.

'Go on with you—' Mary began, but Penny was already reaching for her jacket and standing up.

'You're never coming to work?' Carrie exclaimed. 'You're going back to your digs to rest for today at least?'

'My landlady's out all day. I thought you wanted me to be with people, in case I had some sort of relapse?' Penny challenged with a grin. 'You can't have it both ways, Carrie Anderson!'

So, armed with Alka-Seltzer and aspirin from Mary's medicine cupboard ('Just in case!'), Penny walked to work with Carrie, attracting plenty of funny looks and a few ironic wolf whistles. Bette, seeing them arrive, swept Penny into the tearoom for more tea, toast and tributes, while Carrie got on with the business of collecting the papers and opening up. Only Mr Bayliss was mealy-mouthed.

'Miserable old goat!' Bette told Carrie later. 'Came into the tearoom, didn't ask how she was, just told her she should never have got involved! He's never forgiven her for being a girl and proving him wrong by being able to do the job!'

Carrie had to smile at how Bette, who'd started off

sceptical herself, had come round to Penny. She didn't even seem to mind that Penny was proving herself to be just as good a porter as Eric had been.

But then Bette was convinced that Eric's talents, whatever they might be, were bound to be recognised in the army. Not much of the promised 'training and preparation' had materialised for the 46th Infantry Division. Instead, Eric was digging ditches and building air raid shelters, but his mother was sure that after the war, it could lead him into a career as a civil engineer – or maybe even as an architectural draughtsman. Carrie and Johnnie had always bathed in the glow of their own parents' love, but Bette's devotion to Eric was something else, and very touching.

Mike arrived about midday to tell Penny that the police would be sending a constable round to take a statement.

'Haven't you told them all they need to know?' Penny asked. 'You saw it happen. You were the one who brought him down, after all.'

There was something almost resentful in her tone.

'You don't sound very pleased about it,' said Mike. 'Surely you wanted him caught?'

Penny's mouth twisted.

'I could have had him – he was inches away! I suppose you think I shouldn't have got involved, like Mr Bayliss does.'

'No, I don't think that at all.' Her reaction puzzled him. 'I think you were very brave. You could press charges for assault.'

'What? It was nothing!' Penny huffed. And then, sounding worried: 'Do you think I'll have to go to court?'

Mike shrugged.

'Unless the little rat pleads guilty, which he'd be daft not to. Why, would that be a problem? You'd get the time off.'

'Yes, I know, it's not that . . .' Penny tutted. 'Anyway, like you say, it may never happen.'

'No.'

'OK. Well, thanks for telling me,' Penny conceded. 'I'd better get on, the twelve-fifty's due.'

'Sure.'

Mike watched her go, then strolled over to the bookstall where Carrie was unpacking a box of Penguins. There were murder mysteries and war stories for the troops – three copies of *Patrol* by Philip MacDonald, for starters – as well as novels for the ladies who lunched. *Still She Wished for Company* caught Mike's eye.

'Do you wish for company?' he asked. 'Over lunch perhaps?'

Carrie pulled a face.

'You know I'd love it, Mike. But I can't get away.'

'Don't tell me – the twelve-fifty.'

'Closely followed by the one-oh-five and the one-twenty,' Carrie replied smartly.

'I reckon you go to sleep reciting the blooming time-table,' Mike tutted. 'When you should be drifting off with thoughts about me!'

'Huh!' Carrie laughed. 'Just because you nabbed a thief, you needn't get too big for your boots!'

'No chance.' Mike frowned. 'Penny didn't seem very impressed with my knight-in-shining-armour act. I thought damsels in distress were supposed to fall down in a grateful swoon when you rode to their rescue.'

'In case you haven't noticed, Penny's about as far away from a damsel, distressed or otherwise, as it's possible to be,' Carrie pointed out.

Though Penny's embroidered silk underwear, she thought, might give the lie to that.

Chapter Twelve

The winter seemed endless. Coal was rationed now, which meant that when Carrie came in chilled from work, there was only a meagre fire in the grate. The water pipes froze and the chemist ran out of chilblain cream. If there was any consolation, it was that despite the cold, Carrie couldn't have been happier running her little bookstall. Bette mothered her with mugs of hot Bovril, and Penny often wandered over with a snippet about the war she'd picked up from one of the passengers.

And, of course, in the evenings and on Sundays, unless he had a weekend leave to see his parents, there was Mike and the thrill of their romance. Carrie knew she was falling for him, in love with him, in fact, and from the way he looked at her, listened to her, laughed with her, held her and kissed her, she was sure he felt it too. She could have shouted it from the rooftops, announced it over the Tannoy at the station, seen it in huge headlines in the daily papers. But she didn't say it and neither did he; it was as if neither of them wanted to jinx it.

Following Penny's night at the Andersons', Mary had suggested that she come to tea one night a week. 'Poor girl, stuck in digs. I know how some of those landladies treat their lodgers, pinching their rations for themselves!' Carrie had warned her parents that Penny didn't seem to like talking about her family, and as long as they studiously avoided the subject, Penny was good company. In some ways, thought Carrie, it was like having Johnnie there. It wasn't just Penny's boyishly cropped hair – there was something about the teasing, almost challenging way she talked that reminded Carrie of her brother.

On other nights, they went to the pictures, or joined Mary at her WI knitting circle in the Scout hut. Penny was welcomed by the other women and girls with open arms, but Carrie was amused to see that she was clearly an even less experienced knitter than she herself was.

'This doesn't look right, does it?' Penny said despairingly one night, holding up a distinctly wonky scarf. She'd been set to knit the simplest thing possible. 'Where've I gone wrong now?'

Mary had already had to help her with dropped stitches. Carrie laid aside the balaclava she was working on. She could see the problem at once.

'Well, you've suddenly gone from plain knit stitch to stocking stitch, haven't you?' she said.

'What? Say that again in English, please,' Penny frowned.

Carrie took the scarf from her. 'It's supposed to be every row of knit stitches for a scarf. But for the last four rows, you've done a row of knit stitch, then a row of purl.'

Penny groaned. 'I wasn't thinking! At least, not about knitting. I was thinking how much I'd like a nice juicy steak. With chips cooked in goose fat, peas and maybe a grilled tomato. Some hope!'

Carrie had to laugh. It was funny to see the ever-competent Penny frustrated by something so simple.

'I suppose that means I've got to undo it. Again!' sighed Penny. 'Is it coffee time yet?'

Finally, the thaw came, and the frostiest winter for almost fifty years gave way to a tentative spring. The six inches of snow in Scotland that had frozen the sparrows and snapped the telephone wires finally melted away. Johnnie, who'd been incommunicado for days, rang home.

'Flying again, thank God!' he chirruped delightedly.

But Carrie had known he was flying again even before his call, and not from hearing the weather reports. Some people scorned the idea, or said it only applied to identical twins, but she knew she could sense whenever there was a change in her twin's circumstances. Never mind their mother's sixth sense about her children, this was a sort of seventh sense, just between Carrie and Johnnie. She thought of it as their twin telepathy.

It had started in childhood, one day in the park. They must have been seven or eight. Johnnie was off with his friends and Carrie was with hers, doing French skipping. She'd stopped suddenly in the middle of her turn, the elastic twisted around her ankles.

'Come on!' one of the other girls had urged.

But Carrie hadn't moved. It was hard to explain. The feeling hadn't come in words and it wasn't pictures; it was simply that a sort of dread had descended on her. She untangled herself from the elastic and, without a word of explanation to the others, ran off, calling Johnnie's name. She saw a knot of his friends at the foot of a huge oak tree and headed towards them.

'Carrie!' one of them called. 'It's OK. Someone's gone for your dad!'

Johnnie was lying on the ground, his face ashen. One of his arms was bent at a strange angle, Carrie noticed, the bone of his elbow sticking right out.

'I'm all right,' he whispered, seeing her shocked face.

He obviously wasn't, but her shock was really at how she'd known he wasn't.

After that, the feeling came sporadically, about good things and bad – she knew before he told her when he'd had a caning at school and when he'd got picked for the cross-country team. And though Carrie had never asked him, she knew it worked for Johnnie as well. When her poem about a butterfly had won a prize in a competition, he bought her a little enamel butterfly brooch before she'd even told him.

She'd never mentioned it to anyone, not even Johnnie; there was no need to mention it to him. And she could imagine the laughter from other people who might compare it to supposed mind readers, circus acts or music hall turns. It was much too significant for that.

At the station, troop movements continued, but by now everyone had been lulled into a sort of lethargy about the war. Lost Property was full of the gas masks that people had left on trains, and Norman, with his ARP hat on, complained that people were becoming very lackadaisical about the blackout. It was strange, Carrie thought. The initial fear and panic of the war seemed to have been reduced to petty irritations – gas masks, blackout curtains, cheese-paring rations (literally) and endless knitting. Even her mother didn't seem quite so anxious.

So when, one Sunday of pale sunshine in February, Mike told her that he'd borrowed his friend's car and was taking her for a drive in the country, Carrie was simply thrilled. She suggested her favourite Petts Wood again.

As they strolled arm in arm along the woodland paths, looking for somewhere to have their picnic, she stopped to marvel at the snowdrops poking up through the leaf mould and to listen to the birds. They clearly thought spring had arrived, darting and twittering in the branches above.

She chatted away. Mike laughed when she told him about the woman whose hat made it look as if she had a whole pheasant on her head, and smiled when he heard that Miriam and her mother regularly appeared for more books, Miriam with braces on her teeth.

'Well done, Miss Marple,' he grinned.

'Miriam reminds me of myself when I was her age,' Carrie mused now. 'She asked me what books she could move on to next.'

'And what did you recommend?'

Carrie looked up at him.

'You really want to know?'

'Of course I do! That's why I asked.'

'OK, though they might not mean much to you. *Invitation to the Waltz* by Rosamond Lehmann and *The Crowded Street* by Winifred Holtby.'

Mike nodded, but looked a bit vague.

'Fair enough. I've heard of them, I think, but can't say I know them. What are they about?'

'They're about . . .' Carrie slowed her pace: she had to think how best to put it. 'I suppose they're about young girls growing up and looking around them, working out who they are and what they want from life.'

'Sounds perfect for your young friend.' Mike smiled and squeezed her against him as they strolled on. 'How lucky she's got you.'

'That's what I love,' Carrie enthused. 'Matching books to people, passing on everything I love about reading . . . And when you meet another bookworm like Miriam—'

'Or me?' probed Mike.

'Oh, you! Well . . .' Carrie felt herself colour. 'That's completely different!'

She craned up to kiss his cheek and he grinned down at her. 'I should hope so!'

They strolled on happily. She had her head on his shoulder now. Carrie loved the firm strength of his body by her side, the smell and feel of the cloth of his uniform, the way he held himself so tall. He had his arm around her shoulders; her arm was around his waist. The only sounds were the soft fall of their feet on the path and the chattering of the birds. The war seemed miles away. Carrie felt she could walk like this for ever. But time was getting on: he had to be back at camp.

'Oh, look, what about here?' she said. 'Will this do for our picnic?'

In a little clearing, there was a fallen tree trunk too pitted and rotten to be taken for firewood.

'Perfect.'

Carrie put her basket on the ground. Mike dusted off a

few leaves and they sat down, half facing each other. He took her hands in his. He looked serious.

'Before we eat . . . there's something I've got to tell you.'

It was as if the sun had gone in. Carrie felt her heart and her spirits sink. She realised that she'd been waiting for this moment since they'd met. Never mind twin telepathy; she knew exactly what Mike was going to say.

'You've been posted.'

He nodded.

'Where? Please tell me. There's only the birds to hear.'

'I'd have told you anyway. I'm going to France.'

Carrie said nothing. There was nothing to say, except:

'When?'

'Next week. The rest of my regiment have already gone, but a few of us were held back for . . . well, for further briefings.'

'I see.'

'I'm so sorry, Carrie. I've known for a while,' Mike went on lamely, 'but there was no point in letting it hang over us. I'm sorry if it's a shock. I thought it was better this way.'

'It's not better any way!' Carrie burst out. 'Oh, I'm sorry, I know you've got to go! And I knew it had to happen some-time, I just hoped . . .'

'. . . that we'd have longer. Much longer. Me too. You don't know how much I wanted that.' Mike traced the line of her jaw with his finger.

'Oh, Mike!'

He opened his arms and they clung together, not speak-ing, each sharing the other's anguish. He kissed her hair, and then the tears on her cheeks.

'I'm so sorry,' he said. 'I really am. I don't want to go. I don't want to leave you. But it's this war. You know I have to.'

Carrie nodded. Her heart was too full and her throat too tight to say anything; she hoped he could see from her face that she felt the same. But she had to pull herself together.

'I've just got to be grateful for the time we had,' she said, swallowing her tears. 'And I am, I am!'

'So am I,' said Mike fervently. 'And all thanks to your bookstall!'

'Yes, all thanks to my bookstall. And we do have the war to thank for that.'

'You will still be here when I come back, won't you?' he asked. 'You will . . . wait for me? I need to know that.' Suddenly he was vulnerable, and Carrie knew that despite his years of army training, or because of them, he knew the real danger he'd be in.

'Of course!' she told him. 'Of course I will!' She took his face in her hands and kissed him. 'I'll write,' she said. 'Every day. And your kitbag is going to be stuffed full of books!'

'Oh, Carrie!' He gave a half-laugh, then, full of feeling, his steady eyes looked straight into hers. 'I know it's soon to be saying it, we haven't know each other that long, but I do love you. I love everything about you.'

'Oh, I love you too. So much!' The words burst out of Carrie's chest.

The relief of hearing him say it, and of saying it herself at last, when she'd felt it for so long, was almost overwhelming. And as he kissed her, she thought it over and over again: *I love you, I love you, I love you.*

Chapter Thirteen

When the army moved, it moved quickly. They were at war, after all, and Carrie wasn't alone in feeling the wrench. She only saw Mike again once, briefly, at the station. It was just for long enough to give him the promised books, which she'd agonised over choosing. In the end, she'd selected a murder mystery, a lightweight farce and two rather more serious books – one history and one about the war. Then she'd added two collections of short stories, which would be good, she thought, if he didn't have the time to follow a convoluted plot or was going to be interrupted.

'Thank you,' he said, as he read the back covers one after the other, and then, with a grin: 'Though it's scary how well you know me – they're just what I'd have picked! I can't decide which to read first. But . . .' he selected *The First 49 Stories*, another Ernest Hemingway, '. . . I think for old times' sake, I might start with this.'

He smiled at her, and Carrie glowed at the nod to the writer who'd brought them together, but then a delivery arrived that she had to sign for. After that, a crowd of schoolchildren tumbled off the three-forty-four and formed a scrum around the counter – it was the day *The Beano* came out. As soon as Carrie had dealt with them, a woman was dithering over lined or unlined notepaper, and a man started fussing because the only copy of *Punch* that was left had a torn cover.

All the while, Mike was waiting, checking the clock. His train would be next, and he had to get to the other platform. The bell rang – it was on its way. Cursing this sudden rush of customers, Carrie bit her lip. She knew he daren't miss it.

Mr Bayliss's voice came over the loudspeaker, even more annoying than usual, announcing the next departure – Mike's train to Caterham and beyond. Over the heads of her customers, Carrie looked at Mike. A helpless shrug half formed, while his eyes signalled his desperation. Then they both acted together.

'Excuse me!' Mike pushed between the startled customers at the very same moment that Carrie leaned forward.

'Mike!'

Her hands reached for his, but he'd already grasped her by the shoulders. Across the copies of *Picture Post* and *Reveille*, their lips found each other while the male customer tutted 'Well, really!' and the woman smiled and looked on.

Finally, Mike let her go and Carrie, who'd been almost lifted off her feet, found the floor again. A little knot of passengers had formed, watching the spectacle, and led by a cheeky young midshipman, they burst into a round of applause. But there was no time to take a bow: Mike's train was pulling in on the other platform.

'Run!' cried Carrie, and Mike did, calling, 'Goodbye! I love you! ' and 'Don't forget to write!' over his shoulder.

'I won't! I love you! Stay safe!' Carrie called back as he darted down into the underpass beneath the tracks.

Blushing and pushing her hair off her face, Carrie turned

back to her customers. Seeing she was holding back her tears, the woman patted her hand and bought both writing pads, and the man grudgingly paid for his magazine. Carrie served them in a daze as she saw Mike's train pull out.

Bette joined Carrie later as she closed up.

'Gone, then, has he?' she sympathised.

Carrie nodded. Bette gave her a hug.

'I know it's hard. He's your first love, isn't he?'

Carrie closed her eyes and nodded again. She was not going to cry, not even in front of Bette.

'Don't you worry, sweetheart,' Bette soothed. 'He'll be all right, I'm sure of it.'

Carrie wished she felt the same. With Mike gone, the war had suddenly come much closer.

Sure enough, that night, as they were having tea, the sirens sounded. Carrie and her mother had the usual scramble to get to the shelter, while Norman threw down his knife and fork and ran for his tin hat and ARP armband.

As she sat wrapped in the old tartan picnic rug, playing patience by the light of a storm lantern, her mother trying to knit with shaking hands, Carrie thought about Mike, and how much closer he'd be to danger. She closed her eyes and touched the locket she wore night and day. She prayed like the rhythm of the trains that drummed through her days. *Keep him safe, keep him safe, keep him safe.*

'You'll never believe it!'

This was a favourite opener of Bette's; the other was 'You'll never guess!'

Carrie had started off by obliging. The King was coming to Brockington? An orangutan had escaped from London Zoo and was pelting passers-by with that rarity, bananas? But she'd learned to her cost that the promised excitement usually only revolved around Ruby's new nail polish or the cheek of the baker's boy. Nowadays, she simply raised an eyebrow and let Bette continue.

'They've only gone and posted my Eric!'

It was almost a month since Mike had left. Carrie had written almost every day, writing the way she spoke, about her customers, about her dad and Terry's exploits in the shop, and about Johnnie's progress, or the little that he was able to tell her. She didn't ask where Mike was or what he was doing, knowing he couldn't tell her either, which meant she found herself writing empty phrases like 'Hope you're still safe'. She wanted to write 'not in danger', but even that seemed like fishing for information – and she was determined not to seem needy. She always finished, though, with 'I love and miss you.'

He'd warned her he might sometimes be out of touch and Carrie couldn't help wondering what had been contained in the 'extra briefings' he'd been held back for when the rest of his regiment had gone ahead to France. She might not have known Mike for very long, and caring for him as she did, she realised she might be biased, but she couldn't help wondering if he'd been singled out for some special responsibility, if he was maybe even doing something undercover.

But the wondering would have to continue. The letters that did come described the French countryside, with its straight roads and lines of poplar trees, so different from the winding lanes and mixed hedgerows of England they'd explored in their brief time together. The local café, Mike told her, had a piano on which Sergeant Thompson, the soldier who'd called to him from the train that first day, played 'Roll Out the Barrel' and 'Kiss Me Goodnight, Sergeant Major'. The locals were teaching them French songs too.

Mike's letters always ended:

I miss you very much

All my love, Mike xx

Carrie dragged her thoughts back to Bette – and Eric.

'Posted? What part of the country have they sent him to this time?' she asked. Eric seemed to have been all over the place.

'You'll never guess!' Carrie again employed her raised-eyebrow tactic and Bette continued: 'France!'

'France?' For once, it was something Carrie really couldn't have guessed. 'But what about the training his unit were supposed to be having here?'

'Eyewash!' scorned Bette. 'Can't a trust a word the army says!'

'I see. What does Eric say about it?'

'Well, he's got no choice, has he, it's jump to it, quick march! I don't like it,' Bette added doomily. 'They must think there's something about to happen, for all that we're not told about it in the news.'

Carrie suddenly felt a bit cast down herself. The month

of March had blown in lustily. A cup of tea had a film of coal dust on it by the time she got to drink it, but the trees were greening up properly now and the daffodils starting to poke up in front gardens. You couldn't help but feel hopeful, especially as it was still 'all quiet on the Western Front', as the book title had it. With Mike over in France, it was the hope that Carrie had clung to most of all.

Then Bette seemed to brighten.

'There's one good thing, Carrie. Your Mike's in the 48th Infantry, isn't he?'

'Ye-es . . .'

'Well, since my Eric's in the 46th, they're bound to be near each other! Maybe Mike can look out for him – keep an eye on him, I mean.'

'Well, I don't know about that . . .'

In fact, Carrie was certain. Mike had tried to explain the various regiments, divisions and battalions of the British Army, but he'd also made it clear that in wartime, things were fluid and often unpredictable. Units were moved, attached and merged – and the numbering system meant absolutely nothing.

But Bette needed reassuring. Carrie patted her friend's arm.

'I'm sure if they come across each other, Mike'll do his very best.'

Even by the beginning of April, it was hard to believe they were at war. There'd been various encounters in the air and at sea, but no hint of an invasion or even of air raids. The Prime Minister, Mr Chamberlain, went so far as to stand up in the House of Commons and claim that Hitler had 'missed the bus'.

As if provoked, the very next day, the Führer invaded Denmark, then Norway.

'NAZIS BOMB KING OF NORWAY' yelled the *Daily Sketch*.

At the same time, Carrie read: 'RAF ATTACK SHIPS IN NORWAY PORT'.

Soon a British Expeditionary Force was sent to assist the Norwegians.

'Count yourself lucky "your Mike" and "my Eric", as Bette puts it, were sent to France and not the frozen north,' Penny declared.

She sounded almost nonchalant about it, which was puzzling and almost annoying, because she knew the depth of feeling Carrie had for Mike, and Bette for Eric. She wondered if Penny had ever had a boyfriend or even wanted one. She was a funny girl, and no mistake.

After the night Penny had spent at the Andersons', Carrie had thought they might become closer, and they had, a bit, but Penny still seemed to hold a lot of herself in reserve. The handbag-snatcher had seen sense and pleaded guilty at the magistrates' court, and the matter had been laid to rest, seemingly to Penny's relief. When Carrie had suggested Mr Bayliss might put her forward for a commendation or reward, Penny had promptly squashed the idea.

She reminded Carrie of what someone had said in Parliament about Russia being a riddle wrapped in a mystery inside an enigma, and Penny seemed quite happy to keep things that way. Carrie could feel quite exasperated with her. She admired the way Penny wouldn't be pushed around, but did she have to be so determinedly independent? But Carrie didn't want to gossip about Penny with Bette or Mary, and Mike, who'd met her a few times, wasn't there. Maybe Johnnie would have some thoughts on the matter. And other matters too ... like a bit of inside information about what kind of manoeuvres Mike and his regiment might be on.

Johnnie was nearing the end of his service flying training now, based at Hamble in Hampshire, and nearer home at last. Carrie could hardly wait. She missed him, of course, yet she missed Mike more, and that made her feel almost disloyal. Still, she'd make it up to him. They could pick up their old familiar closeness, the jokes, the easy conversations, once he was home.

But when he arrived home on a week's leave in early May, Johnnie didn't want to discuss Mike, or Penny, or even the bookstall – all he could think about was his posting.

'It's got to be Spitfires,' he declared, perched behind the counter on Carrie's stool one day. 'But that's what everyone wants. They're a dream to fly, once you know how to handle them – so light, so manoeuvrable, like a second skin ...' He sighed. 'I suppose I'd settle for Hurricanes if I had to ...'

Carrie was only half listening as she tidied the counter. All week she'd been selling papers and periodicals hand over fist. It was the same for her father back at the shop, despite the fact that newspapers, already reduced to two-thirds of their size because of paper rationing, had been further shrunk to just a third – about four pages.

The news wasn't good. German troops were massing near the Dutch border, while at home, after a humiliating and costly British retreat from Norway, it looked as if Mr Chamberlain was going to have to resign.

'I think I've done enough to get it,' Johnnie went on. 'And heaven knows, I'll be just in time. Look at what's happening – Hitler's going to go for Holland and Belgium, and then, well, after France, Britain's next on the list. So our air defences are going to be—Oh, Carrie, I'm sorry.'

Carrie had turned, her eyes ablaze.

'Can you just stop talking like that? Do you think I don't realise what's coming, dealing with the papers every day? As if it's not enough worrying about Mike, now there's you as well—'

Johnnie jumped up and took her in his arms. Luckily, it was the mid-morning lull and there were no customers.

'Carrie, I'm so sorry. It was thoughtless of me,' he apologised. 'How is Mike?'

'I don't know. That's the trouble.' Carrie's voice cracked and her eyes filled. 'He's been writing every week, but it's been far longer than that since the last letter.'

'Well, that doesn't mean anything,' Johnnie soothed, 'except the post's all to pot, or he's – well, busy. They'll be shoring up defences, reinforcing troops, getting the supply lines secure. And . . .' he lowered his voice '. . . we're doing a lot of reconnaissance – in the air and on the ground.'

Carrie was silent. Her worries about the special 'briefings' that Mike had been held back for hadn't gone away. He was young, bright and, above all, keen. Reconnaissance behind enemy lines sounded like just the sort of mad thing he'd go and volunteer for.

She pulled away from Johnnie as a couple came onto the

platform. The girl was heaving with sobs, the man, a private in stiff new khaki battledress, looked sad but resigned. Carrie was glad she hadn't broken down completely in front of Mike when he'd told her he was leaving and that her tears had been shed into her pillow. She'd felt she owed it to him to be strong, and now she bit her lip and accepted the handkerchief that Johnnie was offering.

'Sorry,' she said, her voice still slightly wobbly. 'I know you've worked hard for it and it's what you want. But with Mike away – it all just gets to me sometimes.'

'Of course it does.' Johnnie was looking at the couple too. 'I sometimes think – well, I do think that it must be harder to be left behind than to sally off and do your bit.'

'Well, there's not much choice for any of us, is there.' Carrie folded his handkerchief and gave it back. She took a deep breath. 'And I do love what I'm doing here. I truly feel I'm providing a service.'

The couple came up to the bookstall. The girl, still tearful, picked up *Peg's Paper* and *Woman's World*, but the man twirled the carousel, glancing at his wife, whose wedding ring shone so brassily it might as well still have had the price ticket on.

He looked helplessly at Carrie.

'I ain't much of a reader,' he admitted, then, nodding at his wife, 'but Mavis likes a nice story. What d'you reckon she'd go for?'

Carrie had no doubt.

'See that one?' she said. '*Greenery Street*? It's quite a light, easy read. I think she might enjoy that.'

'Yeah? Ta.'

He plucked the little orange Penguin from the stand, handed it to his wife and fished out sixpence to pay. The girl smiled her thanks and they moved off to the far platform. Johnnie winked at Carrie.

'As if in proof,' he said. 'What's the book about?'

'A young couple's happy first year of marriage.' Carrie smiled ruefully. 'They haven't got a war to contend with, though.'

Chapter Fourteen

Usually in life it was the unexpected that happened – this time, at least, it was what everyone was expecting. Mr Chamberlain, the Prime Minister, duly resigned and Winston Churchill, old, wheezy, but a brilliant speaker, became the head of the new coalition government. At dawn on the very same day, Hitler invaded Holland, Belgium and Luxembourg. The phoney war was over.

That night the Andersons gathered round the wireless for the nine o'clock news. There was the familiar crackle and high-pitched whine as the set came to life. Before the time signal, Mr Chamberlain spoke to the nation for the last time.

'*Hitler,*' he said, '*has chosen a moment when, perhaps, it seemed to him that this country was entangled in the throes of a political crisis . . . If he has counted upon our internal divisions to help him, he has miscalculated the mind of this people.*'

'Hear! Hear!' said Norman, tamping down the tobacco in his pipe, putting it between his teeth and lighting up.

Then the newsreader took over.

'*Reports from Holland said German troops crossed the border during the night,*' he read. '*The Dutch destroyed bridges to prevent the advance, but there were reports of fierce fighting at Rotterdam, where German troops landed by flying boat.*

'*Other planes landed at Waalhaven Aerodrome. This evening,*

German forces are occupying the Maas and Bourse railway stations in Rotterdam. There are conflicting reports about whether they are still in possession of Waalhaven Airport. German reconnaissance planes have been seen all day.'

'Tch!' said Norman, and between puffs: 'That Hitler wants locking up!'

'Shh, Dad!'

Johnnie gave a deep sigh and shifted impatiently in his chair. Then Carrie sat up in hers as the announcer went on:

'British and French troops have moved across the Belgian frontier in response to appeals for reinforcements. Reports from Belgium say British troops have been enthusiastically received. Their guns have been festooned with flowers and the soldiers plied with refreshments.'

Mary tutted. 'Poor little Belgium again. Just like in the last war.'

Carrie glanced at Johnnie; the emotional waves passing between them were strong enough to have knocked her off her feet. His leave had barely started, but she could tell he was itching to get back to camp. He looked up and across at her, knowing that she knew. And he knew that for her, no matter how many flowers and refreshments the British troops had been given, nothing could take away her terror that Mike was getting closer and closer to the fighting.

Before anyone could say anything else, the telephone rang.

'This'll be Charlie, I bet. Let's see what he makes of it.' Norman put down his pipe, but Johnnie laid a hand on his shoulder.

'I'll get it, Dad.'

He went out into the small hall and they heard him say the number, then:

'Yes, speaking . . . Oh, good evening, sir . . . Yes, yes, I understand . . . Of course, I was thinking the same . . . No need to thank me, sir, I'll be there, and gladly . . . Goodnight, sir.'

He came back, his face grave.

'All leave cancelled. I'm going to pack.'

'You're leaving tonight?' Mary was aghast. 'There's three days left of your leave! I haven't even made you a cake to take back yet.'

'I'm sorry, Mum, but there it is. The lads'll have to do without.'

Carrie jumped up.

'I'll come to the station with you.'

When they got there, both platforms were busy: who'd have thought there were quite so many soldiers, sailors and airmen on leave and recalled to camp? Not to mention the wives, girlfriends, mothers and sisters waiting with them.

'You should have opened up the bookstall,' Johnnie joked.

They waited in the last dying light of the beautiful May evening, a nightingale singing in the trees at the far end of the platform. With a pang, Carrie remembered Eric sweeping up the fallen leaves and collecting the conkers. Bette would be worried sick. She remembered Penny shovelling grit down in the icy winter. Did she have anyone to worry about? She'd never said. Somehow, with Penny, even Carrie didn't dare ask.

Johnnie was quiet, thinking.

'How many more weeks' training have you got?' Carrie asked, though she knew perfectly well.

'Till the end of the month.'

She'd somehow managed to stay strong with Mike before he left, and again, Carrie made a valiant effort to keep things light.

'Hmm . . . then you get your wings. I suppose you'll be having one of those "Who's a clever boy then?" photos taken?'

Johnnie saw her efforts for what they were, but he played along.

'Pilot Officer Anderson, with a stripe on my sleeve? Oh, yes!'

'And looking pretty smug with it, I bet!'

'And why not?' Johnnie grinned. 'Just make sure you can find room for it, alongside the one of Mike you keep under your pillow!'

'You cheeky—'

But the bell rang. His train.

'Come here.' Her twin caught her in quick hug. 'Don't forget, even after I've qualified, there's still six weeks of operational training before they let me loose in any action. So there's no need to worry just yet.'

Carrie pulled away.

'You clown. I worry all the time!'

'Well, don't!' he scolded. As the train came in, he gave her another quick hug. 'Look after yourself, sis, and the folks.'

'I'll try.'

He shouldered his kitbag, gave her a wave and walked to the train. Ironic, thought Carrie, that she'd had a longer parting with her brother than she'd had with Mike. Was it possible to love two people? It sounded like a letter from the problem page of one of the women's magazines. But Carrie knew the answer – of course it was, in different ways. Her love for Mike was deep and true, but her connection with her twin had been forged at birth and could never be broken.

The sky was ink-dark now, and with the train windows blacked out, there was no hope of waving. But, along with the other women left behind, she watched the train as it jerked into life and chugged away down the track. Then, with a sigh, she left for home.

The so-called merry month of May, the one Carrie usually loved most in the year, was for her clouded with anxiety. The weather was glorious. The bluebells were out, the new leaves shimmered in the trees, the chaffinches and chiff-chaffs sang from dawn till dusk. But all Carrie could think about was what she saw on the newsreels – Dutch cities reduced to rubble and desperate people fleeing with their pathetic belongings.

Brockington Junction was seething again, like at the start of the war, and not just with troops. An invasion of Britain was starting to look like a real possibility again, so mothers and their children were heading off to anywhere they considered safer than the capital, while children whose mothers were doing war work were being packed off with chaperones. And as well as that, on the up platform from the south, came refugees – hundreds of them. Some were shabby, some were smart, but all looked exhausted and numbed by what they'd seen. Those who got off their trains converged gratefully on the good ladies of the WVS. Their tea wagon supplemented Bette's refreshment room, and they'd combed the town to find billets for the displaced people who needed somewhere to stay.

Bette had the wireless on all day now in the tearoom, in case of a newsflash, but Carrie could read the news for herself – almost too much of it – as the papers arrived throughout the day. By the middle of the month, Holland had surrendered, and Belgium by the end.

Meanwhile, the Nazis had managed to get their tanks into France through the dense, supposedly impassable Ardennes forest and were on the march towards the Channel. The news made the most of the splendid job the RAF were doing in bombing bridges, roads and railways to try to halt their advance, but there was no hiding from the facts – the British and French forces were in retreat.

'Retreating to where?' Penny demanded, poring over the front page of the *News Chronicle*. 'He's going to chase them all the way to the coast, isn't he? Are they supposed to swim home?' Seeing Carrie's stricken face, she quickly shut up. 'Sorry.'

'I just can't think about it,' Carrie said. 'But at the same time I can't stop thinking about it.'

'No, well, I daresay I'd feel the same.'

Aha, a chink in Penny's armour? Carrie had to ask.

'Haven't you got . . . anyone out there, or anywhere in the forces?' she said. 'I mean, even if not a boyfriend, you must have friends, cousins, a brother maybe?'

'No brother,' replied Penny, leaving the rest of the question unanswered. 'How's yours, by the way?'

Penny had outmanoeuvred her – again – and Carrie was needled.

'Can't wait to be flying for real and getting himself killed,' she said bluntly.

'Fair enough.' Penny almost shrugged. 'You can't deny we need all the pilots we can get. And flying's all he's ever wanted to do, isn't it?'

Carrie wasn't a violent person, but she could have smacked her.

'Do you have to be so cool-headed and, well, logical about everything?' she exploded. 'Where have you come from, Penny? Did you just drop from the sky? Don't you have any family you care about – or any feelings for anyone?'

Like clouds passing across the moon, Penny's face registered one emotion after another – surprise, resentment and suspicion. Then they were replaced by her usual devil-may-care look as she laughed it off.

'Ooh, never mind me – where did *that* come from, Miss Prickly? We don't all have to wear our hearts on our sleeves, do we?'

And with that she marched off down the platform, leaving Carrie staring after her in frustration.

With no letters arriving from Mike, all Carrie could do was reread the ones he'd been sending since he left. The last was dated Sunday, 28 April.

'My darling Carrie,' he'd written.

*Has spring sprung with you? It's lovely here, with primroses
and lily of the valley growing wild and smelling beautiful —
like the perfume you wear. They call the lilies 'muguets des
bois' in French. Doesn't look so pretty written down, does it,
but very musical when you hear it in a French accent. I think
often of our walk in the woods and the snowdrops. I suppose
they're covered in primroses and violets now, and the bluebells will be out soon — it seems so long since I've seen you.*

She could imagine him pausing there, chewing his pen,
wondering whether to say more, something more intimate
perhaps. But he was a gentleman through and through and
he'd gone on:

*Thanks for your letter. I'm glad there haven't been too many
air raid warnings disrupting your beauty sleep, not that you
need it! Thanks very much for the chocs and toffees — I shared
them round the men and they went very well with our night-
time cocoa. (No boozing allowed on my watch!)*

Carrie turned to the next page. Here it was at last.

*I'm sorrier every day that we didn't have longer together.
Your letters mean so much to me, I have them all, and your
photo in my breast pocket, getting a bit creased now from
looking at it, but you're as lovely as ever.*

Carrie's heart swelled. She'd had the picture taken spe-
cially at the photographer's in the Parade, wearing her best
dress with the sweetheart neckline that showed off Mike's
locket beautifully.

She read on, and her heart swelled again.

A Farewell to Arms *is with me always, and the other books you gave me.*

But then came:

Things may be hotting up here, so if you don't hear from me for a while, don't worry. I'll be fine, I promise. I can't wait to see you and hold you in my arms again.

I love you very much, Mike xx

Carrie could still remember her thrill at hearing him say those words that first time. She'd written back at once, pouring out her heart – how she missed him too, and longed to see him again – and signing her letter in the same way.

If his unit had been on the move, he might not have received it.

Carrie closed her eyes and wrapped her arms around her body, trying to recreate the feeling of Mike's arms around her. It was comforting, but nothing like the exciting, fluttery feeling of being held by him.

With a sigh, she tucked the letter carefully away and picked up his photograph – not from under her pillow, as Johnnie had teased, but in a small leatherette frame by her bed. There he was with his dark hair, his honest, smiling eyes, his firm mouth, which felt so soft when he kissed her. She placed it carefully back on the bedside cabinet so that it was the last thing she saw before she closed her eyes and the first when she opened them in the morning. She prayed again, as she did every night, that he'd be safe.

*

Another night, another evening round the wireless, Norman with his pipe, Mary with her mending, Carrie sewing the fingers of gloves that she and her mother had been knitting for sailors out of thick, oiled wool. Nine o'clock. The time signal, then the newsreader's voice:

'*This is London. Here is the news.*'

A pause. And then:

'*The evacuation of the British Expeditionary Force from Dunkirk is under way.*'

Everyone stopped what they were doing. Evacuation? What evacuation? Norman took his pipe out of his mouth; Mary put her hand to her throat and said, 'Thank God!' Carrie felt the blood-beat in her heart slow, then speed up, then settle. Her mother reached across and took her hand.

'That means Mike, doesn't it? He'll be coming home.'

'Oh, Mum!'

Carrie flung herself against her mother, sobbing away her pent-up anxiety, sobbing her relief. Mary stroked her hair, while her dad patted her on the shoulder and muttered something about putting the kettle on. He was halfway to the scullery when, just as it had the previous time there'd been momentous news, the phone rang.

He retraced his steps and they heard him pick it up.

'Johnnie? Hello, son. Are you ringing about the news? Yes, we heard . . . I know, I know . . . Yes, I'll tell her . . . OK. So how are you? . . . Oh. Oh, I see.'

There was a change of tone.

'Oh, well, that's terrific. I know that's what you wanted, and I know how hard you've worked for it . . . Yes, yes, well done, well done. Do you want to speak to . . . Yes, of course,

152

a few bevvies, yes, I know how it is . . . Well, thanks for ring-ing. You'll keep in touch, won't you? And . . . congratulations. From all of us. Bye now.'

He came back in. The two women raised their faces to him, but they knew what he was going to say. It could only be one thing. And it was.

'He's done it,' he said. 'He's heard where he'll be posted. He's going to be flying Spitfires. Fighters.'

Now it was Carrie's turn to comfort her mother as Mary burst into tears.

Chapter Fifteen

Carrie spent the rest of the evening trying to soothe her mother. There wasn't much time to think about what might be happening to Mike. But the next morning, she couldn't get to the station quickly enough. As the mail train drew in, she was waiting on the platform to get her hands on the papers.

'TENS OF THOUSANDS SAFELY HOME ALREADY' yelled the *Express*, adding reassuringly, in smaller type, '*Many more coming by day and night*'.

All the papers told the same story of the most extraordinary rescue. A so-called 'armada' of little boats – motor launches, fishing boats, pleasure cruisers, paddle steamers and ferries – had set off from the south coast, captained by their brave owners. Protected by the RAF, but under relentless German fire from land and air, they'd supplemented the ships of the Royal Navy in getting troops to safety.

Carrie had been expecting Bette to be in bits, but to her surprise, her friend didn't seem rattled at all. A fervent supporter of 'Winnie', as she called the Prime Minister, Bette was beaming from ear to ear.

'No one but him would have thought of it,' she declared. 'Or dared do it. They'll soon be back, you mark my words – your Mike and my Eric. And won't they have some tales to tell.'

Carrie smiled half-heartedly. Tens of thousands was a start, but there were hundreds of thousands of British troops penned up on the beach at Dunkirk. Still, all they could do was hope. And believe.

'I can't hang about,' Bette clucked. 'I've left Ruby with a batch of rock cakes in the oven, and rock's the word if she drifts off in one of her daydreams. Chatting up a Dutchman, she was, the other day, poor feller, as if he hasn't had enough to contend with.'

And off she bustled. It was obviously business as usual as far as Bette was concerned, and Carrie wished she could feel as hopeful. She'd tried, in the dark watches of the night, to conjure up with Mike the sort of telepathy she had with Johnnie, but there was nothing – not even a crackle of static. She told herself she was daft to have expected it, but the dead nothingness had still given her a sick feeling she couldn't shake.

Days passed and through Brockington Junction they came, the brave soldiers of the British Expeditionary Force, and French troops too. But whoever they were, they were all tired, hungry and dirty, their uniforms sea-stained and torn, the walking wounded limping or bandaged. Carrie gladly handed out newspapers, magazines, pads of paper, envelopes and books, plenty of books, whatever they asked for, to all comers, with no charge. The bookstall had never felt more vital and Carrie had never felt more proud of serving the men who were serving their country.

Bette and Ruby rattled down the platforms with a trolley, giving out tea, while the WVS and Red Cross dished out more tea, sandwiches and chocolate. They were so busy there was no chance for Ruby's usual come-hither head-tossing with the more chipper of the troops, and in any case, even she seemed subdued by the pitiful state of some of the others.

'It's awful!' she wailed to Carrie during a brief break in arrivals. 'They look so – so beaten, most of them. How're we gonna win this war now?'

At that moment, it hardly felt possible, but Carrie wasn't going to give in.

'We have to, Ruby,' she said. 'Our troops will buck up again. They just need a good rest.'

'What, and carry on fighting till they're all dead?' Ruby replied. 'I don't want to end up like my auntie. Lost her feller in the Great War and never been the same since – got six cats, she has, and lives on tonic wine and tablets!'

'Well, at least she's not had to learn to speak German!' Carrie said, more sharply than she intended, but her point seemed lost on Ruby.

Just then, Bette summoned Ruby to get on with the dirty crocks and she trundled her trolley back to the tearoom.

Bette was still amazingly cheerful, convinced Eric would be on the next train, or the next, and that his experience of being evacuated would somehow excuse him from further combat. Carrie didn't like to disillusion her.

The end of May swam into June in a blur of such scenes, until on the fourth of the month, the evacuation was announced as complete. Three hundred and thirty-eight thousand men had been brought home from France – something of a miracle. What was not announced was exactly how many had been taken prisoner, left behind or killed in the evacuation attempt.

Until Carrie heard that Mike was not one of them, and Bette heard the same about Eric, there could be no celebrations for them.

For the whole country, in fact, the silver lining had a cloud. The Nazis were advancing through France: the next country in their sights would be Britain.

Mr Churchill gave a stirring speech in Parliament, which was broadcast on the wireless. It ended with a rallying cry.

'We shall go on to the end, we shall defend our island, whatever the cost may be, we shall fight on the beaches, we shall fight on the landing grounds, we shall fight in the fields and in the streets, we shall fight in the hills; we shall never surrender!'

It had Norman standing up to salute and Mary reaching again for the balled-up hankie that was always in her apron pocket these days. Carrie listened numbly.

What had Mike said, once, when she'd said she'd given up hope of ever seeing him again?

'You mustn't give up on me, ever.'

She'd promised at the time that she wouldn't, though she'd been surprised by his vehemence. Now she understood. And she just had to hang on to that promise.

For the next week, the troop trains passed through or disgorged the same rabble of tired, hungry, tattered men at Brockington to wait for their connection. Still no word came from, or about, Mike or Eric. Bette moved around in a world of her own; Carrie was like a wraith. But their customers, especially the returning troops, needed them: they had to carry on.

One afternoon, Carrie spotted Penny with an armful of what looked like jumble – coats and jackets, boots and shoes.

'What the heck—?'

'Lost Property,' Penny grinned with a gleam in her eye. 'I'm such a clot, I don't know why I didn't think of it before!'

The things that people left behind on trains never ceased to amaze Carrie – parcels, umbrellas, books and briefcases, of course, but also single shoes (how?) and false teeth (surely not!). Someone had once left a full-sized medical skeleton. Even so, it always remained the property of the owner unless it was unclaimed after six months.

'So is this all the over-six-month stuff?'

'Nope.'

'What? What are you doing with it? You're not giving it away? Did Mr Bayliss—'

'Say I could have it? No!' Penny was defiant. 'But I've seen enough. There are men just off this train with no jacket, no shirt . . . A chap down there, he's got to get back to Manchester – he's only got one boot! For goodness' sake, surely even old Bayliss can't complain. Whose side is he on?'

Mr Bayliss wasn't too far away, but thankfully was trapped between an officer, who was barking questions about the next train, and the even more fearsome WVS organiser, who was complaining that the Izal had run out in the ladies' lavatory.

'You might just get away with it,' said Carrie, impressed despite herself by Penny's daring. 'He's busy – look.'

Penny glanced towards the little group. 'That's OK, then—Oh Lord . . . oh no!'

In one swift movement, she threw the bundle of clothes and boots over the counter of the bookstall, a boot almost catching Carrie above the eyebrow. Penny herself shot round the side of the stall and through the little door, slamming it after her. Then she dived under the counter.

'What on earth—'

'Shh! I'm not here, OK?'

'But, Penny—'

'Just get all that stuff off the counter. Chuck it down here with me.'

'You needn't worry. I don't think Mr Bayliss saw you, honestly.'

'Never mind – I'm staying here. Till he's gone.'

'OK . . . whatever you say!' Carrie did as she was told, ever more puzzled by this unusual, impetuous, impossible girl. 'But what about your shoeless soldier?'

'I'll find him in a minute,' Penny hissed from her hiding place. 'His train's not due till after four. What's happening with Bayliss?'

Carrie craned forward over the counter, looking over the heads of the soldiers waiting on the platform. 'He's . . . oh, the officer's gone. He's stuck with the dragon from the WVS . . . Oh, no, the officer's back – the WVS lady's going, and Mr Bayliss is taking the army chap into his office. He's shut the door. So you're safe.'

Penny got to her feet and cautiously peeked out.

'Yes, OK, the coast looks clear. I'm going in the other direction, anyway, to find my chap. Let's hope one of these shoes or boots fits him.'

'I think you might spare him a whole new matching pair.'

'I expect I will.' Penny gathered up the mass of stuff again. 'Can you open the door for me?'

Again, Carrie did as she was asked. But she wasn't letting Penny get away scot-free.

'You've never been scared of Mr Bayliss before. What was different this time? You said yourself even he wouldn't dare complain about . . . well, an act of charity.'

Penny paused in the doorway. She looked at Carrie as if she was weighing something up. Then she said:

'Sorry, no time. Got to go.'

Carrie was left frustrated. What was going on with the girl? She remembered what Mike had told her, how Penny hadn't seemed keen to talk to the police or to appear in court over the bag-snatching incident. Was she really that scared of Mr Bayliss finding out she'd appropriated some lost property? And then, if she couldn't convince him she'd been right to do it, to have him report her to the authorities for theft, which technically it was? It seemed impossible, but surely – surely – Penny couldn't have a criminal record?

With her mum fretting about Johnnie and Bette starting to worry about Eric, there was no one for Carrie to talk to about Penny's mysterious behaviour. When she tried to tackle her about the lost property incident again, and why she'd had to hide, Penny merely laughed it off and said the secrecy had added a bit of spice to the whole affair. She seemed to have got away with her pilfering, anyhow – Mr Bayliss had plenty of other things to think about.

So did Carrie. With no word from, or sign of, Eric, Bette pulled herself together and decided to take matters into her own hands. She was writing letters to everyone she could think of – the Red Cross, who had a Wounded, Missing and Relatives Department, the local MP, the War Office, even the Prime Minister himself. The replies were all the same. They were very sorry, but troops who'd returned from France were still being processed; when they had any information, they'd be sure to tell her. Bette was frustrated, but she aired Eric's bed and hoarded her sugar ration to bake him a cake on his return, which she still, in her heart, had to hope would come.

Carrie had no such comfort. Who could she write to? She'd tried the Red Cross, but sadly they had nothing to tell her. If the War Office communicated with anyone about Mike, it would be his parents, but she didn't know them or their address. She thought of writing to the commanding officer at Caterham, since that had been Mike's last base, but she was sure they'd just tell her to write to the War Office. And frankly, the army had enough to do without acting as an agony aunt for every tearful girlfriend in the country.

It wasn't so bad when she was at work, as she had something else to think about, and on Sundays she tried to keep herself busy. Most of her friends had either joined up or volunteered for war work – her best friend from school was filling shells at a factory in the Midlands. Evie was still in Brockington, but was married now, with a baby on the way. Carrie was pleased for her, of course, and had ambitions to knit a matinee jacket and hat, but Evie's chatter about her extra milk ration or old wives' tales about 'carrying out front', meaning the baby would be a boy, left Carrie feeling even more stranded. Not that she and Mike had been anywhere near marrying, let alone having a baby, but, but . . .

'What shall I do, Mum?' she asked one Sunday. They were in the little backyard, bent over the veg plot. The potatoes and carrots were coming up nicely, but there was always weeding and thinning out to do. 'What *can* I do?'

'Oh, love.' Mary had been pinching out the side shoots from the tomatoes, but stopped to look at her daughter. 'I do feel for you.' She paused, considering. 'I was lucky, I suppose. When Edgar was gassed, we got the telegram at home straight away.'

There was a sepia photo in the front parlour of Edgar, Mary's brother, in his uniform. After the war, Mary had had to watch him decline until he'd died at the age of twenty-two.

'And what about Albert – your fiancé?'

There was no photo of Albert on show, but Carrie knew her mother kept one in her handkerchief sachet – she'd seen it when she was putting the ironing away. Albert had been killed outright, early in the war.

'Well, I knew his mum and dad, of course, so they came round and told me.'

'Right.'

'That's your trouble, I suppose, you've never met Mike's parents. So even if they do hear something . . .'

'. . . they don't know me from Adam. Mike might never have mentioned me – you know what boys are like. Look how closed Johnnie's always been about his love life!' She sighed. 'Anyway, I don't know their home address and even if I found it out, or went to the shop – I can't just turn up there out of the blue.'

'Mike didn't mind doing that here,' Mary pointed out astutely.

'True,' Carrie conceded. 'But the circumstances were a bit different. I just can't see myself doing it, Mum. Whatever they've heard or haven't heard, it must be worse for them. His sister's only young. What's the point of loading my misery onto theirs?'

So she went through the days in a sort of half-life, a vacuum.

They called it 'flaming June' – and it was. Johnnie had started his flying training in blinding snow; now, on his operational training, he was flying for real in the blazing sun. But the fact that his own life was going to plan didn't stop him from realising that his twin was troubled. After all, he had their special twin connection too.

'You've not heard anything, have you?' he asked when he rang.

'Nothing,' said Carrie sadly. 'Sometimes I tell myself he's dead, and that would be something – something final. I'd be let off a hook, if you like. But then I feel terrible. I feel disloyal, and weak, and feeble. But what's the alternative? To go on worrying?'

'You know if he'd made it back he'd have contacted you,' said Johnnie reasonably. 'And if he's alive, well, you know the other option.'

'He's been taken prisoner.'

'Yes. And if that's the case, you will know, in time. I mean, he'll write to you.'

'Yes, I know.'

'Well, that is the better option, isn't it, than the other thing? Don't give up hope, Carrie.'

Mike's words – 'You mustn't give up on me' – rang in Carrie's head.

'I know. I don't want to. But it's easy for you to say.'

'I realise that. But hang in there.'

A klaxon blared at Johnnie's end of the call.

'What's that?' said Carrie, startled. 'You're still only training, aren't you?'

'It's action stations. I have to go.'

She could hear feet running. There was a new note in Johnnie's voice. Crisp, determined, focused. She realised that even if not cleared to fly himself, he'd have some role to play on the ground.

'Oh Johnnie! Take care—'

But he'd already put down the receiver.

Chapter Sixteen

If June had been hot, July started cold, damp and dreary. *Gone with the Wind* was still playing in the West End – Ruby had seen it three nights on the trot, and, she said, got through three hankies each time. Clark Gable was her new passion, and any man with a moustache who passed through the station was 'like a magnet for her', as Bette recounted. Carrie sold endless copies of the book and had been to see it herself, but had been equally struck by the newsreels.

They'd shown German tanks rolling down the famous avenue of the Champs-Élysées and swastika flags draped on the presidential palace. France had fallen and Britain's last ally was gone. As if that wasn't enough, Italy had come into the war on Germany's side. Another enemy to take on – and Britain stood alone.

'The Battle of France is over,' the Prime Minister had admitted gravely when the Nazis entered Paris. 'I expect the Battle of Britain is about to begin.'

For all Mr Churchill's talk of fighting on the beaches, in the fields and on the landing grounds, it was clear that before it came to that – to stop it coming to that – the Battle of Britain would first of all be fought in the skies. By the RAF; by Johnnie. He was still, officially, doing his operational training, so he shouldn't have been in combat. Even so, day and night, Carrie's telepathy senses throbbed with anxiety.

If the atmosphere had been tense since Dunkirk, now everyone was permanently on edge. Rumours spread like wildfire: German spies were posing as Dutch refugees, landing by rubber dinghy in quiet coves, or parachuting into the countryside in disguise, dressed as nuns. Passengers who'd travelled up from the south coast told Carrie about increases in sea patrols and the beaches becoming minefields. The government set up more roadblocks and took down all the signposts. Uncle Charlie helped Mr Bayliss to take down the signs identifying Brockington Junction, leaving scars on the brickwork where they'd always been. Mr Bayliss looked shattered.

'Poor feller. It's like losing his identity,' Uncle Charlie reflected.

Even Penny said she felt a bit sorry for him. It was her job to put up posters at the station and a whole new batch had arrived, warning people to be vigilant about what they said in public in case they were overheard.

'BE LIKE DAD, KEEP MUM!'

Carrie's own dad was out night after night on his ARP patrols. There were constant air raid warnings, the thrum of planes overhead and the retaliatory boom of the anti-aircraft guns. The blackout was even more important. In the evenings, Carrie would have loved to do something more for the war effort herself – be a warden like her father, man the phones at the auxiliary fire station or serve in the WVS tea bar – but her place was at home with her mother, in the shelter, waiting, wondering, wincing until the all-clear.

One day, Carrie was yawning after another disturbed night when she saw Miriam and her mother approaching – the mother and daughter who'd been among her first customers and whom she'd seen regularly since on their trips to the dentist. Miriam still had her braces; her mother had told Carrie she'd need them for another year. Behind the pair of them, Carrie saw Miriam's father and her two younger brothers, Simon and Daniel, who were aged about seven and nine – she saw them occasionally when the whole family took a trip up to town. Today, Miriam's father was weighed down with two large suitcases, while the boys bowed under the weight of bulky rucksacks. Miriam also had a small suit-case with her, and her mother had a cream vanity case.

Carrie stifled her yawn and smiled.

'Hello, this looks exciting. Are you going on holiday?'

Miriam said nothing. She gave Carrie a brief smile and moved off to the Penguin carousel.

'Not exactly,' her mother replied in a low voice.

'You've got a lot of luggage, even for the whole family,' Carrie noted.

'We expect to be away for quite some time.'

'Oh,' said Carrie, suddenly realising. 'Are you moving somewhere further north? To the countryside?'

There'd been a lot of people travelling for that reason: to get away from the London suburbs to somewhere like Shropshire, Yorkshire or the Lake District – anywhere thought to be less dangerous than staying around the capital. With invasion a strong possibility, the southern counties, where people had fled in the early months of the war, were themselves too dangerous now.

'We're going rather further than that.' Miriam's mother smiled sadly. 'I mean, we are going north, initially to Liverpool. We're sailing to Canada, then down to New York.'

'America? Oh my goodness!'

Miriam's mother lowered her voice.

'We have to get away. We can't risk staying here now.'

'I see.'

She didn't really, and Miriam's mother could tell.

'I'm not sure that you do. Our family name is Neumann. We're Jewish.'

It had never even crossed Carrie's mind. Miriam and her mother – the whole family – had striking dark hair, but so did Penny, and she was as English as they came.

'There's no reason why you should realise,' Mrs Neumann said kindly. 'You see so many customers, I don't imagine you give most of them a second thought. You don't have time. But if you think about it, Miriam and I have never taken our trips to the dentist on a Friday. Friday is our Sabbath and we like to observe it.'

She was right. Carrie had never registered the fact, but now she thought about it, it was true. Mrs Neumann seemed to want to explain.

'We've been here for years, my husband's family and mine – both my husband and I were born here. My family fled the Russian pogroms in the 1880s, so in the First War, we were all right. We were on Britain's side. But my husband's family, who are Austrian Jews, had a hard time of it with a German surname. In fact, they were lucky not to be deported. It was only because my father-in-law was a professor of German that he was considered to be useful as a translator.

170

They were still interned, the whole family. And though we have British passports and are patriots, and have no connections in Germany at all any more and consider ourselves very lucky to be here, not there, we know our movements since the outbreak of the war have been monitored – by our neighbours if no one else. And things are only going to get worse.'

Carrie remembered the announcement that had been slipped in at the end of the news one night after the evacuation had started.

'*From Monday, June the third, no alien may have or control a bicycle, motor vehicle, seagoing craft or aircraft without police permission. No alien may be absent from his residence during night hours without a police permit.*'

With an invasion expected any day, it had seemed a sensible precaution – of course you didn't want foreigners who might be Nazi supporters, individually or in groups, fomenting trouble, assisting the enemy or signalling to arriving landing craft or whatever, however unlikely that might be in the case of the Neumanns. Maybe, like the royal family had done during the Great War, they should have changed their name.

'I'm so sorry,' Carrie said. 'You're the last people who'd have any sympathies with Hitler. And you're not aliens!'

'No, it's understandable. It's a serious situation for this island,' Mrs Neumann replied. 'Anyone not wholly British in their heritage could be an enemy alien, or at least have sympathies that lie elsewhere.' She shrugged. 'But if the Nazis come here and see the menorah in our home – the seven-arm candelabra, you know, or our mezuzah by the front door that shows we're a Jewish household, well, we'd be done for.'

Carrie shook her head, trying to take it all in.

'So what about your home here and all your things?'

'We're keeping the house for now. Obviously we hope we'll be back. But we've cleared it, given things away, thrown things away and put the rest in storage. The house is let. Fortunately, there are still people who consider Brockington a safe place – compared with the centre of London.'

'Right.'

'So, all we have for the moment is in these few suitcases.' Mrs Neumann gave a wry smile. 'You can imagine the tussle I had getting Miriam to part with some of her books.'

'Oh, poor Miriam!'

'It's not so bad. At least we have somewhere to go, unlike so many desperate people. Initially, we're going to stay with relatives, who'll have books to lend her. And they have libraries over there, and bookshops, too, I believe!'

'Of course they do.'

Carrie didn't like to ask what they were going to do for money. Both Miriam and her mother had always been beautifully turned out, Mrs Neumann today in a lavender tweed suit, Miriam in a striped dress with a sailor collar, and the boys in smart shorts, ties and jackets. Presumably the Neumanns had managed to get some funds out of England – Carrie had no idea how you'd do this, but it was a phrase she'd read in the papers.

Mrs Neumann looked at her watch, its oblong face on a slim crocodile strap.

'It's nearly time for our train,' she said. She held out her

172

hand. 'Goodbye, Carrie. Thank you for your kindness to Miriam.'

'It was nothing.'

'Miriam!' Mrs Neumann called. 'Come and say goodbye, please.'

Miriam replaced the book she'd been reading and came reluctantly towards the counter.

'Goodbye,' she said obediently.

'Choose a book, Miriam,' Carrie said. 'In fact, take as many as you like. On me.'

'She couldn't possibly—' Mrs Neumann began, but Carrie held up her hand.

'Please. It's the least I can do.'

'May I?' Miriam looked from Carrie to her mother and back again.

Mrs Neumann gave a gesture of defeat and Miriam shot off to the carousel again. She turned immediately with a book in each hand. 'These two?'

'Is that all? Are you sure?'

Miriam nodded. 'I mustn't be greedy.'

She came back to the counter so that Carrie could note down the titles and held out her hand.

'Thank you, Carrie,' she said. 'I want to be a writer, you know, when I'm older, and when I am, I'll dedicate one of my books to you.'

'Oh, Miriam!' said her mother, with an affectionate tut.

But Carrie believed her.

'So many writers begin as readers,' she said. 'I'm sure you'll be one of them, Miriam.'

'I hope so!'

'It makes sense, doesn't it,' smiled Carrie. 'You wouldn't start out to be a plumber without learning about taps – or an electrician without learning about circuits. You wouldn't become a teacher if you didn't like children. If you love books enough to read as much as you do, and like to express your own thoughts too, then it's natural to graduate to writing. And if you want to do that badly enough, Miriam, I'm sure you will!'

The bell rang and Mr Bayliss announced the arrival of the next train to London. Miriam crouched down and opened her suitcase, squeezing her new books on top. Carrie smiled to see that there were at least as many books as clothes inside. Miriam closed the lid and, with a final wave, she and her mother moved off to join the rest of the family.

The train came in, the passengers got off and the little group boarded. This train had its own wheeltapper. He walked the length of the carriages, telling by the sound his special hammer made if a wheel was stressed or starting to crack. Carrie winced as he put his hand on the axle boxes to check if they were running hot – she'd seen a wheeltapper badly burnt once. This time, however, he was satisfied there were no problems. The doors slammed shut, the guard leaned out of his van and blew his whistle. The train pulled out, and with it, the Neumann family left for a new life far away.

Carrie hoped in her heart they'd be back, but she understood their decision. The safety and security of this small island had never been more fragile – and things could go either way.

*

The days went on, the nights went on, the air raids went on. When Carrie arrived at the station one morning, dark circles under her eyes from another broken night, Bette was already there, a good two hours before she needed to be.

'Carrie, hello!' she greeted her, looking surprisingly cheerful. 'Ooh, I haven't had a wink of sleep.'

'Nor me,' grimaced Carrie.

'No, no, not because of the sirens. I've had a letter!'

Carrie's first thought was that the Prime Minister had finally admitted defeat and written back in person, but it was better than that.

'It's my Eric. He's alive! He's a prisoner, love, but he's alive!'

Carrie dropped her handbag and the cardboard box containing her gas mask onto the platform and opened her arms.

'Oh, Bette! That's wonderful. Oh, I'm so pleased for you!'

Bette pushed the official letter into her hands and Carrie took in the brief typewritten words. Private Eric Saunders was being held as a prisoner of war. His address was Stalag XXA. He was reported to be well and was able to receive post.

'As soon as you've opened up, I want two pads of paper and envelopes,' Bette gabbled. 'I've used up all the paper I had at home – I've been writing letters all night and chucking them in the bin. I don't know where to start with all I've got to say to him – and I've got to be so careful. I can't say half of what I really want!'

Carrie unlocked the stall and handed Bette what she needed.

'No charge,' she said, smiling. 'I'm so happy for you, Bette, truly I am. And when you decide what to write, give Eric my best regards, won't you?'

'Course I will,' Bette reassured her. 'I only wish you'd heard the same, my love, about your Mike. But you know what this means, don't you? You'll be hearing from him any day now, I bet! He'll write to you from whatever camp he's in.'

'Yes, well, I hope so. That would be wonderful.'

But Carrie's heart was heavy. Bette was trying to be kind, but even if that were the case, she might still have a long wait.

Chapter Seventeen

Meanwhile, there was Johnnie.

Carrie's twin hadn't just passed all his practical and theory tests – he'd passed with credits or distinctions. There was no such thing as a safe role for a pilot in the RAF, but it was clear that as one of their star pupils, he was going to be on the front line of the fighting, fighting that was getting more intense every day.

Biggin Hill, Kenley and Croydon, all close to Brockington, were the main bases for repelling the German bombers that were coming over the Channel in their droves, set on destroying the entire British air force and its airfields. Sure enough, Johnnie was posted to –

'Croydon!' he told Mary on the phone. 'Nice and near home. I can bring you my washing!'

'Just you make sure it is your washing, and not your things delivered in a box because you're at the bottom of the sea,' Carrie hissed when their mother was out of earshot and she took the receiver.

'Thanks,' Johnnie replied. 'Not got much faith in me, have you!'

He could make light of it all he liked, but the fact that the first thing every pilot had to do on joining the RAF was to make a will wasn't exactly reassuring.

Up in waves, day after day, night after night, went the British fighter planes – Johnnie among them. Their aim was to shoot down the fighters that shielded the German bombers, leaving the bombers unprotected. They could then be taken out by anti-aircraft fire before they reached their targets – or that was the plan. By mid-August, there were constant air raid warnings and the sound of planes over and around Brockington. Wherever Carrie was – at the station or at home, awake or in bed – she'd freeze, straining to try to identify the sound of the engine to tell whether the planes were German Dorniers that had got through, or, thanks be, a group of British fighters taken off from the nearby airfields to repel them. Young Terry had a good ear. If he was in the shop when a raid began, he had to shelter with the Andersons, and he'd curse colourfully if he detected German planes or whoop with delight if they were British.

Mary found it harder and harder to listen to the nightly news – all the Andersons did. Everyone was on edge until they heard the newsreader say 'all of our aircraft returned safely'. Sometimes it was 'one of our aircraft failed to return'. Sometimes it was more.

No one seemed to breathe till the phone rang and they heard Johnnie's voice reassuring them that he was all right. He made a point of phoning after every sortie, or the morning after at least, and his calls were getting more and more frequent. Carrie's twin's antennae were permanently twitching.

One night, she'd just got home when the sirens sounded. Mary was putting their evening meal – liver and onions – on the table.

'Oh blow this!' said Norman. 'Another dinner I don't get to eat!'

He went out for his warden's kit, leaving Carrie and her mother staring at the plates of congealing food.

'Better not risk it,' said Carrie. She was starving; she'd only had a meat-paste sandwich for lunch. The look on her mother's face told her she agreed, so they carried their plates to the shelter.

It was a good job they hadn't risked it. A few minutes later, there was a terrific crump and a tremor and everything shook – the paraffin lamp that swung from the ceiling, even the benches they were sitting on.

Mary clutched Carrie in a panic.

'That felt close!'

Carrie knew it could have been closer, though it was near enough – and too close for comfort. Because ever since the warning had sounded, she'd had a fluttering in her chest, a rolling of her stomach, a prickle of fear down her spine – it was Johnnie. He was in danger.

Sure enough, after hours and hours, when the all-clear had finally sounded and they stumbled back to the house, Carrie sent her mother to bed and stayed up for the midnight news. Gravely, the announcer told her that Croydon Airfield had been attacked.

It was another night of not much, if any, sleep for Carrie. She heard her dad come in at about two in the morning and low voices from her parents' room. It was the same for all of them. It was one thing worrying about her brother when he was in the air, but even if he hadn't been flying that night, he wasn't safe when he was on the ground, trying to relax, trying to sleep, snatching a meal or having a drink in the mess.

Carrie told herself Johnnie wouldn't phone in the middle of the night – that would worry the family even more – but she knew she couldn't leave for work, however late she was opening up, before she heard something, even if she had to call Croydon herself to try to reach him.

At five in the morning, she pulled on her old pink velour dressing gown and went downstairs in her bare feet. Her hand was hovering over the receiver in the hall when the phone rang and made her jump. She snatched it up.

'Johnnie! Thank God!' she said when she heard his voice on the other end. 'I heard on the news last night about the airfield. How are you? What happened?'

'The place is a mess.' He sounded exhausted. 'I'll tell you. I shouldn't, but you'll hear soon enough in the news. Twenty-two of them, Messerschmitts, came over, like a swarm. Damaged the old terminal, destroyed the armoury, two hangars – and about forty training planes have gone up in flames.'

'Forty!' Carrie was shocked.

'That's what I said.'

'Oh, Johnnie! And ... and there must have been ... casualties?' She hardly dared ask about fatalities.

'Too soon to say in numbers, but the worst of it is, they took out a couple of factories nearby as well, that were working night shifts.'

'Oh no.'

'Yup.'

'And what about you? Where were you?'

'I think you know better than to ask.'

So he'd been flying, part of the fighter formation trying to hold off the bombers. And it was ridiculous, but she knew he'd be blaming himself for not personally stopping every single one of the German planes.

'Are you OK?' she asked anxiously. He didn't sound it.

'You know I am. I'm phoning, aren't I?' said Johnnie, rather shortly.

'I mean, are you OK in yourself?' Carrie replied.

'I'm tired, that's all,' Johnnie answered her. 'Wouldn't you be? I've been up all night. So I think I'll go and get some kip, if you don't mind. Bye.'

But Carrie did mind. He must be exhausted, she understood that, but he hadn't sent his love to her, or their mum and dad, which he did without fail at the end of every call. He hadn't urged her to 'stay safe'. He'd sounded so distant and she knew at that moment that he was lost to her. She remembered what Mike had told her: that the army – all the forces – turned boys into men and men into fighting men. That's what the RAF had done for Johnnie. He'd always be her brother, but he was a man now, a proper grown-up doing a grown-up and dangerous job. When he'd put the receiver down as he had, Carrie felt he was telling her that. He'd closed off their communication on the phone, but more significantly, though perhaps to spare her anguish, he'd severed their psychic link.

She stood there in the little hall, her feet getting cold on the worn linoleum. She tried and tried, but she couldn't seem to reach him at all.

*

It was only the bookstall that kept her going. With no news of Mike either, if she hadn't loved what she was doing, and felt so needed by her customers, so many of whom now felt like friends, Carrie didn't know how she'd have coped. She found she was comfort reading, and despite being surrounded by Mr Parfitt's tempting new Penguins, she turned back to the books she'd always loved: *Little Women*, *Pride and Prejudice*, even *Anne of Green Gables*. She deliberately filled her evenings, too, but at night she wanted to howl like the sirens she was always expecting.

The difference in their circumstances also put up a small but significant barrier between Carrie and Bette. Bette didn't have much – so far she hadn't received a single reply to any of the letters she'd sent Eric. Relatives had been told that the Red Cross were sending them on, but whether they ever reached the camp, never mind what happened to them if they did, was anyone's guess. The camp commanders might sit on them for weeks or months. They weren't supposed to, there were rules about that, international agreements, but after the awful things they'd done in the war so far, who knew what the Nazis were capable of? So Bette's life wasn't all roses, far from it, but she did at least have the comfort of knowing that her son was alive. Carrie had a vast, empty silence.

On the other hand, on the plus side (and you had to look for a plus side in everything in wartime), Johnnie was still alive, against all the odds, Mike might still be – she had to hang on to that – and Carrie was finding that she'd drawn closer to Penny.

'It's just a bit awkward,' she confided to her. 'It's more on

Bette's side, really. It's as if she's embarrassed because she's had news and I haven't.'

'Well, you'd be a saint if you weren't a bit jealous,' Penny replied. 'And you don't want to be one of those – very dull! You need cheering up. How about the pictures tonight?'

Penny seemed to have unbent as the months passed and summer had unfolded. She came over to chat more often, and as long as Carrie bit back her curiosity to know more about her background, Penny was warm and friendly. Just the other week she'd said sympathetically that Carrie was losing her bloom over the situation with Mike, and had brought her a little gift of some new hair ribbons to cheer her up.

There were now quite a few women porters up and down the country – there'd been a programme on the wireless about them – and the train companies had had to come up with a uniform that fitted. Penny had a smart white shirt, a tailored waistcoat, a better-fitting jacket and trousers in navy serge, serviceable shoes and a cap. Her dark hair had grown, though she still tucked it under her cap for work, and all in all she cut a striking figure.

One afternoon, Penny was standing at the bookstall leafing through *Picture Post* when Carrie noticed Mr Bayliss.

'Enemy at six o'clock,' she hissed, using the military term she'd learned from Mike and Johnnie.

Penny glanced behind her and straightened up, putting down her magazine. Mr Bayliss was marching up the platform from his office.

'Nothing to do, Edwards?' he barked as he got closer.

'Waiting for the two-oh-five to come in, Mr Bayliss, sir,' Penny replied, laying it on thick with his name and a 'sir'.

Since their first run-in, she'd made a point of being over-polite. Mr Bayliss was so full of his own importance, he didn't seem to realise that it was all tongue in cheek. 'Two crates of chickens to unload for the Acme Insurance Company's Fowl Club.'

Mr Bayliss sniffed and consulted his fob watch.

'Very well. Have you watered the pelargoniums today?'

Mr Bayliss brought them in himself every summer from his greenhouse to decorate the hanging baskets near the ticket office and the raised beds at the end of each platform. Woe betide anyone who called them geraniums – Mr Bayliss was very particular about the difference. Geraniums were 'hardy', apparently, while his pelargoniums were 'tender'. So there!

'First thing, sir,' said Penny meekly. 'Before the sun got on them. That's best, I believe. Otherwise they scorch.'

But no one could tell Mr Bayliss anything about his precious flowers.

'Don't be clever with me, young lady!' he snapped. 'I've been growing pelargoniums since you were in the nursery. Just ask anyone in the Brockington Horticultural Society.'

'I'll do that, sir.'

Mr Bayliss harrumphed and strutted on. Penny met Carrie's eye. They were still giggling about the pompous old fool as the train puffed in alongside the up platform.

Carrie straightened her periodicals and papers for the expected customers while Penny moved towards the train's goods van. The train ground to a halt: the doors opened and passengers began to get off. The guard lugged open the heavy wooden door of his van, and Carrie saw Penny heave two crates of squawking birds onto the platform. Then Mr Bayliss called her from a couple of carriages away.

'Edwards! Stick those against the wall and come over here to help this lady, please!'

'Just coming, sir!'

Carrie watched as Penny did as she was told with the birds, then moved towards an elderly lady cautiously descending backwards from the train, as if she was coming down a ladder. With a gap between the step and the platform, it was the safest way to get down if you were a bit unsteady on your feet. Mr Bayliss was holding out a sheltering arm in case she missed her footing anyway.

'There we are, madam, safe and sound!' he boomed as the woman stepped backwards on to the platform. He turned to Penny. 'Edwards, there's a small brown leather suitcase in the rack – in the third compartment along, wasn't it, madam?'

'That's right. A very kind young sailor put it up for me—'

The woman turned and faced Penny for the first time.

'Oh my goodness! Oh, bless me!' she exclaimed. 'Miss Penelope! What on earth are you doing here?'

Carrie was watching open-mouthed. 'Miss Penelope' – what? Surely even Penny, mysterious, secretive, closed-as-an-oyster Penny, couldn't get out of that one! Fortunately, at that moment, the guard called Mr Bayliss over and he scurried off. Penny got into the train, fetched the case and hustled the old lady quickly out through the ticket office to the taxi rank and out of Carrie's hearing. But when she came back through, Carrie was waiting to pounce.

'You can forget the pictures tonight,' she told her. 'We're going to the Kardomah. We need to talk!'

Penny held up her hands in submission.

'You win,' she said.

'Come on, then, "Miss Penelope",' Carrie began when the waitress had taken their order. 'Confession time. Tell all!'

Penny sighed and took a long swig of her lemonade.

'OK. Full disclosure. What I told you in the beginning is true. I am from Norfolk. I was brought up there. But I'm not Penny Edwards. Well, I am, now.'

'I thought you were going to explain!'

'Give me a chance! Do you want to hear this or not?'

'Yes. You know I do.'

'Well, shut up then!'

Typical Penny! Carrie made a zipping-up-her-mouth gesture. Penny made a face at her, took a deep breath and went on:

'My real name is Penelope Eversleigh. The Honourable Penelope Eversleigh, if you must know. And the old dear on the train – and she is a dear, she pretty much brought me up – she was my old nanny.'

Carrie had been about to take a sip of her own drink, but she put it down so fast it splashed onto the table. Forgetting the promise she'd made just a few seconds ago, she spluttered:

'What?'

'I ran away from home,' said Penny simply, as if it was something as everyday as putting on your socks or cleaning your teeth. 'My mother died when I was a baby and my father – well, let's just say he's rather old-fashioned. In fact, someone ought to notify the Natural History Museum that one of their dinosaurs has escaped.'

Carrie laughed and Penny continued.

'He had my name down for Eton before I was born. He was so disappointed that I wasn't a boy, he didn't register me for anywhere else. He didn't – he doesn't – think girls are worth educating.'

'That's ridiculous—' Carrie began, and received a warning glance.

Penny went on.

'So, I was never sent away to school. I had a nanny and a governess, and I was due to go to finishing school in Switzerland when war broke out. That's all girls are good for in my father's view. Being charming, and finding a husband. I've got nothing else to thank Hitler for, but at least he saved me from that!'

Nannies . . . finishing school . . . so much now made sense to Carrie. The initials on the silk camiknicks – not from a jumble sale at all, but out of the Honourable Penelope's underwear drawer, laundered by the housemaid, no doubt. The fact that Penny didn't really have an accent; in fact, sometimes she'd sounded quite posh. The fact that she didn't bite her nails any more – maybe that had all been part of the act, part of her disguise? Which had been pretty good. With the way she'd mucked in and taken on all the work Mr Bayliss had thrown at her, no one would have thought she'd been brought up a . . . well, a lady!

'OK . . . I see all that,' Carrie said, 'but running away from home and pretending to be someone else is still pretty extreme!'

Penny straightened the cruet and the little vase with its carnation and spray of fern.

'You should meet my father! Or maybe not. He's ex-army himself, probably a big cheese in the Home Guard by now, bossing them all about. Like he thought he could boss me. Because finishing school wasn't the end of it.' She blew out such a big breath that a lock of hair lifted off her forehead. 'There was this boy, you see, local, a neighbour. We'd known each other since Pony Club. He's always had a thing for me, but he was a horrible little squirt then and he's not much better now. Talks about nothing but hunting and shooting. Boring as hell, but loaded. And since our place is entailed—'

'Entailed!'

'It means it has to go to a male relative. I told you I have no brothers. And I can't inherit.'

'I know what entailed is,' said Carrie. 'Like in *Pride and Prejudice*. Mr and Mrs Bennet only had daughters. Hence the need to marry them off.'

'Exactly.'

'So your father wanted you to marry this bloke, and then what? Go off and live on his family's estate? I assume he has an estate? Or his parents do.'

'They certainly do, a large one. And yes, Giles will inherit his family pile, while the house I grew up in is due to go to a second cousin in Australia.'

'That's so unfair,' muttered Carrie.

'You're telling me! But my father thought that if he could marry me off to Giles, and if maybe the Australian cousin didn't want our place, because he's got a life in Australia, he might sell it, then Giles's folks would buy it, as it neighbours their land. They're seriously well off, you see.'

'Right . . .'

'And with me married to Giles, I might get to live in our old house, at least till he took over his parents' place, and our bloodline would still sort of have a stake there. Which might sound OK in theory, if you're my father. The snag for me being that I'd have had to live there with that goon Giles.' She shuddered. 'The thought of him touching me – yeuch!'

Carrie goggled at what she'd learned. It was so far removed from her experience, she could hardly take it in. It really did sound like something out of a nineteenth-century novel.

'But it's all so . . . calculating!' she exclaimed. 'As if you're something to be – well, practically bought and sold.'

'Hmm. That's what I thought. I mean, you'd think we'd have moved on a bit from the *Pride and Prejudice* era.'

Their food – Welsh rarebit – arrived, but neither girl even glanced at it. Carrie was still agog.

'You'd have hoped so. But it was that important to your father?'

Penny shrugged.

'Well, the house has been in the family since some ancestor picked the right side to be on in some old war or other. If I was being kind to my father, I'd say he saw it as my duty, really.'

Carrie picked up her knife and fork, then promptly put them down again.

'OK, so far, so awful. But how come you decided to be a

porter, and how did you change your name and end up in Brockington?'

Penny had started eating and finished her mouthful.

'Eat while it's hot. It's not bad.'

Carrie did as she was told and Penny continued.

'I wasn't going to hang around while my father scrambled about trying to marry me off before Giles went off to the war – he was a reservist, of course. There was so much confusion and panic, and so many people moving here and there, I knew if I could just get away, I could reinvent myself. I went to London, asked around, got myself a new identity card. It's not difficult if you can pay. And then I picked Brockington by sticking a pin in a map, came here, got myself digs, and went to the Labour Exchange to see what work was on offer.'

'But why didn't you just join one of the services?' asked Carrie. 'They'd have had you like a shot and you could have got miles away without all the cloak-and-dagger stuff.'

'Didn't I say my dad was ex-army? He's got all the right contacts. He'd have tracked me down.'

'Of course.'

'But by doing a dirty, menial job – that's not how I see it, but it's how he would – by doing a job that he'd never think of me touching, I felt I could hide away. And till today, it's worked, hasn't it?'

'Well, yes,' Carrie admitted. 'Though I was a bit suspicious about the monogrammed camiknickers.'

'Ah, yes, those,' Penny smiled. 'I was pretty impressed with the story I came up with, given that I was concussed at the time!'

Now even more was falling into place for Carrie.

'And there were other things! Like why you didn't want to go to court over the bag snatch. I suppose the police might have looked into your background and checked your identity and somehow found out who you were.'

'That's exactly why. Well done, Sherlock.'

'And was that the same with the lost property? When you had to hide? In case Bayliss had you prosecuted?'

'Hah! You think I'm that scared of Bayliss? He was just a handy excuse. It was the officer he was talking to that panicked me. It was Giles!'

'Oh my goodness! Your heart must have stopped.'

'It very nearly did. I don't know what I'd have done if you hadn't hidden me.'

Carrie sat back and puffed out a breath, she didn't know of what. Astonishment, yes, but admiration, mostly.

'Honestly, Penny, your life. It's like ... *The Thirty-Nine Steps*!'

'There you go again,' grinned Penny. 'You've got a bookish reference for everything.'

'I'll take that as a compliment,' Carrie smiled.

'You should. You're someone who's definitely in the right job.' Penny smiled too. 'But the biggest irony is that it was Nanny Hargreaves – the lady on the train – who finally exposed me. She's the sweetest person. She was so kind to me. I loved her to bits. So of course my father got rid of her and got a dreadful old dragon instead.'

Carrie put her hand across the table and squeezed Penny's.

'I'm sorry. I'm sorry you've had such a hard time.'

And she was. There was Penny, born with the proverbial silver spoon – big house, land, money and a title, all of that – yet her childhood had been nothing like Carrie's in a warm, loving family in a modest newsagent's shop.

'Oh please don't feel sorry for me,' Penny said at once. 'I had every advantage. And I still feel myself pretty well off. Dear Nanny Hargreaves isn't going to tell my father where I am. I had to tell her the truth, I wasn't going to lie to her. But she's safely on her way to stay with her sister in Woking. It was nice to see her, though.'

'But what about Mr Bayliss? He was right there when she called you "Miss Penelope". Hasn't he asked you about it?'

'Nope.' Penny shook her head. 'He's so wrapped up in himself, he's not going to bother. And if he does, I'll have to tell a white lie. Say she was confused and I wasn't who she thought I was.'

'Do you think he'll believe you?'

'He'll have to. I feel safer with him these days. I think I've proved myself enough in the work. He's not going to get anyone better to do the job now the war's really taken off. And Eric, bless him, isn't coming back anytime soon, is he?'

Carrie shook her head. 'No, he's not.'

It was Penny's turn to put her hand out to Carrie.

'I'm sorry I couldn't tell you before. I nearly did, a couple of times. I felt I could trust you, but . . . I don't know. I've got used to holding it all in, I suppose, to protect myself. Sorry. You deserved better.'

Carrie was touched.

'I did wonder why you still seemed a bit stand-offish, even when we got to know each other better. Anyway, it's water under the bridge. The Brockington Junction railway bridge!'

Penny grinned, then her smile faded.

'I want to say something else as well. I can't imagine how ghastly it must be for you, not knowing about Mike for all this time. I'm glad I haven't got anyone I really care about who's fighting. I hope you hear something soon. Either way.'

'Yes. So do I,' said Carrie. 'Thanks, Penny. And thanks for telling me . . . well, who you really are. I won't breathe a word.'

'No, please don't. Not to Bette, not even to your lovely parents, or your brother.'

'I won't, I promise. But can I ask you something?'

They'd both finished their rarebits by now. Penny was studying the little menu card.

'I fancy a knickerbocker glory. I suppose the cream'll be ersatz, but even so . . .' She looked up. 'Yes, ask me anything. We have no secrets now. What?'

'Have you got a tiara?'

Penny threw back her head and hooted with laughter, so loudly that a man at the next table almost choked on his soup.

'Several!' And when Carrie's face registered amazement, she said, 'Joke! But there's quite a nice set of emeralds in the safe.'

Chapter Eighteen

After the astonishing revelation about Penny (or 'Miss Penelope', as Carrie now thought of her, and teasingly called her when no one else was around), Carrie expected everything to calm down. But they say buses come along in threes, or at least they had before the war, and now, in the same way, everything suddenly started happening, like an avalanche that couldn't be stopped.

First, Hitler upped his bombing raids. His plan to put the RAF out of action hadn't worked, so he switched his attention to the major cities, trying to knock out their factories or vital services. But since people lived near where they worked, what it really meant was that when the Luftwaffe targeted London's or Liverpool's docks, or Birmingham's armaments factories or gasworks, row after row of terraces – people's homes – got wiped out too, as well as churches, shops and offices. Brockington had no heavy industry worth targeting, but the bombers flew over it relentlessly to London, the Midlands and the North.

Everyone was exhausted.

'Even Ruby hasn't got the energy to dye her hair,' Bette reported. 'And her nail varnish is chipped! She's never been the same since the Bourjois factory got bombed – worried she'll never get any more of that Evening in Paris scent she douses herself in. I said to her, if that's all you've got to worry about, my girl, you're on velvet!'

Carrie nodded wearily. Even Penny seemed worn down by the constant air raids and had to peel herself off the wall where she'd been almost asleep on her feet when a train came in on the down platform.

'I'd better drag myself over and see if anyone wants any help,' she sighed. 'No sign of Bayliss, I note. Snoozing in his office with his feet on the desk, I presume!'

Carrie watched dully as the passengers from the train streamed through the tunnel to emerge on the up platform before heading out through the ticket office. A few came over to buy a paper or a magazine, a couple even bought books, but for once Carrie couldn't stir herself to say anything about their choices, to ask if they'd read any others by the same author, or if they'd recommend it if, unusually, they chose a book by an author she'd never read.

Out of the corner of her eye while she served people, she noticed a short, stocky man, late forties or fifty perhaps, in a sergeant's uniform. He lingered nearby, and when her customers had gone, he stepped forward, taking off his cap to reveal salt-and-pepper hair, smoothed down and neatly parted.

'Carrie, isn't it?' he said. 'Carrie Anderson?'

'Yes . . . ?'

'I don't suppose you remember me. No reason why you should,' he added swiftly.

'I'm afraid I don't,' Carrie frowned. 'I see a lot of soldiers pass through. Did you buy a book?' Sometimes customers came back to tell her they'd enjoyed her recommendations. 'Or, sorry, have we met?'

196

The sergeant shook his head.

'No, not exactly. Not at all, in fact.'

'So how do you know me?'

'I served with your boyfr—well, with Lieutenant Hudson. From the start of the war. In this country and then in France.'

Now it came back to her.

'I remember you, I do! You called him from the train and he had to go.'

It had been the very first day she and Mike had met.

'That's right.' He held out his hand. 'Stan Thompson.'

Carrie shook his hand.

'Well, it's nice to meet you properly. But please, I – I've been desperate to know. I've heard nothing. Where is Mike? What's happened to him? Do you know?'

The questions tumbled out one after the other, like balls rolling down a slope.

'Well, that's why I came.'

'So? Oh please tell me!'

He looked awkward.

'Erm . . . you mean 'ere? What if you get customers? I'm not in a rush. Can you get off for a bit?'

'Just tell me, in a word! Please! Is he alive or dead?'

'I don't know.'

Not aware she was even doing it, Carrie had been straining forwards across the counter. Now she sagged back.

'All I can tell you,' Stan said, 'is what I do know. If that's any help.'

*

Carrie didn't want to take him to the tearoom, with Bette looking on curiously and Ruby earwigging, so she locked the stall. This was one time when disappointing any customers who might come in on the next train didn't matter. To think she might learn, once and for all, something of what had happened to Mike – good or bad. So she took Stan Thompson to The Ginger Cat.

On the way, because she couldn't bear for him to start telling her what he knew about Mike in the street and for it to be drowned out by a passing bus or a car backfiring, she asked him about himself.

'Well, as you can probably tell, I'm a Brummie by birth,' he smiled, referring to his accent. 'Been in the army almost all me life, man and boy, like my dad before me and his dad before 'im. I could've retired, I suppose, being as I'm over the age, but it's all I know.'

'I bet you know a lot. I bet you've been invaluable in this war.'

'Well, I've picked up a few tips over the years. How to make a decent brew in a billycan and soap your boots to stop the blisters.'

'I suppose you've seen a lot as well,' Carrie probed.

'Oh, ar. I've seen it all.'

They were at the café now and Sergeant Thompson ('Call me Stan') held the door open for her. The waitress knew Carrie and waved her to a table by the window. Stan ordered them a pot of tea.

They sat in silence till the waitress brought it over, then Stan poured them each a cup.

'You don't want to hear about me, anyway,' he said. 'You want to hear about the Lieutenant.'

'Yes. Please tell me – whatever it is, I have to know!'

'I'm sorry I couldn't come before,' Stan said. His warm brown eyes, full of compassion, met hers. 'I 'ad a bit of a rough time meself after Dunkirk, but . . . any road, I'm on light duties now, clerical, at Caterham. We've had a lot of letters from people like yourself, not relatives –'cos if there was news, they'd hear through the official channels, eventually – but friends, young ladies, I mean, frantic to know about fellers they've not heard from.'

'I almost wrote myself,' Carrie confessed.

'It wouldn't have done no good,' Stan shrugged. 'We couldn't tell 'em anything – they could have been anyone, masquerading as a friend, you see.'

'What? Who? Like spies?'

'Spies, fifth columnists, anything to winkle out some gen.'

Carrie was horrified at the thought, but she couldn't wait any longer.

'But Mike – tell me about Mike, please.'

Stan took a sip of his tea.

'Well, when we first got over there, we had a pretty decent time of it. The French treated us like kings. The exchange rate was about a hundred and seventy-five francs to the pound, and if I tell you a whisky down the local caff was a couple of francs, and a slap-up meal with wine was about seven . . . well, you get the picture! Plus the French said no one'd ever get through their Maginot Line – you know, the fortifications between France and Germany – so we thought we was safe as houses.'

Carrie's tea was untasted in front of her. She just wanted him to get on with it!

'But the German tanks broke into France through the forest, didn't they,' she prompted.

'Spot on,' said Stan. 'There was only a few French troops there, 'cos that was supposed to be impassable as well, owing to the up-and-down terrain and the trees and that, and from then on – well, France had had it, basically. Any road, we'd gone ahead into Belgium, 'cos of Hitler massing his troops on their border, and suddenly our orders was to retreat, which was one thing till it became another – when we realised the Jerries in France weren't heading for Paris.'

There'd been enough maps in the papers; Carrie knew northern France almost as well as she knew the lanes to Petts Wood.

'They came north and west, not south and east,' she said.

'Yeah. So in effect, we was marching towards 'em. And it wasn't just us – it was absolute bloody chaos, excuse my French. The roads were thick with cars, carts, lorries, anything that moved. And hundreds, thousands of 'em on foot, all they could carry in suitcases, in prams, and pushing granny along in a blinking wheelbarrow.'

Carrie shook her head sadly. She'd known all this from the papers, the wireless and newsreels, and she'd seen the refugees who'd made it out passing through the station, but hearing it directly from someone who'd been there made it horribly real. But she had to get Stan back to the point.

'And you and Mike were still together?'

200

'Oh yes, him and a captain in charge.'

Carrie nodded encouragingly – surely they were getting closer to what she most wanted to hear. Stan resumed his tale.

'So we're on the march, going west, and blow me, if it isn't getting worse. As well as the Dutch and Belgians going the same way as us, we'd got French refugees coming towards us, and the flaming German planes strafing us with bullets. Didn't bomb us, but only because they wanted to keep the roads in good nick for their tanks! So Lieutenant Hudson and the captain had a bit of a conflab and decided we'd march across country. We split into two parties, about twenty each – we'd lost a few by then, what with the bullets and that – and I was with the Lieutenant. God, did we march, day and night! We was clapped-out, hungry, drinking from streams, swarms of bombers and fighters looking for anything that moved. We lost a few more men that way.'

He paused for a moment, obviously reliving it, thinking back.

Carrie realised there was no point in trying to hurry him: Stan needed to tell the tale in his own way. For all she knew, it was the first time he'd told it, and she'd read somewhere that once a man – or woman – who'd seen action started to talk, it was important not to interrupt, but to let them have their say.

'When the bombers appeared, you made a run for it to a hedge or trees. If you was out in the open, you ran like the clappers.' Stan sighed. "Course we had a couple of walking wounded by then as well, and poor old Brooksy, one of the men, we were half carrying him between us . . . Anyway, to cut a long story in half, we finally got near the coast – we'd seen it from miles off 'cos of the fires from the incendiaries and the bombing of the ports . . . Dawn was breaking, and I think we thought this was it, we'd be going home. Little did we know!'

He took another sip of his tea and shook his head.

'Three days we waited on the beach at Dunkirk. If we thought the bombing and the machine-gunning on the roads was bad, that was a kiddies' party. On the beach there was nowhere to hide – well, you had the dunes, but they were NBG.'

Carrie knew from the soldiers' slang she'd picked up that meant 'no bloody good'.

'But Mike was still with you?'

Stan smiled and sighed at the same time, remembering again.

'He'd go round the men, give 'em a little pep talk, tell 'em to keep their peckers up, say our turn would come. We could see the ships offshore, and the little boats coming in, but you had to wait your orders, see. But the ships was being bombed as fast as they came in, and we was torching equipment and petrol dumps – you don't want to leave that sort of kit for the enemy.'

Surely, Carrie thought, surely now he must be getting to the vital part? As if reading her mind, Stan seemed to pull himself together.

'So finally we get the call: down to this sort of jetty, only a narrow thing, a groyne almost, stretching out into the water, and blow me if this thing that's like a blinking paddle steamer's come for us. Anyway, whatever, it was a boat! So

Lieutenant Hudson and me hang back, obviously, to get the men on first. Brooksy and the other two injured, then the rest – another eight men. The German planes are swooping down, machine-gunning, there's noise and shouts and curses and spray, and I don't know what all. My turn comes – I scramble on, and then—'

'Yes?'

Carrie leaned forward, but Stan shook his head sadly.

'Then I don't rightly know what happened. I got flung into the water, got a knock on the head, the next thing I know is I'm in a military hospital in Poole. Seems I got hauled into another little boat – a fishing smack, I think – and from there onto a destroyer that was anchored offshore. I've tried and tried to find out what happened to the Lieutenant. As far as the army's concerned, he's MIA – Missing in Action. We've had no news he was took prisoner.'

Carrie swallowed hard.

'So that's what his parents have been told – that he's missing?'

'Yes. And that's how it'll stay until . . .'

Carrie knew the answer. It had happened to a family in Harold Road; their son's ship had been torpedoed early in the war.

'Unless we hear Mike's a prisoner, after six months he'll be presumed dead.'

They sat in silence for a moment. Carrie found her eyes were full of tears – not even for herself, but for Mike's mum and dad and his sister, Jane. There they were in Leamington, animal-mad Jane at school, the parents going every day to their shop, dealing with customers, politely fending off questions and concerned looks, selling buttons and thread and measuring out material by the yard, booking in sewing machines for a service, going through the motions, just as she had been, with the awfulness of not knowing, and the even more awful prospect of having to accept something worse.

'I'm sorry, love,' said Stan. 'I'm sorry to be the one to tell you. And not to have anything concrete to tell you after all. Maybe it was a mistake to come—'

'No, no, please, you mustn't think that!' Carrie exclaimed. 'It was so kind of you. And it's been really helpful.'

'Really?'

'Really.'

They finished their tea; there didn't seem much more to say. Stan paid the bill and they left the café. He was going back to Caterham, to his clerical work, or 'bottom polishing', as he called it. Carrie had to smile. She could imagine him and Mike getting along a treat.

'We'll walk back together, shall we?' he asked. 'I guess you're going back to work?'

But Carrie shook her head. Bette and Penny would have noticed her unexplained absence. They'd be sure to find her on her return and she wasn't ready yet for their sympathy or concern. It was almost five o'clock, a busy time, but for once her customers would have to do without.

'Actually, I'd like to be on my own for a bit,' she said.

Stan nodded and they shook hands.

'Fair enough. But . . . I ain't got much family – married to the army, don't you know.' He made a comical face. 'But I've got an old auntie up Lewisham way and I nip up to see her when I can. Perhaps you won't mind if I come and say hello again when I'm passing?'

'Please do! I'd like that.' He was a live link with Mike, after all, her only one. 'And thank you, Stan. I can't thank you enough.'

'Nothing to thank me for, bab. And if we do hear anything back at base, you'll be the first to know.'

'Thank you,' Carrie said again.

But somehow, she didn't think there'd be any more to tell.

Chapter Nineteen

She walked aimlessly for what seemed like hours, reliving her time with Mike. She travelled back through every precious moment. The Sunday afternoons when they'd walked in the countryside, their cheeks pink from the cold, then thawed out over ginger wine in a low-beamed pub or tea and scones in a tea shop. The evenings in the smoky dark of the cinema, or swaying close at a dance: the rough feel of his uniform, the firmness of his arms around her, the faint smell of shaving soap and a peppery cologne. The locket he'd given her; the awful day when he'd told her he was leaving . . .

She went back over what Stan had told her, forcing herself to picture him in France: the desperate march to escape, scavenging for food, footsore and weary, but having to appear cheerful and determined to urge the men on, only to find chaos on the beaches and a terrifying wait, which in his case hadn't even proved worthwhile. She saw in her mind's eye those final moments on the jetty, the boat and freedom just a footstep away, only to be gunned and bombed, thrown into the water, or back onto the sand, and then . . . tears were coursing down her face and she had to grope her way to a wall and sit down.

'Are you all right, love?' a passing woman asked her with concern.

Carrie nodded, shaking tears onto her lap.

She got home somehow. Mary was rubbing suet into flour for dumplings and the homeliness of home, her mum's flowered pinny, the battered kettle beginning to whistle on the stove, a handful of Michaelmas daisies in a jam jar by the sink – the ordinary sights and sounds that Mike might never see or hear again – set off her tears once more.

'Carrie! What's happened?' Mary turned, sticky dough clinging to her fingers, and called, 'Norman! Norm!'

Carrie's dad appeared in the doorway, the evening paper in his hand. Carrie flung herself at him and sobbed out all she'd been told.

'I've tried and tried to believe he's alive, but Bette's known for ages about Eric – if Mike was alive, there'd have been definite news about him by now. But at the same time, I can't give up hope, I just can't!'

Her parents let her cry.

'Better out than in,' said Norman later, when they'd sat her down and she'd had a cup of tea with a capful of brandy in it.

Carrie nodded dumbly.

'I've just got to get on with it,' she whispered. Her eyes stung and her throat was sore from sobs. 'It's not as though I'm the only one. There's thousands living with the uncertainty. And thousands more who've had definite news – and not the news they ever wanted to hear.'

Her mum squeezed her hand. She didn't have to say anything. Carrie knew she'd lost those she loved in war as well. She understood.

'You've always got us,' Mary said. 'I know it's not the

208

same, but we're here. And we always will be when you need us. That's what family's for.'

It was what friends were for as well, and Carrie knew both Bette and Penny would rally round. But they each had very different reactions to the news Stan had brought.

Penny, characteristically forthright, offered her advice.

'I can't tell you what to do, but I can tell you what I'd do,' she said after Carrie, twisting her hankie, had blurted it all out. 'And I'm sorry if it sounds brutal, but you know me, penny plain, they say, don't they, and twopence coloured, and I have to say what I feel. I should tell yourself he's dead. Then if in the next few months you get good news, won't that seem like the most wonderful surprise?'

Carrie could see her logic and was almost convinced, until she settled down for a cup of tea with Bette. Still writing faithfully to Eric, still not having had one single reply, Bette took the opposite view.

'Never give up!' she said. 'He's out there, I can feel it. Tell you what, shall I ask Madame Celeste to see if she can tune into him when I next go?'

Bette had taken to visiting a fortune teller whose crystal ball had revealed, variously, that Eric had 'a bit of a cold', was sleeping badly, was sleeping better, and would welcome a parcel of toothpaste, chocolate and socks.

'A standard-issue Red Cross parcel, in other words,' Penny had said scathingly, when Bette was out of earshot.

But Madame Celeste had also revealed that a side order of his mum's flapjacks would be especially well received, a detail that had convinced Bette of the woman's uncanny gifts.

'Anyone who's ever passed through the tearoom'd know those are Bette's speciality!' Penny scoffed. 'Honestly, I think I'll dress myself up in some old drapery, get hold of an upturned goldfish bowl and fleece a load of mugs! I could make a stash.'

So Carrie smiled politely at Bette, but declined Madame Celeste's intervention. It was kind of her friends; in their different ways, they were both trying to be helpful. But from day to day, Carrie still veered wildly between the two extremes: remembering what Mike had said about not giving up on him and castigating herself if she ever had a moment's doubt, then berating herself for being so ridiculously hopeful. But at least living on this sort of see-saw was what she knew, rather than having to plump for one alternative or the other.

And so September arrived, and with it the first anniversary of the war. Johnnie came home that very day for a brief leave and Carrie was shocked at the change in him.

He looked fine: he was definitely an inch taller from all the drills, and a bit broader too, but in a good way; his hair was crisply cut and his skin was tanned. But he'd flown nine sorties in a fortnight – there'd been more anxious waiting for his phone calls in the Anderson household. It seemed a miracle he was still alive, even though he was a sort of hollowed-out version of his former self. There were shadows under his eyes, and the eyes themselves were dull. They all noticed it, and Mary remarked on it.

'I'm just tired, Mum,' he said, just as he'd said to Carrie on the phone that time, then, bucking himself up, added, 'Now, what have you got for me? The food in the mess isn't bad, but it's your steak and kidney I've been dreaming about.'

Mary had anticipated this and obliged with his favourite, but after tea and a bit more chat, instead of the walk-and-talk Carrie had hoped for, Johnnie retreated to his room to sleep. He only had twenty-four hours and she'd left for work before he was up the next morning. Their twin bond hadn't been restored, and she felt uneasy.

They called it, afterwards, 'Black Saturday'. If they'd thought the bombing was bad before, the onslaught of the seventh of September was something else. Carrie was at the station when, in the late afternoon, the sirens went off. With the other staff and travellers, she was about to scuttle into the usual place, the tunnel under the tracks, when the local ARP warden appeared, blowing his whistle. He shooed them all to the public shelter on the corner of the road.

'They're heading for London, no doubt about it,' he said, running alongside Carrie and the others. 'Hordes of the blighters coming over the Channel. You can forget the tunnel – they're going to be looking for railway lines, aren't they?'

'What, bomb Brockington Junction?' Carrie panted, disbelieving.

'I don't think they're that fussy, love, especially when they've dropped their payload further in and want to off-load any bomb that's left to get them home quicker! Now hurry along, please!'

Then he charged off to help a mother trying to corral two toddlers while holding a screaming baby to her chest.

Parted from Penny and Bette, and even Ruby, Carrie squeezed onto a bench in the shelter between an elderly woman who smelled of mothballs and a shabby fellow with bad BO. Carrie thanked the Lord that she had her lifesavers with her – books.

These days she carried not one but three books in her bag, and through this particular long night, she had three of her beloved Penguins. There was an old favourite, a comfort blanket, if you like, and two that were new to her – one she was sure she'd like by an author she knew, and one she felt she ought to try. Whatever was happening outside, above and all around, Carrie could try to immerse herself in another world.

And so she tried, not always successfully, for twelve long hours. It was a fearful night of terrifying roars, whines, thumps and crumps, which they later learned had been the docks, but which had sounded as though the bombs were falling right outside. If that was what it had been like in Brockington, what it must have been like for the terrified residents of Stepney, Mile End or Bethnal Green was unimaginable.

Stiff and tired, but at least alive, Carrie emerged blinking into the dawn and headed back to the station. It wasn't worth going home only to get up again in less than two hours. Instead, she curled up on a bench in the ladies' waiting room – but she couldn't rest.

The RAF would have been in the thick of it. If she'd been terrified and felt drained, what must it have been like for Johnnie, desperately trying to hold back the bombers? Again, she tried to tune in to him, but there was still nothing; there'd been nothing since he'd cut their connection so abruptly in the phone call at the start of the Blitz. But surely after such a night ... Maybe she was too tired; maybe he was. She had to believe that was the reason. The blank silence couldn't be anything else ... could it?

At six she gave up the struggle to sleep and rang home from the call box outside the station. The phone was snatched up on the first ring.

'We thought you were Johnnie!' her mother exclaimed, then quickly said: 'But I'm glad you're all right, of course, love.'

'He's not rung yet, then?'

'Not yet.'

'He will, Mum,' Carrie said with more conviction than she felt. 'He's probably exhausted.'

'Yes, I daresay that's it.'

Mary had learned, day by painful day since Johnnie had got his wings, to sound confident even if she wasn't.

'Will you let me know when you hear from him?' Carrie asked. 'Phone the station – Mr Bayliss's office.'

'Is that allowed?'

'It had better be,' said Carrie defiantly. If Johnnie had taken down their special link, she didn't care what she had to do to establish a connection.

When the papers arrived for the bookstall, the early editions had some, but not all, of the story. It was days before the full extent of the destruction could be tallied, but the dead were known to be in their hundreds, the injured in their thousands, and entire families, hundreds more of them, had been made homeless. The massive fire the bombs had caused that night had done more damage than the Great Fire of London in 1666.

Bette and Ruby arrived together at about seven, and Penny not long after, bleary-eyed. They'd been directed to a different shelter from Carrie, where, Penny reported, she'd had to sit right near the toilet area.

'There was this chap with a harmonica,' she explained, wrinkling her nose, 'and when the lavs were in use, everyone said, "Play up!" and he did, to cover the sound.'

'Useful,' said Carrie.

'Yeah, trouble was he only knew about three tunes. If I hear "Danny Boy" one more time in this war, I swear I'll scream. And it didn't do much for the pong.'

As Carrie sympathised, Mr Bayliss came up the platform towards them. Even he looked dishevelled, with his waistcoat crumpled and his bowler hat askew on his head.

'Precious few trains today,' he informed them shortly. 'In or out of the city. You can guess why.' Penny and Carrie exchanged glances. 'Oh, and Miss Anderson – a telephone call came for you. Your brother's safe.'

It had never happened before, and probably never would again, but Carrie could have hugged him. Mr Bayliss seemed subdued. He didn't even say anything about the telephone being for important railway business only.

So it went on for the next few days. By day, the bombers crossed the coast in waves. The ack-ack guns around the suburbs and Inner London rattled and clattered away, while the Spitfires and Hurricanes from the airfields near Brockington – Johnnie, in other words – went up to meet the bombers and the enemy fighters that protected them. At night, the same thing happened as searchlights probed the sky like wands. Norman was out patrolling, but Carrie and her mother lay in their beds, wakeful, tensed for the alert that meant the night-time bombers were on their way. And all the time, fearful as she was for herself, Carrie was even more fearful for her twin.

Her parents, both of them, were grey with worry. Her dad's hands shook as he lifted down the big jars of humbugs and aniseed balls. On top of everything else, he was worried about sweets being the next thing to go on ration and how the shop would survive. He relied on the sweet tooth of the locals to keep the place going.

'It's amazing people still buy papers when they're down to only a few pages, and half the time they're not allowed to print what we want to know,' he complained.

Carrie understood. She'd been worried for her book trade, but so far, at least, the stock kept coming. The Penguin rep said that the government recognised that books were vital for morale – for soldiers and civilians alike. Anyway, Penguin had access to additional supplies of paper because they sent special editions to the forces and prisoners of war.

Johnnie's calls home now were nothing more than a quick 'I'm OK.' He wouldn't be drawn into anything resembling a conversation. 'There's no more I can say,' he'd snap, if pressed, and Carrie felt guilty for even trying – but she didn't stop trying to reach him in their special way.

'Crikey, that was a day and a night of it, wasn't it?' one of Carrie's regular customers greeted her one Monday in mid-September. 'Our boys did damn well, though.'

The *Mail*'s banner headline told it all:

'GREATEST DAY FOR RAF – *Half of Raiders Brought Down*'.
The *Daily Herald* had the figures:

'175 NAZI PLANES DOWN – *RAF Triumphs in Biggest Air Battles of War*'.

'I think I'll take three papers today, there's that much news,' the chap said eagerly, handing over his coppers for *The Times*, the *Daily Express* and the *Daily Mail*. 'They say one plane crashed right in the middle of the city – the army defused that time bomb under St Paul's just in time! And apparently there's bits of German planes all over Sussex and Kent.'

Carrie took his money with a nod. She'd had a sick feeling, that feeling of dread she recognised, the twin telepathy feeling, all the previous day and all through the long night; she had it still. Against all that, the fact that the RAF had miraculously lost only thirty planes should have been a triumph, but all she could see in the papers' reports were the bare typeset words saying that of those thirty losses, 'ten of the pilots are safe'.

And the other twenty? she screamed silently. And that was when Johnnie came through. She saw him suddenly, his eyes screwed up, his face contorted. 'Help me!' he seemed to be saying. What did it mean? Had his plane been hit? Had it crashed and he was lying injured in the wreckage? Had it – God forbid – caught fire? Or was he one of the twenty who hadn't made it back at all?

She had to sit down abruptly on the stool her dad had made, eyes closed, fists clenched, her nails digging into her palms.

'Where are you?' she asked Johnnie in her head. 'Tell me!'

'Oy, wakey-wakey, before Bayliss sees you!' It was Penny. Then she seemed to realise. 'Hey, are you all right? You're not ill?'

'It's Johnnie,' Carrie told her friend. 'Something's happened to him, I know it.'

'Go home,' Penny said decisively. 'If there's any news, that's where you'll hear it. I'll square things with Bayliss. And don't even think about the stall. Just lock it up and go!'

Chapter Twenty

And so Carrie went, hurrying past knots of people discussing the news, jubilant at what was seen as a great battle won.

'That'll show 'im,' she heard one woman say. 'Hitler's bit off more than he can chew with our boys!'

Back home, she went in through the shop. Her dad was there behind the counter, listening patiently to old Mrs Harrison telling him how 'my Bertie' had been so terrified in the night he'd wet his bed, not once, not twice, but three times. Bertie was her dog.

'How do you do it?' Carrie asked when the old woman had gone. And before her dad could ask what she was doing home, she jumped in with: 'Has Johnnie rung?'

The look in her dad's eyes told her exactly what she'd been dreading.

'Oh, Dad!' As Norman opened his arms, she went round the counter for a hug. 'How's Mum?'

'Sat at the table. Not moved since six. She wants to be near the phone.'

'I'll go and sit with her,' Carrie offered.

'Thanks, love. She'll be glad you're here.'

So the long day, the longest of Carrie's life, passed. She'd thought she'd got better at living with uncertainty after Mike, but her fears for him had receded into the far distance in the last twenty-four hours. Try as she might, she couldn't conjure up Johnnie again, and she dreaded to think what that meant – that she might never be able to, because he just wasn't there.

At noon, simply obeying the clock, not because anyone felt any hunger, she made some sandwiches for them all. Her mother nibbled a corner, her dad ate a couple, and Carrie forced one down, then covered the rest with a tin plate and put them in the larder. She made a pot of tea – the third, or was it the fourth?

When the phone rang mid-afternoon, they all scrambled for it and collided in the tiny hall. But it was only Penny, ringing to see if they'd heard anything. It was a relief and a disappointment all at once. It wasn't the RAF, telling them the worst, but it wasn't too late for it to have been Johnnie ringing to say he was all right . . . or was it?

Finally, at eight in the evening – Alf Warburton had let Norman off his ARP rounds – there was a loud knock on the shop door.

'If they think I'm opening up, tonight of all nights, because they're out of Gold Block ready rubbed . . .' muttered Norman, pulling aside the chenille curtain that separated their living quarters from the shop and going through. 'All right, all right, I'm coming!'

They listened as the bolts were drawn back and the door was unlocked, then heard the tinkle of the shop bell as it opened. A deep voice – not one they knew.

'Mr Anderson? I'm sorry to disturb you. May I come in?'

And then Norman's rather muted reply:

'Please. Go on through.'

Carrie and her mother jumped to their feet as a tall man in his early forties came into the living room. He swept off his cap and held out his hand.

'Mrs Anderson? Miss Anderson? I'm Squadron Leader Sheridan. I'm Johnnie's CO.'

Carrie and her mother looked at him dumbly. It was left to Norman, coming back in, to say, 'Please, have a seat. Can I get you anything?'

'No, no, but thank you.'

He sat down and placed his cap on his knees. He was good-looking – almost a requirement in the RAF – with a narrow, intelligent face and a small moustache. He cleared his throat.

'Can I say at the outset what a fine young man your son is.'

'Is?' Carrie leapt on the word. 'So he's not—'

'No, no. I'm sorry, I should have said straight away. Johnnie returned safely.'

'Thank God!' breathed Norman. 'So why are you here?'

'Why hasn't he rung?' squeaked Mary.

Squadron Leader Sheridan exhaled.

'Look. The situation is this. Johnnie is one of our best and brightest – he's the second-youngest Spitfire pilot we've got. And he's shown capability and maturity beyond his years this summer. Which doesn't look to be letting up.'

'So . . .' began Norman.

'Johnnie's been pushing himself,' Sheridan admitted. 'Some blame attaches to us, to me and his immediate superiors for letting him do it, but I'm sure you understand the pressure we've been under. The attrition rate's been high. We've been desperate for pilots willing to go up and hold them off. Even so, we urged Johnnie not to fly yesterday. He'd flown too many sorties already in the last ten days – we were worried he'd be holding his eyes open with his fingers. But he insisted.'

'Please just tell us what's happened to him? Is he hurt?'

It was an unusual outburst from Mary, but her nerves were stretched to breaking point. Norman got up and sat on the arm of her chair. He put his arm round her shoulders.

'No, no, it's not that either,' Sheridan apologised. 'He was fine when he landed – well, as good as you'd expect physically. But mentally . . . Basically, he's pushed himself too far. He's flown too much, seen too much, had too many narrow escapes. Johnnie's gone AWOL – absent without leave.'

'Where is he?' floundered Norman. 'Where can he be?'

'I don't know.' Sheridan spread his hands. 'I hoped you would. I came to ask if you had any ideas. But if you haven't seen him . . . ?'

'No, of course we haven't!' Carrie burst out. 'Do you think we're hiding him in a cupboard? We've been out of our minds with worry. We're not hiding him – I only wish we were!'

'Carrie!' Norman reprimanded.

Carrie sank back in her chair. 'Sorry.'

The Squadron Leader gave her a sympathetic smile.

'Please don't be. I understand the strain you're under. But the reason I'm here is because we – I – value Johnnie so highly. I should call in the Military Police, but I don't want to, not yet anyway.'

'But how will you explain . . .' Norman began.

'I can fudge things,' Sheridan said. 'I've come to appeal to you. If there's anywhere you think he might have gone, or might be hiding out, well, can you just have a think about it and let me know?'

'Of course – of course we will!' Carrie was on his side now.

'How long have we got?' Norman questioned.

'I can stall them for twenty-four hours, but that's about it, I'm afraid.' Squadron Leader Sheridan took a card from his pocket. 'Here's how to reach me if you have any ideas, or even if you don't. Let me know by tomorrow evening, all right?'

Norman took the little piece of pasteboard before passing it to Mary and Carrie to examine. They, and Johnnie, had been thrown a lifeline, that was for sure. And Carrie for one was determined to make the most of it.

She and her father spent the rest of the evening on the phone to Johnnie's friends. Their story was that they'd expected him back on leave and wondered if he'd called in on one of his pals first to say hello. But no one had seen him.

'Where can he be? Why hasn't he come here?' Mary wailed. 'This is his home, we're his family, this is where he should be if he's in trouble!'

'I know, love, I know, but from what Sheridan said, the lad's not thinking straight right now, is he?' Norman soothed.

'But where else would he go?'

Carrie had been asking herself the same question since Squadron Leader Sheridan had first outlined the problem. And suddenly, in the middle of the night, it came to her. She waited till dawn – there was no point trying to do anything in the blackout, not where she intended to go. But as soon as she heard her father stirring in her parents' bedroom, she tapped on the door.

'I've had an idea!' she told her bemused parents. 'It's just a thought, but it's worth a try.'

'What? Where are you going?' Mary had raised herself up in bed on one elbow.

'Honestly, Mum, I can't stop. I just . . . I have a feeling I might know where he is!' And she was off.

She'd barely got to the end of the street when she met Penny.

'I had to come!' exclaimed her friend. 'I've been awake all night worrying about you. Bette's been worried too. We both came in to work early because we knew if you'd had good news you'd be in, you're so bonkers about your book-stall. But you didn't and – oh, Carrie, it's not bad news, is it?'

'I can't stop. Sorry.' Carrie hurried on as Penny turned and trotted alongside her.

'What? Where are you going? Are you coming to work?'

Carrie kept walking. Now she'd started, the urgency of her mission had taken hold of her.

'Johnnie's done too much flying,' she said. 'He's gone AWOL, and it's a long shot, but I've had an idea where he might be!'

Penny took all this in with impressive speed.

'I'm coming with you!' she said impulsively. 'I mean, can I? If you don't mind?'

'What about your work?' said Carrie, stopping. 'I've got an excuse, but you know what Bayliss is like about you—'

224

'Stuff work, and stuff Bayliss. This is far more important!' declared her friend.

Carrie flashed her a smile. In the few minutes since leaving
the house, she'd started to wish she wasn't going alone and
had almost turned back for her dad. But now . . . Thank goodness she had Penny, thank goodness Penny had found her!

'Oh, Penny, thank you,' she said wholeheartedly. 'I'd
love someone with me . . . just in case.'

She didn't say just in case of what, but Penny seemed to
understand. If they did find Johnnie, who knew what state
he'd be in?

Penny reached out and touched Carrie's arm.

'That's what friends are for.'

Chapter Twenty-one

They were in the posh part of Brockington, the part known as 'Poets' Corner' because the roads were named after poets – Tennyson, Longfellow, Wordsworth and Kipling, though the grocers' delivery boys, labouring up the hill on their bikes with laden baskets, called it 'Writers' Block'. The houses had been built in Victorian times: huge turreted and balconied piles of terracotta brick, put up by and for wealthy industrialists or City men, stockbrokers, lawyers or accountants. The people who lived here now were still that sort: Carrie saw them at the station, bowler-hatted, with furled umbrellas and briefcases. They bought *The Times*, the *Financial Times* or the *Daily Telegraph* from her with a brief smile of thanks, their minds already on some deal to be done, some document to sign, a meeting with a government minister maybe.

But on one side of Longfellow Road – the more desirable side – there was still a wooded area behind the houses and, for those in the know, a public footpath that led to it. Carrie and Johnnie had discovered it as children, brought there on a picnic one Sunday by their mum and dad. It had become one of their favourite places to come on their own.

With Penny in tow, Carrie made her way down the footpath. But the path had been neglected; the council were too busy painting white lines on the kerb and putting up 'YOU NEVER KNOW WHO MAY BE LISTENING' posters to cut back vegetation.

'Crikey, if I'd known we were going into the jungle, I'd have brough a machete!' Penny exclaimed as Carrie led the way into what had become a dense thicket. She untangled her hair from some brambles. 'Ow! Where the heck are we? I had no idea these woods were here.'

'Not many people do,' Carrie replied, moving a branch away from the track and holding it back for Penny to pass. 'It's more overgrown than I remembered – mind you, I've not been here for ages.'

'I don't think anyone's been here since the start of the war!' Penny retorted. 'I'm surprised, because these nettles'd make great soup.'

'We're not here for a cookery class,' hissed Carrie, then stopped. 'Shh! Look!'

Ahead of them, on a path that crossed theirs, branches were broken, nettles trodden down and some twigs snapped. Someone had made their way through from another direction, and recently. Penny nodded that she understood. Carrie indicated that they should turn right and, trying not to make a sound, they crept forwards over the leaf mould beneath their feet. The way dipped and twisted through mud and snaking stems, but they could see that someone had pushed away the foliage at head height. Someone had been through ahead of them.

'Nearly there!' Carrie turned and whispered. Penny, still with no idea what or where Carrie was leading her to, gave a thumbs up.

Even more stealthily, Carrie parted another couple of branches. Penny's eyes widened. There, in a clearing, stood what looked like a tumbledown stone hut, though the amount of fallen masonry showed that it had once been something much more substantial. It had been roofed with slate, much of it also scattered around, and the wooden roof spars had rotted away, but enough of a roof remained to give shelter to someone who might want to hide away for some reason. Like going AWOL, perhaps?

Carrie moved towards the little doorway that still remained. Penny touched her arm.

'I'll hang back,' she whispered. 'If Johnnie's there, it's you he'll want to see.'

Carrie had introduced her to Johnnie at the station back in May when he'd been home on leave, and she'd seen him come and go on other occasions, but if he was distressed and upset, disorientated maybe, this wasn't the moment to be confronted by someone he barely knew. Carrie nodded. She stepped away, creeping forwards as quietly as she could and crouching as she peered in through the low doorway. Penny saw her shoulders start to shake and almost moved forwards. What had Carrie seen?

But then her friend turned, her face bathed in tears – and a smile.

'He's here!' she said in a loud whisper. 'Asleep!'

They waited for almost an hour, Carrie on guard in the doorway, Penny sitting with her back to a hazel tree, before Johnnie began to stir. Carrie didn't want to startle him, so as he came round, she gently called his name. He was startled, even so, and no wonder – and he didn't seem very pleased to see her.

'Carrie,' he said flatly.

'Hello, you.' Carrie tried to keep the wobble out of her voice.

He raised himself up wearily on one elbow.

'I don't suppose you've got a cigarette? Or any water?'

'Er, no. Sorry.'

She'd left home in such a hurry, she hadn't thought to bring anything. Johnnie sank down again.

'Did you have to come? I'm so dog-tired. I just want to sleep.'

'Oh, Johnnie.'

Carrie crawled towards him. He'd made himself a sort of bed of brushwood and, careless of her own clothes, she lay down beside him. 'Please come home. You can sleep at home. In a proper bed.'

'I can't go home. The MP will come for me. I'll be chucked out. I've blown it.'

'No, you won't, and you haven't blown it!' Carrie urged. 'Far from it! Squadron Leader Sheridan's been round.'

That woke Johnnie up, so much so he half sat up again.

'Sheridan! Bloody hell!'

'It's not like that,' Carrie insisted. 'Listen, he wants you back, but not till you're feeling better. He says he's to blame, and the other officers who've let you fly too much. You need a rest. A proper rest, away from it all for a bit. And they should have made sure you had one before it came to this.'

Johnnie shook his head. He slumped back down.

'I've let them down, all of them. The RAF, my pals, Mum, Dad, you, everyone who believed in me.'

'Nonsense! That's not what anyone thinks, not Sheridan, not your friends, not any of us! You're a hero, Johnnie, you and all the others. Everyone says so. The Prime Minister says so! You heard what he said, surely? "Never in the field of human conflict was so much owed by so many to so few." That's you he was talking about!'

To her horror, tears began to leak from her brother's eyes. She'd never seen him cry, not that day when he'd fallen out of the tree and broken his arm, not when – oh, no, actually, maybe once, when their pet rabbit died. But Johnnie had only been six at the time.

'Oh, Johnnie. Don't, don't, please. It's all right, it's all right. Come here!'

She wrapped her arms around him and he sobbed into her shoulder.

'I can't take any more! I can't do it! I can't!'

'Shh, shh.'

But now Johnnie had started, it all spilled out.

'I saw him come down – my friend, Bruce, a really good mate. We'd been together all the way, all through training, we had this sort of . . . well, we always flew together if we could. We geed each other up – who'd got the most kills, you know? We were on our way home, right beside each other, then he gave me a thumbs up – he was always a cheeky beggar – and he shot ahead, and then this—'

He broke off.

'Yes?' Carrie prompted softly.

'They got him.' Johnnie still sounded disbelieving. 'This

Bf 109 just . . . came from nowhere. Shot away the fuselage, sent him spinning down right into the sea.' He gulped. 'There was nothing I could do. I barely had enough fuel to get back myself. I had to get back to save my own kite, get it back in one piece.'

His voice broke again and Carrie hugged him tighter.

'Oh, Johnnie. I'm so sorry. I'm so sorry for your friend. And for you.'

She paused while he sniffed and wiped his eyes on his sleeve.

'What a display. No, I'm sorry, sis. What a wimp you've got for a brother.'

'Of course you're not! You're not! Sheridan doesn't think so – you should have heard what he said about you! Best and brightest, he said.'

'Huh! Snivelling wreck, more like.'

'Oh, shut up, for goodness' sake,' said Carrie with a flash of their old relationship. 'If you're fishing for compliments, you've come to the wrong pool!'

It had just come out, like a lot of Carrie's thoughts did. It wasn't a conscious change of tack, but it had a miraculous effect. Johnnie actually gave a half-laugh.

'Huh, no change there. Your sympathy didn't last long!'

'Well . . .' Carrie began in her defence. And then: 'Hey, do you remember when we came here – oh, years ago, we must have been about eight? There was a lot more roof then, and you climbed up and your foot went through? And it was like that joke about putting an umbrella up a chimney down, but not down a chimney up, or whatever it is . . . Anyway, I had to climb up, too, and work away some more tiles to free you.'

'I remember how long it took you to get up there, you were that scared!' Johnnie retaliated. 'You'd rather have pretended to cook us a meal out of acorns and serve it on leaves for plates – typical soppy girl's stuff!'

At that, Carrie heard his stomach rumble.

'You're starving,' she said. 'What were you going to do for food, by the way? Acorns are for squirrels and pigs. They'd poison you, probably.'

Her brother had no answer and she drove home her advantage.

'Come home,' she said. 'Think about Mum and Dad. They're desperate about you. Sheridan's given us till tonight, so let's not waste any more time. He's not going to punish you, that's what he came to say. The Military Police aren't involved. But he can't hold them off for ever.'

Still Johnnie hesitated. Carrie made one final appeal.

'Johnnie, all you've ever wanted to do is fly, but no one ever thought you'd be pitchforked straight into a war, not like this one, anyway! Everyone understands that it's been a bit much. You'll get back to it. But you need some proper time off.'

Johnnie appeared to consider this.

'And Sheridan's definitely not going to have me court-martialled?'

'He gave us his word.' And then: 'Oh please, Johnnie, can you just come home with me? For one thing, you stink, frankly, and for another, I'm getting awful cramp lying here!'

Chapter Twenty-two

When Carrie emerged with a dishevelled Johnnie in tow, Penny tactfully tried to excuse herself, saying she'd go to work after all.

'I'll tell Bayliss I overslept,' she said. 'And take my punishment on the chin.'

'No, you won't!' Carrie replied. 'You remember Penny, Johnnie?'

Her brother nodded.

'Hello.'

'She wouldn't let me come on my own, bless her!' Carrie added. 'Perhaps she thought you'd gone completely crackers and might need pinning down or something.'

She grinned as she said this, and Penny issued a hot denial.

'No, I'm teasing,' Carrie went on, more confident now that she could say anything in front of Johnnie without him overreacting. 'She came to support me. She'll have her wages docked for this, so the least we can do is give her some breakfast.'

Johnnie gave Penny a fleeting smile.

'Sorry to be meeting again like this,' he said. Johnnie and Penny had met a few times on the station. 'I hear a lot about you, though. It's a good job someone's around to keep Carrie in line.'

'Hah! It's the other way round!' Carrie retorted, as Penny shook her head.

Then the three of them made their way back through the sunlit woods and along the still-quiet streets.

Mary fell on her son with tears of joy, while his dad, breaking off from serving in the shop, wrapped him in a huge bear hug. Johnnie took himself off to phone Squadron Leader Sheridan, who told him he had two full weeks' leave, and more if he needed it. Sheridan also told him directly just how highly valued he was by the squadron.

So the morning passed and it was now almost noon. Mary had gone off to find a fatted calf, or the nearest thing she could, for the Prodigal Son's return, and Norman had had to return to the shop. Johnnie, Carrie and Penny were still sitting round the table in the back room with the remains of a huge breakfast in front of them.

Johnnie had washed, shaved and changed, and looked much more like himself in his old fawn drill trousers and a pale blue flannel shirt. He wasn't his old self, though, not by a long way. His eyes were clouded with everything he'd been through and Carrie noticed that his hand was shaking as he lit his cigarette. She saw Penny clock it too. Would Johnnie ever be his old self again, or anything like it? They could only hope.

'You still haven't explained how you knew where to find me,' Johnnie began.

'Yes, I wouldn't mind an explanation too,' Penny added. 'I just followed her blindly, Johnnie – she could have been taking me anywhere!'

'How to find you?' Carrie gently replied to her brother.

'Don't you remember when you found me on the bridge at Brockington Junction the day war broke out, the day I had the idea for the bookshop?'

'Quite a lot's happened since then,' said Johnnie mildly.

'Well, I'll remind you. You said you'd tried all our old childhood haunts. Like the old oak tree in the park? Well, that's still there, and the hollow at the bottom we used to squeeze into till we got too big. But you were never going to fit through that tiny gap, were you?'

'I get it,' said Johnnie. 'The next place you'd try would be the old folly in the woods.'

'Is that what it was?' Penny asked. 'It's hard to tell, the state it's in now.'

'It was a sight more luxurious back in the day,' Johnnie told her. The food and the cigarette were taking effect. 'And it's got a romantic history. Some noblewoman in the 1800s had it built as a hideaway where she met her lover, a local man of more, shall we say, lowly status.'

'Wow, that was pretty bold. What happened to them?' Penny asked. 'I hope they eloped and lived happily ever after.'

'Sadly not.' Carrie took up the story. 'One night her brothers lay in wait and killed him.'

'Oh no! And her?'

'Oh, they married her off to some local bigwig.' Johnnie tapped the ash from his cigarette into his saucer – it was a good job his mother was out. 'That's how things were done in those days. Marriage was a contract, nothing to do with feelings.'

Penny raised her eyebrows, and Carrie knew why – in her experience, things hadn't changed much.

'Well, our story had a happier ending,' said Carrie squeezing Johnnie's hand. 'Thankfully.'

Johnnie was home for a blissful fortnight. Mary fussed over him and fed him the most nourishing food she could muster. Margarine and tea were rationed now, but Mary, canny housewife that she was, had set aside a store of tins. Carrie revelled in tinned salmon one night and chicken and ham roll another. She didn't even mind (well, not much!) when she was denied the top of the milk with her apple pie. That had to be saved for Johnnie's morning porridge.

'Red carpet or what?' she teased her brother. He was still quieter, older, a bit withdrawn, but she hoped she could at least try to jolly him up a little. 'We've been living on scraps till you came home!'

'Nonsense!' chided Mary. 'I hope I always manage to make you and your dad something tasty.'

'Course you do, love,' said Norman soothingly, holding out his plate. 'Any more potatoes?'

Johnnie's appetite still hadn't quite come back, and when Bette heard, she immediately came round with a Victoria sponge. Penny popped by a couple of times to check on his progress.

'You'll be in line for a medal or three before the war's out, I bet,' she told Johnnie with her trademark directness in the second week he was home. '*Per ardua ad astra* and all that.' It was the RAF's motto, and meant something like 'Through adversity to the stars'. 'Where's mine and Carrie's for our daring rescue of you, I'd like to know?'

Johnnie said nothing, but, like his sister's gentle teasing,

Penny's challenge turned out to be a help in nudging him back to life. The next time Penny called, he presented both her and Carrie with a couple of medals he'd planed out of balsa wood in his workshop and painted silver-grey. On them he'd inked 'Per ardua ad fratrem'.

'Er . . . lovely,' said Carrie, baffled. 'Meaning . . . ?'

' "Through adversity to the brother",' grinned Johnnie. 'I think. I went to the library and looked it up, anyway.'

He solemnly hung the medals round their necks.

'Thanks, I'll treasure it,' said Penny, and it didn't even seem as if she was being sarcastic. Though she did add with a grin, 'Worth a fortune one day, I expect.'

Carrie thought of the heirloom emeralds that Penny had left behind in the safe when she'd run away from home, and smiled to herself.

Johnnie had had a couple more telephone calls with Squadron Leader Sheridan, who reassured him once again that he was not in any trouble.

'He says I can see the MO when I get back if I want to,' he told his family. 'But honestly, I think I'll be fine. Turns out everyone else was right, and I was being pig-headed about flying so many missions.'

'Hmm. Who'd have thought it?' teased Carrie.

'Ha ha,' said Johnnie, but he grinned. 'I just needed a break.'

Even in Brockington, though, Johnnie couldn't get away from the war entirely. The bombing raids were relentless. Whenever the siren sounded in the weeks he was home, everyone in the Anderson household held their breath.

Carrie saw her mum and dad exchange glances, while she flicked her eyes towards her brother, worried, as her parents were, that it might upset him again.

The first few times, he had seemed jumpy. His eyes darted around as Carrie helped her mum to gather up her knitting and ran to fetch everyone's hats, scarves and coats, stuffing whatever novel she was reading in a pocket. Norman collected blankets and the haversack containing the flask of tea that Mary made up every evening, a torch, candles, matches, chocolate and a tin of Smith's crisps from the shop.

'The fire pail's by the back door,' he said, and they all trooped out to the shelter.

There they hunkered down for what might be hours, sometimes a whole night. Johnnie tensed as the ack-ack guns started up and the planes went over. He could identify them all, of course, far more swiftly than the less finely tuned ears of his family. But during successive raids, his nerves gradually improved. Carrie felt that identifying the planes restored his confidence and made him realise the value of his training and experience, for all the hardship and heartbreak they had brought him.

'It's done me good to understand what you go through,' he admitted when they got back indoors after one raid. 'I got far too wrapped up in my own war.'

'Of course you did. We understand,' said Carrie, fetching the biscuit barrel. Mary was making them each a restorative cup of cocoa before bed.

'No, it was selfish,' Johnnie contradicted her. 'Along with what Sheridan said, tonight has made me realise I've got to be sensible. It's annoying, but I can't win this war single-handed.'

His mother broke off from stirring the milk pan with the smile that turned her from a tired, middle-aged housewife into the pretty young girl she'd once been.

'I've been acting as if I was completely indispensable,' Johnnie went on. 'Well, tonight proves I'm not. The RAF's managed perfectly well without me, so if they tell me I need a couple of days off in future, I'll be taking them, you can be sure.'

'A outbreak of common sense in this family? That's a novelty,' joked Norman, but Carrie could see it was his way of covering his relief. She took the lid off the biscuit barrel and peered inside, then offered it to Johnnie.

'There's only one Bourbon left,' she said. 'I'd usually wrestle you for it, but in view of what you've just said – it's all yours!'

The night before Johnnie was due to return to base, he and Carrie went for a drink at the Rose and Crown.

'I feel I've hardly seen you,' he said as he passed her a glass of port and lemon.

'Well, that's hardly surprising, you getting as much rest as you can, and the hours I work,' Carrie replied. 'Work, eat, sleep, that's my routine.'

'Yes, I've noticed.' Johnnie took a sip of his beer. 'Why is that?'

'That's what I do.' Carrie was bemused. 'I wanted to make a success of the bookstall, and I am, so . . .'

'Yes, you are, and that's great. But what about all work and no play?'

'I do play,' Carrie insisted. 'I go to the cinema with Penny, I go to the WI and the knitting circle with Mum, I go with Bette to pack Red Cross parcels—'

'Thrilling! How do you stand the excitement?'

'What do you want me to do? In case you haven't noticed, there is a war on! I'd do more if I could.'

Johnnie had been about to light up, but he put his cigarette and lighter down.

'I don't mean war work, worthy as it is. And I know you enjoy the bookstall, but what do you do for fun outside of it, Carrie?'

Carrie had no answer to that. She enjoyed her evenings out with Penny, but she knew that wasn't what he meant.

'It's about Mike, isn't it?' Johnnie said gently. 'You're waiting for him to come back.'

'Of course I am! Well, I – I'm just not . . . I refuse to give up hope. Not yet. What's wrong with that?'

Carrie tried not to talk much about Mike these days, and she felt the tears begin to prick her eyes. She blinked to stop them and Johnnie noticed.

'Don't cry, sis, please. Look, I'm sorry, but someone has to say it. It's been what, four, five months now? You know what that nice sergeant who came to see you said about what happened at Dunkirk. It really didn't sound too good.'

Carrie had written to him about Stan Thompson's visit.

'I'm not giving up on Mike,' she insisted. 'I can't. I won't. I'm just not!'

Johnnie sighed. 'Carrie, surely if Mike's alive, he'd have

got word to you. He'd have written from wherever he's being held.'

'You don't know that!' Carrie insisted. 'Bette heard Eric was taken prisoner back in July and she hasn't had a single letter from him yet.'

'Yes, but she did at least have confirmation of what happened. If the Red Cross aren't able to tell you anything . . . and Stan Thompson hasn't come up with the goods . . .'

Carrie twiddled the stem of her glass.

'So what are you saying? Give up all hope?'

'Oh, Carrie. I know how you felt – feel – about Mike. But you've got to be realistic. I'm going to say this, because maybe no one else will, or can. But what else are you going to do for the rest of your life? Take a vow of chastity and become a nun?'

'Don't be so flippant!' Carrie flared.

'I'm sorry, I'm sorry—' Johnnie backed off.

'I do know,' Carrie said in a low voice, 'that I can't go on like this for ever. I'm not stupid. And if they haven't – if I haven't – heard anything by the New Year, then, OK, maybe I should give up hope. But not yet.'

That was when, after six months, Mike would officially be declared dead. Johnnie lit up his cigarette and exhaled. He covered her hand with his.

'OK. I'm sorry for bringing it up. It's just that . . . I care about you. I don't want you pining away.' Carrie gave him a fleeting smile and he went on: 'I was going to suggest you come out with a group of us, some of the lads and a few WAAFs we knock around with. But I can see you're not even ready for that.'

Touched, Carrie squeezed his fingers. She could see Johnnie's concern was sincere. It would have been nice to meet the pals he was closest to, but she knew what it would mean. She cringed at the thought of joining a jolly crowd in the pub, being introduced, making chit-chat, going through all the basic 'getting-to-know-you' stuff of family and work and likes and dislikes . . . She couldn't do it. She didn't want to. While there was still even a glimmer of hope that Mike could return and she'd feel his arms around her, look into his steady eyes, hear him say again that he loved her, Carrie was going to keep the faith. She'd made him a promise not to give up on him, and she wasn't going to break it.

'Never mind,' said Johnnie. 'If you ever do want male company, you've always got me.'

'Yes, I know. Thank you.'

'Stick with me, kid,' he grinned. 'Better the devil you know, eh?'

Chapter Twenty-three

The day came for Johnnie to leave. Seeing him again in his cleaned and pressed uniform, boots polished, hair cut to regulation length, Carrie felt a pang. In this past year of the war, since she'd started her new venture and Johnnie had been flying, they'd each grown up and into different people. Johnnie was a man now, and Carrie a young woman with her own life. It would always have happened, she knew that, as their lives diverged, but the war had speeded it up. She knew she could never fully appreciate what Johnnie's life was like in the RAF, and, older and wiser herself through the people she'd met and what she'd seen and heard on the station, she accepted that. Their special bond would always be there, but Carrie knew that she had to let him go. She had to stop fretting about him and trying to summon it up, and trust that the bond would spring to life again if it was needed.

So Johnnie rejoined his squadron and the rhythm of normal life resumed. She just hoped that he would stick to his promise of not overdoing things.

In any case, Carrie had plenty of things of her own to think about. It was October, the nights were drawing in, the blackout was lasting longer and she was having to walk to and from the station in the dark.

There were few people about on the streets or at the station at that time of the morning. Penny clocked on at seven thirty; Bette and Ruby started at any time between seven and eight, depending on whether it was a baking day. Mr Bayliss, important as he was, or thought he was, wasn't usually seen till eight. The main doors, though, were never locked these days – you never knew when a train would pass through in the middle of the night, with troops coming and going.

Even so, Carrie was astonished and not a little worried when she turned onto the up platform early one morning. In the light of her torch, she could see that the stall was already open, with the shutter up. Not even stopping to think whether it was wise to investigate on her own, she quickened her step. What puzzled her was that the shutter looked neatly rolled up – if the bookstall had been burgled at dead of night, surely it would have been smashed in with a sledgehammer?

Even so, she cautiously crept forward, wishing she had access to the big fire axe that Mr Bayliss kept in his office. She was about thirty feet away when she almost fell off the edge of the platform onto the track.

'Surprise!' shouted Uncle Charlie as he popped up from beneath the counter, flanked by Penny on one side and Bette on the other.

'What . . . you . . . what's going on?' stuttered Carrie.

'Don't you know what day it is?' demanded Penny.

'Er . . . Wednesday?' Carrie answered.

'Very good!' chuckled Uncle Charlie. 'And exactly a year since you opened!'

'Is that what this is about?' said Carrie, bemused.

'No, I really wanted to get up at this ludicrous hour,' retorted Penny in her usual sarcastic-but-I-don't-really-mean-it tone, while Bette smiled and scolded.

'Come on, Charlie, what are you hanging about for – open that fizz!'

Uncle Charlie ducked down again, there was the pop of a cork and, sure enough, he had somehow acquired a bottle of champagne – real champagne! Bette produced four tumblers and Uncle Charlie poured them each a glass. The three conspirators came round and stood with Carrie, looking at the stall.

'Speech!' cried Penny after they'd all chinked glasses and taken a sip, Carrie coughing as the bubbles hit the back of her throat. Penny might have drunk champagne as a matter of course in her previous life, and she had no doubt Uncle Charlie had indulged in a celebratory bottle when car sales had gone well, but she was more used to tea at this time of day, or at any time, come to that.

'Yes, come on, Charlie,' said Bette, who seemed to be making short work of her glass. 'You're the one with the gift of the gab!'

'I'll take that as a compliment,' said Uncle Charlie, putting down his glass on this week's *Woman's Own*. 'Right, here we go.' He cleared his throat theatrically. 'When Carrie came to see me last year, I thought she was paying a visit to her lonely bachelor uncle out of the kindness of her heart. Little did I know she was going to tap me for an investment – that is, present me with a gold-plated business opportunity!' He paused and put his arm around his niece. 'Now, I may have given her a bit of a boost to start her off, but the reason this stall's a success is entirely down to her hard work and her . . . I can only call it her instinct for what the customers want and, frankly, need right now. Books, books and more books.'

Carrie could feel her cheeks going pink, and it wasn't just the effect of the champagne.

'Hear, hear,' said Penny and Bette together.

'So, to sum up,' said Uncle Charlie. 'Congratulations, Carrie, from your mum and dad – they're planning a little celebration for you this evening, by the way – from us three here, and I'm sure from all your grateful customers, wherever they may be, at home or abroad, in uniform or not, on the first year of what I think we can safely call the amazing, extraordinary, one and only Carrie Anderson Penguin Bookshop!'

'And here's to many more,' Bette chimed in.

'I don't know what to say,' said Carrie, blinking back tears as Uncle Charlie refilled their glasses. 'Except thank you. I couldn't have done it without all of you, in different ways. I'm so lucky – I love what I do. I couldn't be doing anything that suits me better or, as it's turned out, that's actually vital for morale in this war. To escape into a book, to let it take you into another world for a while – it's the greatest thing on earth.'

Embarrassed, she looked down at her feet, then at her watch.

'Crikey, we'd better pack up. I've got a stall to run!'

'You see, dedication to duty!' Uncle Charlie drained his glass. He crooked his arm and offered it to Bette. 'If I might escort you to your place of work, madam? And did I hear you promise us all a bacon sarnie?'

'I never did. What sauce!' exclaimed Bette, but she took his arm, which was just as well. She lurched a little as they set off down the platform.

'I hope she doesn't set the place on fire,' Carrie fretted. 'She seemed a bit tipsy to me.'

'I think she's taken a bit of a shine to your uncle,' Penny observed shrewdly. 'Quite . . . coquettish, she was, when we were huddled down under the counter.'

'Bette?' Carrie screwed up her face in disbelief. 'With Uncle Charlie? He's years younger than she is!'

'That doesn't stop film stars, does it?' challenged Penny.

'This is Brockington, not Sunset Boulevard!' protested Carrie. 'Anyway, I've asked Bette before if she'd ever think of, well, finding herself a man. I mean, she's so lovely, it seems a waste. She said she hasn't got time for "all that malarkey".'

'Not what it looked like to me,' declared Penny. 'Your uncle Charlie had better keep his hand on his ha'penny!'

'Penny!' said Carrie, shocked. 'If your posh friends could hear you now!'

'Oh, I've learned far worse than that working here!' grinned Penny. 'It's been an education, I can tell you. Better than any finishing school.'

There was no time for further chat. The milk train arrived on the up platform, so Penny scooted off to deal with the churns, and the mail train came in on the down platform, so Carrie had to trundle off with the sack truck to get the papers.

Another day had begun. And it wasn't just the champagne that made Carrie feel emotional. No one remarked on
it, because no one would have realised, but the day she'd
opened the bookstall was the day she'd first met Mike. It
was their anniversary, too, and he wasn't there.

Where are you? she cried silently as she served her customers with books and papers, parcel string and magazines.
But she'd been through every possibility a million times –
he was dead, he was alive, he was a prisoner, he wasn't a
prisoner, he was injured and in such a bad way he didn't
want her to know about it, he was in a coma, he'd lost
his memory ... There was still no satisfactory answer she
could come up with.

But as she locked up, looking forward to the 'little celebration' waiting for her at home, she reflected that she had
much to be grateful for. She was young and strong. She had
a loving family and friends, and work she loved. She'd had a
few magical months with Mike, more than some people had
in a lifetime. She should concentrate on what she had and
not what she'd lost. And one day, perhaps she could look to
the future.

When Johnnie next rang, Carrie didn't have much to tell him
that wasn't about sewing gloves, pinning up posters urging
people to give blood or, one ghastly time, helping her mum
weigh babies at a WVS clinic. Nappyless, the little darlings
had piddled all over the floor, splashing her shoes and
stockings.

'Anyway, how are you?' she asked.

'Since you ask, I'm pretty teed off,' Johnnie replied.

'They've still got me nannying the new recruits. I'll be wiping their bottoms next and asking if they've got a clean hankie.'

Carrie laughed. She and her parents were all for Johnnie's new role: it took him right out of the fray. She repeated what she'd said before.

'Don't be daft, you're training them, not nannying. And it's a compliment, Johnnie. They must think you know your stuff if they want you to pass it on.'

'Yeah, yeah, rhubarb, rhubarb,' Johnnie grumped. 'I'd much rather be putting what I know into practice! I just want to get back in the cockpit. I'm nagging them about it, don't you worry.'

'I'm sure you are.' Carrie felt quite sorry for Squadron Leader Sheridan.

'I need to be back with my mates, flying, not with these youngsters,' Johnnie went on, and then, sounding as if he was thinking it out as he spoke, 'No, they're good kids, but it's not the same. All of us who trained together, who've been stationed together, fought together . . . we've shared it all, good times and bad, having a laugh, having a beer, sharing the sick feeling and the silence when one of us didn't come back . . . In the air, on a mission, we know each other, we trust each other, we rely on each other. They're like brothers to me. Your friends – comrades – I suppose they're your family in a war.'

'You're right.' Carrie nodded slowly. 'It's the same for me, in a way.'

Carrie was thinking of Bette. Without replacing her mum, Bette was another mother, plying her with tea and treats, always there with a shoulder to cry on if needed. As for Penny – with her fierce independence and her madcap ways, she was the naughty little sister Carrie had never had. And there was Ruby too – she felt like the baby of the station family, one who still had a lot of growing up to do.

'I suppose it's partly . . . well, I spend more time at the bookstall than at home, and when I'm at home, I'm asleep,' Carrie reflected. 'And you . . . I can see that. When you were on active service, you pilots were together twenty-four hours a day, seven days a week. All the excitement – and all the danger too. It's bound to feel intense. Mad, in a way . . .' And reluctantly she admitted: 'I can sort of see why you'd want to get back to it, though.'

'Thanks,' Johnnie agreed. 'It was mad, but . . . I knew you'd understand.' He paused, then added: 'If you ever do meet any of my pals, though, don't you dare tell them what I've said. They'd rag me from here to kingdom come!'

'Ha! You're a hostage to fortune now,' Carrie teased.

'Watch it!' warned Johnnie.

Carrie felt a warm glow. He had other brothers now, brothers-in-arms, but he'd always be her brother too. They could still talk about anything, and always get back to their familiar, jokey relationship. Their bond was still there, quieter now, but there.

Chapter Twenty-four

'I wrote my twentieth letter to Eric last night,' Bette told Carrie as she placed a sausage roll on a plate. Carrie was having a rare lunch break – Uncle Charlie was minding the stall.

'Oh Bette.'

'And still not a dicky bird from him!' Bette lamented. 'I try to write him something to cheer him up. I mean, however fed up I am, poor Eric's got it a lot worse, hasn't he? But I dunno . . . I ended up telling him about the feller who had hiccups the entire hour he was in here, do you remember?'

'Indeed I do.'

'Couldn't shift them, could he? Not with us patting him on the back, not with drinking a glass of water backwards, nor puffing into a paper bag and holding his breath . . .'

'I wonder if he ever got rid of them?'

'Who knows?' said Bette dully. 'But when I'd finished, I thought to myself, what does Eric care? And anyway, isn't it all just a waste of ink?'

'Bette! Of course not!'

'You reckon? Is he even getting these letters? Or is some jumped-up Nazi – "Commandant" they call them, don't they? – is he just using them to wipe his behind?'

'Now, come on,' said Carrie, roles reversed. 'Think about it the other way round. What if Eric is getting your letters and they're what's keeping him going? How's it going to make him feel if they suddenly stop?'

Bette didn't say anything. She straightened the doily under the macaroons and rubbed at an imaginary smear on the counter with the corner of her apron.

'I know it's hard, hearing nothing, but I'm sure he'll be writing back. Maybe his letters to you are just held up for some reason . . . I'm sure the Red Cross do their best, but it can't be easy, with Europe in the state it's in. Have you thought of that?'

'I've thought of everything! I just get so . . . sometimes I get . . .'

Tears pooled in her eyes and the corner of her apron came in handy again. Carrie's heart went out to her, and her hand went out, too, to touch Bette's plump arm.

'Of course you do. Of course.'

Bette sighed, then she pulled herself together.

'Right,' she said, 'I'm better now. Show's over! Move along, please!'

Carrie smiled.

'That's the spirit.'

'And I shan't stop writing really, of course not.' Bette sniffed. 'That'd be giving Adolf what he wants, wouldn't it, and we're not having that!'

'Quite right! What are you always telling me? What does Mr Churchill say? Never give up!'

Bette lifted her eyes to the three photographs that graced the wall behind the refreshment-room counter: the King, the Prime Minister and, just as Carrie had predicted when he was called up, Eric in his uniform.

'Never!' she declared.

Their eyes met in solidarity.

'Hug?' said Carrie.

Bette came round the counter.

'Hug,' she said.

There was one thing to be grateful for. After fifty-seven con-secutive nights – Carrie hadn't been counting, but the newspapers had – the intense bombing of London seemed to be easing off a bit. The results were shocking: bombs had hit the Tower of London and the Houses of Parliament; they'd even hit the Palace. Massive areas of the city were nothing but ruins of dust and rubble, pitted roads and twisted ironwork.

As if anyone wanted any more bangs, flashes and flames, Bonfire Night would soon be coming up. Outdoor fireworks and bonfires were banned, of course, but the Andersons' shop had its usual cabinet of indoor fireworks, always some-thing of a damp squib in Carrie's view. Terry, as enterprising as ever, had made a guy with his scruffy little pals and was extracting pennies from passers-by. He wasn't the only one to take Hitler for his model. There were a lot of toothbrush moustaches on flock-stuffed pudding cloths on the streets.

One late-October day, a cheeky little tyke wheeled his guy onto the station platform and began tapping up the waiting passengers for change.

'You'd better get out of here, quick, before the station-master sees you,' Carrie said, parting with a couple of coppers.

'I ain't scared of 'im!' pouted the urchin, but he jumped a foot in the air when a voice behind him said:

'Are you bothering this lady? Now beat it!'

The lad shot off as if he had a rocket behind him. But it wasn't Mr Bayliss, it was Stan Thompson, Mike's sergeant. Carrie smiled, delighted.

'Stan! How lovely to see you!'

But she was confused: there'd been no train in. Stan saw her puzzlement.

'I'm in a lorry,' he explained. 'Volunteered to deliver a couple of bicycles and some odd bits of equipment to the Home Guard. So I thought I'd combine business with pleasure. Can you get off for a bit?'

'Oh, yes – why not!' said Carrie. 'Though not for as long as last time. Shall we just go to the tearoom here?'

'As long as they serve something hot and wet, I don't care where we go,' grinned Stan.

'Oh, Bette will do you rather more than that. It's Monday, so there should be Eccles cakes.'

They were another of Bette's specialities.

Stan whistled. 'My favourite. Well, one of 'em!'

Carrie locked up the stall and they walked down the platform. When they got to the tearoom, though, there was no sign of Bette. Ruby was there with her back to them, examining her appearance in the etched mirror behind the counter. She had an unfortunate new spot erupting on her chin, Carrie had noticed earlier, and she was giving it a tentative prod with her forefinger. At least the Eccles cakes were made, sitting plump and inviting on the glass-domed cake stand. Thank goodness Bette insisted on cake tongs!

'Afternoon, Ruby,' said Carrie briskly. 'No Bette?'

Meeting Carrie's eyes in the mirror, Ruby jerked her head to indicate the empty refreshment room.

'Dead quiet, so she's nipped home,' she turned round to explain. 'She hung her washing out this morning 'cos it was nice and blowy, but it looks like rain, so she's gone to take it in. Said she wouldn't be long. Did you want her?'

'What we want, love, is two teas and . . .' Stan turned to Carrie, indicating the Eccles cakes. 'Will you join me?'

'Oh, go on then,' smiled Carrie. 'But it's my treat – you paid last time.'

'Don't be daft. What kind of feller do you think I am?' protested Stan. And to Ruby: 'Two Eccles cakes, please.'

Stan paid and they carried their cups and plates to a table in the corner. Ruby returned to contemplating her face.

Carrie sat down and said, she hoped brightly, 'No news, I suppose?'

'I'm afraid not.'

Carrie let her face fall.

'I didn't really expect any.'

'No, well . . .' Stan rubbed his nose. 'There is one thing, though, you might like to hear about. I had a couple of days' leave owing, so I called in on my auntie up Lewisham – I told you about her – and then I decided I'd go to Leamington.'

'To see Mike's family?'

Stan nodded.

'I took an afternoon train, went to the house in the evening. I didn't want to disturb them at the shop. I wasn't sure about it, I mithered all the way on the train. But in the end I felt I should.'

'Oh, Stan, good for you – I'm so glad.' Lately, Carrie had been more and more tempted to do just that herself. 'So . . . it's the silliest of silly questions, I know, but how are they?'

'Struggling, to be honest,' Stan replied. 'I'd not met his mum before, but I'd seen photos, you know, and this hasn't half aged her. His dad too, I think, but he's got more to occupy himself, running the business and all. I didn't meet Jane, the sister. She was out on salvage collection with the Girl Guides, bless her.'

'Right.'

Stan took a bite of his cake.

'It's sad,' he said when he'd finished chewing. 'There's photos of the Lieutenant all over the house. But ... you know, they had the letter from the CO ages ago, saying he was missing and ... it's like a light's gone out for them.'

Carrie nodded. 'It must be terrible.'

She knew how she felt after knowing Mike for such a short time; she could barely imagine the torture it must be for his family. His mother, who'd prepared his baby bottles and treated his grazed knees, nursed him through any childhood illnesses, and marvelled over his first scribbled drawings and stabs at joined-up writing. His father, who, Mike had told her, had patiently bowled him cricket balls when he was trying to make the school team and stood on freezing rugby touchlines with a loyal Jane, who apparently idolised her brother. And the generous great-aunt, who'd paid for his schooling – was she going to have to bear another loss?

'They showed me his room,' Stan said sadly. 'It's just as he must have left it. His books in the bookcase, his sports cups from school, his passing-out photograph ... They go in to dust and sweep it round, that's all. They're just waiting for the final letter now, really.'

The letter that would say Mike had officially been declared dead.

'I'm sorry I haven't got better news.'

'It's not your fault,' Carrie assured him. 'I'm glad you've seen them. I'm sure Mike had told them about you, so to meet you, someone he'd served with, and hear how brilliant he was, keeping everyone's spirits up, and how right at the end he put the men's safety before his own – it paints a picture. It's not a complete black hole. Because when you don't know, you imagine all sorts of things. Worse and worse things.'

She'd done it herself. She still had nightmares about Mike's final moments.

'Yeah, well, I hope so.' Stan wetted his finger and mopped up the pastry crumbs. 'That was delicious. My compliments to the chef.'

'I'll pass them on.'

But there was no need. At that moment, Bette burst through the door like a human hurricane. She flopped on to a chair at the first table she came to and put her hand to her heaving chest.

'Carrie! Oh, I'm so glad you're here! I went to the book-stall and – get me a glass of water, Ruby, there's a good girl – I've run all the way from home!'

Carrie jumped up and crossed to Bette's table. She pulled out a chair and sat down.

'Bette! What is it? Whatever's happened?'

'It's come! It's come! I've had a letter! A letter from Eric!'

Seeing it was a moment for friends and not for a stranger, Stan made a tactful, or tactical, withdrawal. He placed a

259

hand on Carrie's shoulder and, mouthing 'I'll keep in touch,' went quietly out. Carrie was sorry not to be able to thank him properly, at least for the tea and her untouched cake, but Bette needed her full attention.

Ruby brought over Bette's glass of water. Even she'd been roused from her usual state of self-absorption – she didn't spill a drop.

'What's he say?' she asked eagerly, sitting down un-invited at the table.

Bette was so wrapped up in her news, she didn't even order her back to the counter.

With trembling fingers, she opened her handbag and drew out a flimsy envelope covered with stampings and frankings: it had obviously passed through several hands before getting to Brockington. She took out an even flimsier single sheet of paper and passed it to Carrie. Ruby craned round to see.

'Dear Mum,' Carrie read.

Thank you for your letter, I was glad to get it I'm glad you are OK. I am fine I really am I had a spell in the hospital when I first came here but I am fine now. The camp is OK there are some good blokes here, and a lot of foreigners too. We got some Red Cross parcels yesterday. I hope we will get more. We have a lot of drills to check we are all still here, that's all we do really. It's dead boring. We were deloused last week. We had to go to XXX and the stuff they used XXX

Heavy crossings-out obscured any details.

The letter concluded:

Give my best to everyone at the station I miss it like I never thought I would. Stay well Mum.

Your loving son
Eric

Carrie found her eyes were full of tears. The writing was untidy and there was not much punctuation, but Eric was alive, and surviving. Too full to speak, she put her hand over Bette's.

'Thank God,' she said finally.

Bette nodded.

'I have, oh, trust me, Carrie, I have, from the minute I saw the letter on the mat!'

Ruby had taken the letter from Carrie and was studying it minutely.

'What do you reckon was crossed out?' she asked, passing the letter back to Carrie.

Carrie shrugged.

'I suppose they didn't like what he said about the delousing, where it happened and the stuff they used – the chemical. I don't know, maybe they didn't want us knowing what it was, or him saying it stung or something. But they didn't want that either.'

'Miserable so-and-sos.' Ruby stuck out her bottom lip.

Bette was studying the letter again, her face rapt.

'Worth waiting for, Bette?' smiled Carrie. 'At least you know your letters are getting through – and you'll get a reply eventually.'

Bette nodded mutely. She was holding the letter like a holy relic.

'And,' Ruby added with unusual perceptiveness, 'it might be that he gets a whole load of letters all at once, mightn't it? And we – you – might get a whole load of his letters back the same way.'

'That's right,' Carrie agreed. At Bette's request, she'd written Eric the odd letter herself. Prisoners of war could receive any number. 'So it was worth keeping on writing, wasn't it?'

'Oh yes,' said Bette fervently. She glanced at the photographs behind the counter – the King, the Prime Minister, and her son. 'Like Winnie says – "Never give up!" '

Chapter Twenty-five

Bette's joy transformed her and lifted everyone else's spirits. Even Mr Bayliss managed a gruff 'I'm pleased you've heard. Give the lad my regards.'

As Ruby had predicted, more delayed post arrived from Eric: two postcards and a letter in one day! Carrie received a dog-eared epistle too, saying much the same as he'd said in his letter to his mum, but what else did he have to say, poor thing?

With Bette relieved, everyone was relieved, so Carrie was surprised when Ruby came to find her, her face anxious. It was one of Uncle Charlie's days on the bookstall, but he was helping Bette out. Her till drawer wasn't shutting properly, and taking advantage of another body in the tearoom, Bette must have sent Ruby on her break. Chewing her lip, Ruby asked:

'Can I have a word? It's about Mrs Saunders.'

Carrie put down her Penguin – something that always made her smile, as if she was a keeper at London Zoo. The amateur sleuth Lord Peter Wimsey was about to reveal the murderer in *The Unpleasantness at the Bellona Club*, but his clever deductions would have to wait.

'Of course, Ruby. What is it?'

Ruby looked over her shoulder like someone in one of

the 'WALLS HAVE EARS' or 'YOU NEVER KNOW WHO MAY BE LISTENING' posters that had mushroomed since the summer.

'I've had a letter.'

'Ye-es?' prompted Carrie.

'From Eric.'

'Oh!' Not what Carrie had been expecting. 'Right! Is it . . . why did he . . . is he worried about his mum or something?'

If so, Carrie wondered why Eric hadn't asked her, though she'd made a point of telling him in her letter that Bette was doing fine and, as promised, she was keeping a good eye on her.

'No, he isn't, but I am. Worried about her. Thing is,' Ruby confided, 'I wrote to him, see, off me own bat. I got the address off of one of Mrs Saunders' letters to him.'

'I see.'

Off her own bat! There was more to Ruby than Carrie had ever suspected.

'I wasn't sure, 'cos I hardly know him,' Ruby went on. 'I mean, he was called up so soon after I started. But I knew you were writing to him and I thought, why not?'

'I think it was very nice of you, Ruby.' Carrie was confused. 'I'm sure as far as Eric's concerned, the more the merrier. But what's the problem about Bette?'

'I didn't tell her I was doing it, see. I know what she thinks of me – she thinks I'm no better than I should be.'

'No, she doesn't think that!'

Ruby sniffed, not in a haughty way, but more pathetically.

'She may not have said as much, but I've seen the way she looks at me, just 'cos I like talking to people. Well, OK, to men.'

'Well . . .'

'It's just . . . it never comes to anything, I swear! Even that Dutch feller that used to come in, I told him about my afternoon off and where I'd be, and it's the only time I ever did that, honest. I thought I was doing him a favour, seeing as how he's stuck in a bedsit in Orpington, not knowing a soul. You'd have thought he'd like someone to go around with, but he never turned up, and then he stopped coming in the tearoom altogether.'

'Oh, Ruby!'

Ruby's mouth turned down and her eyes filled with tears.

'And the thing is, Carrie, I only started chatting to fellers 'cos . . . well, I'll tell you if you won't tell anyone. It was all because of Eric!'

'Was it?' Carrie was truly baffled now.

'Yes! I . . . Tell you the truth, I liked him from the start. But he seemed to like you . . . but then you got with Mike, and I thought Eric might notice me then, but he didn't seem to.'

No, dear Eric, thought Carrie, he wouldn't. It was obvious he'd never had anything to do with the opposite sex. He might have crushes, like he'd had on her, but it wouldn't occur to him that anyone beyond his devoted mum might take an interest in him.

'I only started chatting to other blokes 'cos I thought it might make him sit up and pay attention if I was walking out with someone,' Ruby went on pitifully. 'But then he got called up, and after that . . . well, it had become a sort of habit.' She sighed. 'I dunno what's wrong with me. I know

I'm not pretty like you, Carrie, but I ain't a complete ugly bug, and I do try!'

'No, of course you're not ugly! And anyway, Ruby, life isn't about how you look on the outside, it's about the inside – what kind of person you are.'

'I'm a person who'd like someone to call a boyfriend, that's all,' Ruby tailed off sadly. 'Someone to treat me nice, and be kind to me. From the way he treats his mum, I think Eric would.'

'I'm sure he would.'

One of Mary's firm convictions was that you could judge a man by how he treated his mother, and no one could fault Eric on that.

'I feel he'd treat a girl like a lady,' said Ruby, echoing Carrie's thoughts. 'And he's got lovely eyes.'

Carrie felt guilt-ridden at this heartfelt confession. She'd raised her eyebrows along with Bette at some of Ruby's more obvious attempts at flirting, and she'd joined Bette in warning Ruby about it, although their motives had been different. When the Dutchman had looked like becoming a regular visitor, Bette had asked Carrie to have a word.

'Me? I thought you were going to speak to her about it,' Carrie had replied.

'I've tried!' Bette protested. 'She doesn't take a blind bit of notice, says she's only being pleasant with the customers and wouldn't I want that, the cheeky minx! Well, it looks like more than that to me. I've got the tearoom's reputation to think of. I can't have people thinking it's nothing but a knocking shop!'

'I don't think they'd think that . . .' Carrie began, but she did think Ruby should be a bit more careful. She was more concerned for the girl's own reputation – and her virtue. It was a miracle some Tommy hadn't taken advantage before now. But when she spoke to Ruby, the girl had been adamant.

'She's put you up to this, hasn't she? Mrs Saunders. I'm only being friendly and there's no harm in it, so there!'

Carrie now realised she needn't have worried. All the time, the real object of Ruby's feelings had been Eric.

'You should have told Eric how you felt before he left.'

For someone who managed to simper at complete strangers, Ruby looked horrified.

'Oh, I could never do that!'

'Why not? We're modern women, aren't we?'

'You might be . . . I'd be too embarrassed. What if he'd said get lost?'

'I can't imagine he would have.'

Now that Ruby had admitted her feelings, Carrie could actually see her as quite a match for Eric. With dye becoming harder to get hold of, she'd stopped colouring her hair. Its real colour was mouse, but it had a natural wave that a lot of women would have sold their rations for, especially since perming lotion had all but disappeared. Her skin was improving – Carrie had recommended witch hazel for spots – and if she was what you might call well proportioned, that had never done Mae West any harm! And anyway, as Carrie had said, life – and love – wasn't, or shouldn't be, about looks. Ruby also had some very good qualities.

She was at heart a decent girl. She'd been moved to tears by the plight of the refugees ('Them poor little kiddies!') and she was as honest as the day was long. She always put any small change that customers had dropped on the floor onto the tips plate to be shared between herself and Bette, though it must have been a sore temptation, on her wages, to pocket it for herself. And she was reliable, despite Bette's doubts in the beginning. She'd hardly missed a day's work in all the time Carrie had known her, coming in panda-eyed after the worst nights of air raids when many girls in her position would have skived off. Under Bette's tutelage she'd turned into a handy little baker: as well as her surprisingly dainty icing skills, she had a light hand with pastry.

Yes, Ruby had been snide about Penny in the beginning, but no one had known what to make of Penny, who was about as far away from Ruby's attempts at beauty and femininity as it was possible to be. What Penny had in bucketfuls was confidence – even her tyrannical father hadn't knocked that out of her; in fact it had made her even more determined.

Carrie had never realised till now what an important quality that was. She was sure of herself, too, which stemmed from her secure and loving home. But from what she knew of Ruby, the eighth of nine children and the seventh girl, she doubted she'd ever had any encouragement to boost her self-esteem.

'So what shall I do?' Ruby appealed. 'How am I going to tell her? Mrs Saunders, I mean.'

Carrie sighed. She couldn't help feeling Ruby was making a mountain out of matchsticks here. And they needed to go back to the beginning.

'Can I see the letter, Ruby? Eric's letter? Do you mind?'

'No, you're welcome! Here.'

268

Ruby took the letter out of her cardigan pocket and handed it over. Carrie unfolded it and read:

Dear Ruby

It was a surprise to hear from you and no mistake but a nice surprise. I'm glad you and everyone at the station is well. You made me laugh about that film, I like Charles Hawtrey too, and Laurel and Hardy. My favourite is The Music Box I'm sure you've seen it. They showed us A Chump at Oxford, not here, I mean before when I was with the XXX.

Perhaps Eric had named his regiment; the censor had crossed it out.

Saps at Sea sounds good too please write again and tell me about more films I don't mind that I can't see them maybe I will one day. I hope so and that you'll keep writing.
Yours
Eric

The simple innocence of the letter, and what had obviously been the simple innocence of Ruby's to him, moved Carrie almost to tears. She folded the letter and handed it back. Ruby stuffed it in her pocket.

'Well, there's nothing there that Bette could possibly object to. In fact, Ruby, you must have written a lovely letter. To give Eric a laugh, when you think about where he is, that's quite something – and he obviously wants you to write again. That's great!'

'Not if Mrs Saunders is going to go mad at me for it! And I don't want to keeping writing on the sly.'

'No, you mustn't,' Carrie agreed. 'I think you've got to be brave and come clean. Tell Bette you wrote, tell her Eric's written back and show her the letter, if you like. There's really nothing she can be cross about. You just wrote a nice, chatty, friendly letter, and he's written back in the same way.'

'You reckon?'

'And you must keep writing. It never occurred to me to write to him about films, and you know his mum only tells him stuff about the tearoom and worries about him getting enough to eat and keeping warm. You're telling him the things he wants to hear.'

Ruby still looked horror-struck.

'I'd get all tongue-tied trying to tell Mrs Saunders, I know I would. And it'd come out wrong!'

'Look.' Carrie gave her a smile. 'Would you feel braver if I was there?'

'Oh, yes,' Ruby replied fervently. 'You could weigh in on my side.'

'OK,' Carrie agreed. 'Go back to work. As soon as Uncle Charlie gets back, it's my turn for a break. I'll come down and we'll tell Bette together. How's that?'

'Oh, thank you, thank you, yes, please!' Ruby's eyes shone. She seized Carrie's hands. 'You are kind. And I've never said, not really, but I heard you with that sergeant in the tearoom the other day telling you he hadn't got any more news, and I want to say it now – I'm ever so sorry about your Mike. I thought you was a lovely couple. You looked so good together. And so happy.'

'We were,' said Carrie simply. 'But it wasn't to be. Thanks, Ruby.'

'Blimey, Bette. I have to say, next time you've got a pig of a job like this, can you find a farmer to fix it?'

Shirtsleeves rolled up, Uncle Charlie had one arm groping inside the empty cavity of the tearoom's till drawer.

'I'm sorry, Charlie, but—'

'Ah. Hang on. I think that's got it!'

He screwed up his face as he fiddled with the mechanism at the back of the drawer, then emerged holding a small pipette of oil.

'Phew! Right, pass us the money drawer. Let's see what happens now.'

Bette passed him the drawer, emptied of its small change for the operation.

Uncle Charlie inserted it carefully back on its runners and pushed it cautiously to and fro before shutting it with a ting.

'Now the acid test,' he said, ringing up 'No Sale' and waiting for the drawer to open. Out it shot like a bullet from a gun.

'Oh, that's so much better!' exclaimed Bette.

'Hold your horses. Let's try it a few more times.'

Uncle Charlie did so, and the drawer behaved perfectly every time.

'What a relief!' exclaimed Bette. 'You can't get an engineer for love nor money, you know. The nice feller that used to service the till is on bomb disposal now.'

'I should think that's a picnic compared to fiddling with this thing!' Uncle Charlie rolled his sleeves back down and Bette handed him his jacket. 'Right, I'd better get back to Carrie. She'll be wanting her lunch.'

'Thanks again, Charlie—And where've you been, miss?' This last remark was addressed to Ruby, who'd just come in.

'I was on my break, Mrs Saunders.'

Bette huffed.

'You never usually go out, just sit in the back reading your *Picturegoer*! Now you're here, there's a delivery of dry goods needs putting away.'

'Right you are, Mrs Saunders.'

Ruby came round the counter, but as she passed, Bette caught her arm.

'What's that you've got there?'

Ruby glanced down, a look of horror creeping over her face. Eric's letter with its German franking was clearly visible in her cardigan pocket.

'That's my Eric's writing!' Bette gasped. 'You've never – you've never pinched one of my letters from him to read?'

Before Ruby could protest, Bette had plucked the letter from her pocket and was studying the envelope. Her face changed from shock to outrage to amazement – and back again.

'It's addressed to you at your house! What's he doing writing to you?'

'I – I – I wrote to him!'

'You what?'

Ruby hung her head. This wasn't how it was supposed to be!

'I got his address off of one of your letters to him. I—'

'Well, you sneaky little thing,' Bette fumed. 'What an imposition! And you never said a word. What made you think he'd want to hear from you? I've never heard the like!'

Huge tears welled in Ruby's eyes and spilled down her face.

'I'm sorry, Mrs Saunders, I never meant nothing by it, and I was going to tell you. I—'

'Here!' Bette stuffed the letter back in Ruby's pocket. 'Take it. Take your letter and get out of my sight!'

'But—'

'Don't you answer me back, my girl. I can't look at you. I don't want to see you again!'

'But—'

'No, I don't want to hear it. Just go. Now!'

Ruby's tears turned to full-blown sobs and she fled into the back. There was the sound of her locker door opening, a scuffle as she got her things, then the sound of the trades-man's entrance opening and closing.

Bette, bosom heaving, turned to Charlie.

'The little minx!'

Chapter Twenty-six

'I told her she was being harsh,' Uncle Charlie told Carrie when he got back to the bookstall. 'I told her the girl most likely didn't mean anything by it. But Bette wasn't having it. Steaming, she was!'

'Oh no!' Carrie had been listening in horror. 'Poor Ruby. She gave up her break to come and talk to me about it – that's the only reason the letter was even in her pocket.'

'What did she expect you to do?' queried Uncle Charlie.

'She'd got herself in such a stew over telling Bette, I said I'd go down and be with her when she did. Ruby thought I could be a sort of . . . I don't know . . . a mediator, I suppose.'

'More like a fire blanket, the way Bette blew up!'

'Ruby was terrified Bette would react like this. I told her it was nonsense – but she was right all along.'

'Good to know you haven't got the monopoly on wisdom,' said Uncle Charlie with a wry smile.

'OK, point taken, but it doesn't help Ruby, does it? I'd better go and talk to Bette now and see if I can calm her down. I mean, Ruby's done nothing wrong.'

She took a step towards the door, but Uncle Charlie held her back.

'Do you know what, I should leave it for the moment,' he

advised. 'Bette's up to high doh, she's in no mood to listen to reason. She's told Ruby to get out of her sight—'

'What?'

'It was just in the heat of the moment. So Ruby's gone home – but best you leave Bette to cool off. I wouldn't go near her while she's like this.'

'If you think so . . .' Carrie replied doubtfully.

'I do. But I also know it means you missing out on your lunch.'

On Uncle Charlie's cover days, Carrie didn't bring sandwiches; he insisted she had a proper break and something to eat in the tearoom.

'That doesn't matter.'

'Yes, it does. We can't have you fading away, or living on chocolate out of the machine – if you can call it that!'

It was true – a bar of Dairy Milk wasn't the same now they'd had to cut the sugar in it.

'So,' Uncle Charlie delved in his jacket pocket and produced a greaseproof package, 'here's a cheese scone, and it's even got a smidge of butter on it – well, marge, but anyway . . . Bette sent it for my tea, but you can have it.'

'Ooh, are you serious?' And when he nodded: 'Thanks, Uncle Charlie!' Carrie fell on it delightedly.

'You enjoy it,' said Uncle Charlie. 'Brain food, isn't it? You'll need your wits about you when you do see Bette, even once she's calmed down!'

They didn't see Bette again that day. Carrie and Uncle Charlie stayed late to stocktake, and Bette must have left by the tradesman's entrance herself, as they didn't see her pass.

It was almost ten by the time they finished. The streets of Brockington were increasingly deserted, and she was glad of a lift home in his car. Uncle Charlie had given up his Rover for a Baby Austin that was more economical on petrol; as a private citizen, he was lucky to have a car at all.

Carrie still worried about paying him back the money he'd put in to help her start her little enterprise, and she raised it again as he pulled up outside the Andersons' darkened shop. Just as he had before, Uncle Charlie waved her concerns away.

'What you're giving me to pay off the bank loan is quite enough for me,' he said. 'We've had a bit of a boost at the garage, thanks to me being in the Home Guard.'

'Oh, what's that? Surplus army ration packs? All the bully beef you can eat?'

'You can mock!' chided Uncle Charlie. He added with undisguised pride: 'We've got the maintenance and repair contract for the vehicles belonging to the local militias round our way, about twenty in all, so it's an ill wind, as they say!'

Carrie shook her head and smiled. As her dad often remarked, Uncle Charlie really did seem to have the Midas touch. Or, as her mother added on the quiet, the luck of the devil.

'Well done you,' Carrie said now, gathering her bag and gas mask and opening the car door. 'I'm glad someone's having a good war! Thanks for the lift, Uncle Charlie, and for the help with the stocktake. Night-night.'

'Cheerio, love,' Uncle Charlie replied, leaning over as she got out and adding: 'And good luck with Bette in the morning!'

The next day, Carrie had her usual routine – the early-morning papers and her regular customers. Then, in addition to the normal timetable, two unexpected trains puffed in. They'd been shunted into sidings during a night-time air raid and disgorged hundreds of tired, fed-up, hungry and thirsty passengers to cater for.

'To think we called it the Bore War at the start when nothing was happening,' yawned Penny. She'd sauntered over to the bookstall when the rush had subsided. 'I'm bored of it now, with the air raids, I can tell you.'

'I don't suppose the people who were bombed out last night or any other night feel that way,' Carrie replied tartly. 'We're lucky nothing's hit Brockington yet, intentionally or not.'

She was on edge after too little sleep and at the prospect of her talk with Bette. She dreaded to think what the atmosphere in the tearoom would be like between the two women there, but just then, Penny, blithely unaware of what had gone on, said:

'Ructions in the tearoom when I went in for my cuppa. Ruby hasn't turned up.'

'What?'

'Bette's not herself either,' Penny went on. 'I said Ruby had probably overslept because of the raid, and she nearly bit my head off.'

Yes, she would, thought Carrie, given how Bette had bawled out poor Ruby the previous day.

'Can you keep an eye on the stall for a bit?' she asked.

'What, now?'

'Sorry, but it's urgent. I've got to see Bette about something.'

'Well, OK,' Penny agreed, 'but you can explain to Bayliss. He's not going to be impressed by me selling mags with the ten-twenty-three due.'

'I will, I promise.'

'Go on, then,' grinned Penny. 'I wouldn't mind a rest. There's no freight on the ten-twenty-three and people can jolly well carry their own cases for once. Shift yourself.'

'I'll be as quick as I can. Thanks, Penny!'

And off she flew down the platform.

In the tearoom, the early rush had subsided and from the clattering out the back, Bette was dealing with the aftermath. Clearing away and washing up were Ruby's job, so the girl clearly still hadn't arrived. Bette had had to put the little brass bell on the counter with a luggage label tied to its handle saying 'Please ring for service', but Carrie ignored it. She went straight through to the back.

'Need any help?' she asked.

Bette was at the draining board, unloading crocks from a tray.

'Carrie!'

'I hear you're short-handed today.'

Bette didn't reply. She ran water into the sink and added a torrent of soda crystals. While the big stone sink filled, she turned round and folded her arms across her chest defensively.

'I suppose Charlie told you what happened.'

'He did. And that you told Ruby to go.'

'Yes, all right, so I did. I didn't expect the silly girl to take it like this. I never said she was sacked!'

'Maybe not, but from what I can gather, you gave her quite a roasting,' said Carrie mildly. 'Perhaps it's no wonder she took it that she was.'

Bette heaved a huge sigh.

'Oh, Carrie. It was just – well, I dunno.'

'Tell me. Try.'

'All right.' Bette puffed out a breath. 'I suppose it's just – I've been so used to having Eric to myself, I – well, it took me by surprise, that's all, her writing to him like that. And anyway—'

'Bette,' Carrie interrupted, 'hang on. That's completely illogical! You didn't mind me writing to him, did you?'

'That's different,' Bette defended herself. 'I asked you to! It was her doing it on the sly, behind my back, that got to me.'

'Oh come on. Ruby, sly? She couldn't be sly to save her life! Look, Bette, she came to me about it because she was worried you'd take it like this. She wanted me to be a sort of mediator when she told you. She knows how . . . what a . . . what a special relationship you and Eric have.'

What had almost slipped out, and was the truth of the matter, was 'how possessive you are about Eric', but that would only have made things worse. Carrie's tact paid dividends. Bette's lip wobbled. Seizing the advantage, Carrie continued:

'And Ruby didn't say as much exactly, but from what she did tell me about herself, there's another reason she wrote to Eric without telling you.'

'What's that, then?' Bette was curious now.

'She's got so little faith in herself, so little confidence, she wasn't sure he'd write back. And then, well, she wouldn't have needed to tell you, would she? That sink's nearly full, by the way.'

Tutting, Bette turned and snatched off the taps. She stuck a pile of cups and saucers into the suds and turned back to Carrie. But she wasn't done yet.

'Well, I can't believe that! Are we talking about the same girl? With the way she paints herself up and throws herself at anything in trousers? No confidence, you say?'

'Yes, I do. It was sad, to be honest,' Carrie said, reflecting on her conversation with Ruby. 'All that chatting up of men, that's not what she's like – it was all put on! She told me so. She just wants someone to notice her, someone to be nice to her, and make a bit of a fuss of her. I don't imagine she's ever had that at home, poor girl.'

Finally, Bette's expression seemed to soften, and Carrie certainly wasn't about to mention that the person Ruby had really wanted to notice her was Eric. Instead, pressing her point, she went on:

'You've said it yourself, she's not a bad worker, and you've turned her into a very useful baker. Think about it, Bette. If she doesn't come back, who are the Labour Exchange going to send you now? Anyone half-decent is busy doing war work. And since you admit you didn't mean her to leave for good—'

'Oh no,' said Bette, wagging her finger. 'No, no, no, no! I can see where you're going with this and it's a no! If you think I'm crawling round to her house to apologise, you've got another think coming!'

'No one said anything about you crawling—'

'Even so,' Bette sniffed. 'If she wants to come back, the job's still here. That's as far as it goes.'

'And how is she supposed to know that?'

'You're going to tell her, of course!' Bette sounded positively smug. 'You said she thought you could be a – what did you call it? A mediator? Go round to her house, then, and do a bit of mediating!'

Chapter Twenty-seven

Ruby lived in a part of Brockington that Carrie knew only by reputation – and it wasn't a particularly good one. Ethel Street and Harold Road, which flanked the Andersons' shop, were nothing special, just two ordinary streets of terraced houses, though Harold Road liked to think of itself as superior since its houses had bay windows and were three-up two-downs. Carrie felt perfectly at home there, but even a stranger in town would have had nothing to fear. By contrast, in the pitch-dark of the blackout, she felt uncomfortable and positively unsafe in Ruby's part of town.

The area was also made up of rows of terraces – two-up two-downs – but even in the feeble light of Carrie's torch there was something mean and cramped about them. More than a few had a neglected, uncared-for look – Ruby's home being one of them. The paint on the front door was blistered and peeling, and the half net in the front window drooped dingily. The dull door knocker would have had Carrie's mum reaching at once for the Brasso and a pound of elbow grease. Carrie raised it and let it fall. Inside, a small child began to wail. Surely, thought Carrie, Ruby's mother hadn't had a tenth baby? Ruby would have said, wouldn't she?

'Who the blazes is that?' shouted a male voice. 'Trevor! Get your nose out of that comic and go and see!'

'Why me?' came a loud, petulant whine.

'Just go, before I leather yer!'

There was a pause, the sound of dragging feet and the door was opened a crack by a lad of about twelve – presumably the unfortunate Trevor – accompanied by a waft of stale air and the smell of cabbage. Now the door was open, Carrie could hear more noise from inside – dance music on the wireless and female voices raised in an argument.

'Yeah?' Trevor asked sullenly.

'Who is it?' called the same male voice, presumably Ruby's father. 'If it's for the rent, he'll have it when I'm paid, end of the week – he knows that!'

'Who are yer?' repeated Trevor. 'You're not from the rent, are yer?'

'No, I'm a friend of Ruby's from the station,' said Carrie patiently. 'Is she here?'

'Nope,' said the lad, and yelled into the depths of the house: 'It ain't the rent man, Dad!'

'Right,' said Carrie, trying not to get distracted by the two conversations Trevor was managing to sustain, or the background noise. 'So where is she, do you know? And when will she be back?'

Trevor shrugged.

'She's gone up the Co-op for Mum. Ain't long gone.'

'OK.' Carrie sighed. She'd passed the Co-op, which was open till eight, on the way and wished she'd known Ruby was there; she could have saved herself this encounter. 'I'll find her there or hope to meet her on her way back.'

'Suit yourself.' With that, Trevor closed the door, keen to get back to his comic.

Carrie retraced her steps and was glad when she came to the wider main road, where she'd passed the Co-op. Like all shops, its windows were blacked out and latticed with criss-cross tape. She pushed open the heavy door and shut it behind her quickly, so as not to let out any light.

It was a big, old-fashioned shop with a high ceiling and dark wooden shelves. They weren't anything like as well stocked as they once had been, but even at this hour there were housewives at the cheese and meat counters. Ruby was at the dry goods counter: she was putting a few things into a basket as her purchases were rung up.

Carrie waited beside a meagre display of tinned pil-chards and caught Ruby's arm as she turned for the door. Ruby was so startled she nearly dropped her basket.

'Carrie! What are you doing here?'

'I've come to see you,' Carrie smiled. 'Can your mum wait for her groceries? And is there anywhere we can go to talk?'

Ruby seemed befuddled by two questions at once, so Carrie waited while she processed them.

'Ye-es. I suppose,' she stuttered finally. 'It's only a bit of baby rice and rusks for the baby's breakfast.'

So there was a baby! Carrie nodded encouragingly.

'If we're quick . . .' Ruby went on. 'There's the pub down the road here. It's quite . . . OK.'

Carrie had noticed it in passing. It had looked quite respectable, so she was happy to agree.

Carrie was glad, in the end, that they wouldn't be having their conversation in the hurly-burly of Ruby's home, which sounded chaotic, and she gave the girl even more credit for

285

turning up to work on time and well presented each day. Quite apart from air raids, it was hard to see how anyone could get a moment's peace or a wink of sleep in that noisy household. But then, if it was all you knew, presumably you got used to it.

At the pub, settled in a corner with a lemonade each, Ruby said shyly, 'It's nice of you to come. I didn't think I'd ever see you again after yesterday.'

'That's why I'm here,' Carrie said. 'It's nice to see you too, but actually I'm here on Bette's behalf.'

Ruby shrank back into the corner like a frightened foal.

'Mrs Saunders?' she said nervously. 'Why? Did she send you? Has she sent my cards?'

'No, quite the opposite,' said Carrie soothingly. 'You're not sacked, Ruby. She never meant that. She wants you to come back.'

The pantomime of emotions that Uncle Charlie had seen cross Bette's face when she'd found Eric's letter in Ruby's pocket was repeated, though taking different forms, on Ruby's face now. Disbelief turned to delight, and then to doubt.

'Are you sure? She really said that? How do you know?'

Carrie couldn't lie. Bette had said nothing of the kind; she'd never have lost face.

'I went to talk to her,' said Carrie simply. 'Bette – Mrs Saunders – realises she went too far, it was just that she was taken by surprise. I think she accepts now there's no harm in your writing to Eric, and there never was.'

'No, I know that, I never meant there to be!'

'She'd have liked you to mention it to her before you did,

that's all, but that's not what happened and we can't change that.'

'So is she saying I can write back to him and keep writing and she won't mind? She's not going to be all nasty to me about it again?'

Ruby's eyes filled with tears as the hurt and humiliation of the previous day came back to her. Carrie put a hand over hers.

'I think we can all agree the whole thing's best forgotten. And yes, of course you must write back. Eric's asked you to, apart from anything else! What's he going to think if your letters dry up?'

Ruby rubbed her nose as she considered this.

'So can I come to work tomorrow like usual?'

'Yes.' Carrie grinned. 'I think Bette's realised today how much work you actually do! To be honest, Ruby, you're far too much of a good thing for her to lose.'

Ruby blushed.

'No one's ever said that to me before.'

No, thought Carrie, and there lay part of the problem.

'Well, I've said it now. And Bette realises it. So come back tomorrow morning, and you'll be very welcome.'

Ruby gave a huge, happy sigh.

'I can't believe it,' she said. 'It's like a fairy tale. And you've made it happen, Carrie.'

'Oh, come off it!'

'No, really, you've saved my life! I didn't dare tell Dad I'd lost me job, he'd have given me such a larruping! I pretended I'd come home a bit early yesterday with a sick 'eadache and I've had to pretend to be poorly all day. This evening's the first time I've been out.'

'Oh, Ruby!'

'Tomorrow I was going to get up and pretend I was going to work and go down the Labour, see if they'd got anything for me. I suppose I could've got summat else quick enough, but I like that job at the tearoom. I don't want another.'

'Well, that's all right, then. Everyone's happy.'

Ruby beamed. 'I am. I could kiss yer!'

'Well, maybe not here, Ruby,' Carrie smiled, but she was moved. Poor Ruby, what a life she had! 'Now drink up, and tell me a bit about your family. Who was the little one I heard crying?'

'Oh,' said Ruby dismissively. 'That's our Vi and little Ron. Left her husband, she has.'

'Oh no!'

'Oh, he's all right really, her feller, it's only when he's been on the drink. I dunno how long she'll stay with us this time. Not long, I hope, 'cos they're bunking in with us, Ron's teething and there's three of us girls that box and cox in that room already.'

'How many of you are there at home?'

'Only four of us kids now. Vi's married, so's Elsie, Bernard's in the army and Maggie's in the ATS. Pat's in a munitions factory, digs provided.'

'That's still quite enough in one house! I suppose you all have to muck in?'

'Yeah.' Then Ruby added with a rare show of humour, 'I come to work for a rest, tell you the truth, but don't tell Mrs Saunders that!'

They finished their drinks and parted outside the pub, Ruby giving Carrie the promised kiss on the cheek. Carrie felt guilty that she'd never bothered to find out more about Ruby. From her unpromising start in life, she had overcome even more than Penny had. Carrie walked home in the virtuous glow of a good deed done, and with a new fondness for her.

Carrie made sure she was in the tearoom when Ruby arrived the next day, going down there especially to tell Bette to expect her. She was standing at the counter with Bette when they heard the tradesman's door, then the sound of a locker door opening and closing. Carrie pulled an expectant face; Bette was impassive. Then Ruby came shyly through from the back, tying the strings of her crossover apron around her.

'G'morning, Mrs Saunders,' she said meekly.

'You're back then,' sniffed Bette. 'Let's see your fingernails!'

Some welcome, but the fingernail inspection was a ritual Bette insisted on every day. As Ruby held out her hands, Carrie marvelled at how the girl got to the sink in the early-morning mayhem at home, fighting for space with her parents, sisters and younger brother, never mind the addition of Vi and little Ron.

Bette nodded her approval and without further ceremony, or acknowledgement of what had gone on, said, 'Right, the kitchen floor needs mopping, the tables need polishing and there's a delivery needs putting away. Then you can start on a batch of rock cakes.' There was a minuscule pause before she added: 'Please.'

'Yes, Mrs Saunders.'

'And just so we're clear,' Bette went on, 'I can't stop you writing to Eric, and I'm not going to. If he wants to write back to you, that's his own affair.' She paused and swallowed. Humble pie can stick in the throat, but she managed a little smile. 'It was kind of you to think of him.'

'Thank you, Mrs Saunders,' said Ruby meekly. 'I'll go and get on then.'

'And I'd better get back to the stall before Mr Bayliss arrives,' said Carrie. Penny was minding it for her again. 'But save me a rock cake for later, please – the one with the most currants in it!'

She felt she deserved it.

Chapter Twenty-eight

Bonfire Night came and went and one evening towards the
end of November, Carrie stayed late at the stall. Inspired by
the government's Mass Observation project, which was
recording the feelings of ordinary people in their daily lives,
Mr Parfitt had asked her and a few other booksellers on his
patch to keep a note of what he called the 'feedback' they got
from customers. It was his own initiative, but he intended to
pass it on to the management as a tool, separate from sales
figures, to guide them in what was popular – or not. He'd
typed out and cyclostyled a special form, and Carrie was
transcribing her jotted notes onto it.

It was almost eight o'clock when she emerged onto the
darkened platform. She pulled up her coat collar and switched
on her torch, only to see a blurry shape emerge from Mr
Bayliss's office and hear the door slam behind it. Carrie
stiffened. What was Mr Bayliss doing there late into the
evening? And who'd been in there with him? She stayed in
the shadow of the stall, but as the shape hurried towards
her, she realised it was a woman's footsteps, a woman who
was snuffling and crying. What's more, she knew at once
who it was.

'Ruby?'

Ruby jumped in shock. 'Carrie! Oh, thank God!'

'Ruby? What's the matter?'

No reply, just more tears.

Quickly, Carrie unlocked the stall again and drew Ruby inside. She switched on the dim bulb, sat her down on the stool and fished a handkerchief out of her bag. Ruby was a mess – her hair disarranged, her makeup smudged.

'What's been going on? Is it Mr Bayliss? What's he said to you? What were you doing in his office?'

'Oh, Carrie!'

Carrie looked on, mystified, as Ruby dabbed her face and struggled to control her tears.

'It's not what *I* was doing!' Ruby burst into a fresh bout of crying. 'It's what he tried to do to me!'

'Oh, Ruby!' breathed Carrie. 'You don't mean—'

Ruby sniffed.

'Mrs Saunders left me to lock up tonight, and I was about to when he come in the tearoom, said he had something for me. Well, I didn't know what he meant, but he's like the boss of all of us, ain't he, and I thought it might be a Christmas bonus, like, so . . . so I went with him.'

'Right,' said Carrie grimly. She had a nasty idea of what was coming next.

'We gets in there and he's got two glasses out, and a bottle of cherry brandy. Well, I still didn't think anything of it, it's getting to Christmas, after all, so he sits me down and gives me a glass and he says cheers and that, and he's, like, perched on the edge of his desk. And he starts by saying I'm a good girl and good worker and that, and I'm thinking, so it is a Christmas bonus, but then – then—'

She gulped.

'It's all right, Ruby. I think I can guess.'

But Ruby, it seemed, wanted to tell her.

'He made this kind of lunge for me, and he grabs me by the shoulders and he's trying to kiss me and I'm ... I'm frozen. I can't believe it's happening, and then I come to my senses and I try to twist away, and he – he gets a bit rough, and he tells me not to be silly and he starts – he starts . . .' She gulped. 'He starts pawing at me, at my chest, and he – look!' Ruby opened her coat to reveal her blouse. 'He's tore off one of my buttons, and another's hanging by a thread . . . Oh, Carrie, it was horrible!'

Carrie had to swallow her revulsion at the thought of Mr Bayliss's slug-like lips anywhere near her face and his pudgy paws scrabbling at her.

'He's disgusting! You poor thing. But, Ruby, has he ever tried anything like this with you before?'

'No, no. Not like this, any road. He's ... I suppose he has . . . paid me a bit of attention. Said me hair looks nice, or that pink suits me and that. But I didn't think anything of it.'

'No, no, of course not.'

Though given what Carrie had clocked as Mr Bayliss's weakness for young girls, anyone but Ruby might have seen it coming.

'Well, we can't leave it there,' Carrie said. 'He'll have to be reported to the railway management.'

'Oh no! No!' Ruby jumped up. 'He'll only deny it, say I made it up! Then I'll get the sack and you know I don't want that, I've only just got me job back.'

'What about your blouse? That's proof!'

'No, it's not – I could have lost that button any old how and ripped the other. Oh please, Carrie, just leave it.'

Carrie chewed her lip. Ruby was right. If it came down to her word against Bayliss's, who would the male managers of the railway believe? For all Carrie knew, they were at it themselves – that sort of behaviour wasn't uncommon in workplaces. She knew as much thanks to the conversations of typists and shop assistants as they bought their books and magazines – another valuable lesson in life thanks to the bookstall. And there was another problem. Because of the way Ruby had flirted with men in the tearoom in the past, Mr Bayliss might well say she'd been 'asking for it' – as if that was a defence! Carrie wasn't going to let it rest.

'I'm sorry, Ruby, I'm not leaving it like this.'

'What are you going to do?'

'Never you mind.' She glanced at her watch – she was due to meet Penny soon; they were going to see a picture at the Rialto. 'Seriously, Ruby, leave it to me. Are you all right to get home? I can walk into town with you.'

Ruby looked down at Carrie's damp and smeared handkerchief. 'Yes, please, I'd like that,' she said. 'And I'll wash your hankie and iron it.'

'Don't worry about it,' smiled Carrie. 'And don't think about this any more, Ruby. It won't happen again. I'll make sure of that.'

Waving Ruby on her way as they parted, Carrie thought fast. She wasn't scared of Mr Bayliss, so it wasn't that there was safety in numbers, but there was strength in depth. Strictly speaking, Bette was Ruby's boss; she ought to know about this.

And if Bette was going to be involved, Penny should be too. Between them, they could surely give Mr Bayliss what for!

She hauled Penny out of the queue for the pictures, refusing to tell her why till they were seated round the table in Bette's cosy living room.

Bette poured them each a cup of tea and passed round the inevitable plate of home-baked biscuits.

'Lovely to see you and all that,' Bette said, shrouding the teapot in its knitted cosy, 'but to what do I owe the pleasure?'

'I wouldn't mind knowing either,' Penny chipped in through a mouthful of biscuit. She'd taken two; her landlady really didn't feed her. 'She kept mum all the way!'

'I'm afraid it's work, not pleasure,' Carrie admitted, and went on to tell them about Ruby's ordeal.

Penny made retching noises and Bette shook her head gravely. Carrie held her breath for Bette's response. Bette had only just accepted Ruby writing to her precious Eric – was this going to set her back off on her 'that girl's no better than she should be' tack?

'I was worried something like this might happen, wasn't I, Carrie?' Bette began, her mouth tight. 'I told her, and you told her, that she'd get herself into trouble!' Oh no, thought Carrie, here we go. But Bette went on: 'Still, I never thought for a minute he'd dare try it on with her, the dirty devil!'

Carrie felt her shoulders relax – Bette had taken Ruby's side.

'So, what do we do?' Penny demanded. 'We can't let him get away with it. I mean, it might be Ruby one day, and who knows what other poor girl the next!'

'Exactly!' Bette agreed.

'I know,' Carrie nodded. 'So I think we confront him, the three of us.'

'All for one, and one for all!' declared Penny, lifting her teacup in a toast. 'Let's put the old goat in his place!'

The next morning, as soon as Mr Bayliss arrived, they marched into his office. Mr Bayliss was still taking off his overcoat.

'Yes?' he barked, turning round from the bentwood hat-stand. 'Why aren't you at your posts?'

'I'll give you posts!' Bette began. 'You'd be losing yours if I had my way!'

'I beg your pardon?' Mr Bayliss puffed himself up to his full height of five feet and four inches.

'You lured Ruby in here last night, plied her with drink and assaulted her,' Penny said coldly. 'You probably thought she wouldn't dare say anything. But we know.'

'I don't know what you're talking about!' Mr Bayliss replied, but his ruddy cheeks went even ruddier. 'Is that what she's saying? Silly girl. She's making it up!'

'Really?' said Carrie. 'There are two glasses on your desk, one of them still half-full of what looks like cherry brandy. And then there's this.' She bent down to the floor. Penny and Bette's eyes followed her, puzzled, as she straightened up, holding a small, round, pearl button. 'Looks to me like a perfect match for the ones on the blouse Ruby was wearing yesterday. Do you want me to ask her to bring it to work, and we'll see?'

Penny and Bette looked at her admiringly.

'That could have got here anyhow!' blustered Mr Bayliss. 'There must be thousands of buttons like that!'

Carrie shrugged.

'Maybe, but only on women's clothes. Are you in the habit of entertaining women in your office after hours? Women who unaccountably lose buttons off their clothing?'

Mr Bayliss's eyes narrowed, making him look even more unpleasant.

'That's a slanderous allegation, and I won't have it!'

'Well, nor will we,' declared Bette. 'You know it happened like Ruby says. You're a dirty old man, that's the top and bottom of it!'

'Yes, you are,' echoed Penny. 'We've all seen you leering at any pretty young passenger, but you've gone too far this time.'

'Looking at people? What are you going to do about it, eh?' sneered Mr Bayliss. 'It's not a crime. It's a free country – still!'

Carrie held up the button between her thumb and forefinger and nodded towards the glasses on the desk. She was having to work hard to hold in her disgust at what he'd done and his trying to wriggle out of it.

'Looking may not be a crime, but what you tried on with Ruby is different. Who knows how far it might have gone if Ruby hadn't managed to get away, and who knows how many other girls you've accosted on or off the station – or still might, if you keep getting away with it? We could report you to your superiors, and you know it.'

He had nothing to say to that, so he said all he could.

'Get out!' he snapped. 'Go on, out of my office!'

Carrie, Bette and Penny looked at each other. His dismissal of them proved their point. He had no defence at all.

'We'll be glad to,' said Bette. 'Being in here with you, even with the others for company, is making me feel quite sick. We've got your number, Mr Bayliss, and don't you forget it! We'll be watching you.'

Outside, on the platform, they hugged each other in glee.

'Well done, girls!' said Bette.

'All for one, and one for all!' Penny said again. 'But it was down to Carrie, really, spotting Ruby's button. Well done, you!'

Carrie smiled. 'I didn't.'

'What?' squeaked Penny.

'Ruby's button's somewhere in that office, of course,' said Carrie, 'but it could have rolled into a corner or under a piece of furniture. What I showed him is one of my own I cut off a blouse last night. I had it in my pocket all the time and just pretended to find it.'

'Whatever gave you that idea?' asked Bette.

'I've read enough detective stories between trains,' grinned Carrie. 'Take *The ABC Murders*.'

'You've lost me, duck.' Bette shook her head.

'Poirot pretends to have found a fingerprint on a typewriter, and that flushes out a confession,' Carrie grinned. 'So don't give me the credit. Thank the bookstall!'

Chapter Twenty-nine

After a further rumpus with Ruby, who had to be reassured all over again that no one blamed her for what had happened and she wasn't going to lose her job, there was barely any time for things to settle down before Christmas was galloping towards them.

Bette got out the Christmas decorations and had Ruby and Penny shinning up ladders to hang strips of lametta and paper chains all around the tearoom. She stuck cotton wool over a football and an empty catering-size tin of custard powder to make a snowman, which she filled with sweets for the children. Wonderful smells wafted from the kitchen: she made flapjacks, shortbread and a dozen extra mince pies, using her own hoarded rations, and sent them off to Eric.

'I don't care if he doesn't get them till Easter, I'm darn well going to try!' she declared.

But on the home front, the festive season wouldn't be all about merry gentlemen resting and geese getting fat. Last Christmas, the fighting had hardly begun; this year, there was no doubt that the country was properly at war.

The Andersons' shop had some special Christmas tins of toffees and boxed chocolates for sale, but the contents were getting meaner or the sizes of the containers smaller, and

Norman had ordered fewer this year. Sweets themselves weren't rationed ('Yet,' he said darkly), but the rationing of butter and sugar meant that manufacturers had already adapted their recipes. Butter toffee was less buttery, and sugar mice less sweet.

The Christmas cards in the rack were smaller and flimsier too. There was no jolly Santa or robin redbreast wrapping paper to buy, apart from last year's leftover stock, and no wonder, when even brown paper and paper bags were in short supply. Many shops had already stopped wrapping customers' purchases.

But none of that affected Carrie's trade. Mr Parfitt's Penguins and other books suitable for gifts had arrived in good time, and the *Radio Times* was already promising 'a feast of entertainment' on the wireless over the holiday, along with messages to and from the troops.

Carrie loved the lead-up to Christmas almost as much as the day itself. She loved planning what she'd buy for family – and this year, for her new friends. No one knew what next Christmas would bring, where Johnnie would be, or where any of them would be, for that matter. So she was determined to make this Christmas one to remember for those she was closest to.

Uncle Charlie had agreed to 'mind the shop' and he watched in amusement as she checked her list.

Snowed in in Scotland, Johnnie had missed out on leave last Christmas, so he was certain of getting a couple of days off this year, especially as, to his frustration, he was still not flying combat missions.

'They're talking about putting me in the control room

now, presenting it as a chance for promotion!' he'd huffed on the phone to Carrie. 'And don't you dare tell Mum, or she'll be writing to the Air Vice-Marshal in support. I'm digging my heels in. I'm not being stuck on the ground for the rest of the war, talking the other bods in and out. It's not as if I'm injured. I want to get back in the air!'

'I know you do,' Carrie sympathised. 'But the RAF knows best. For now, I'm sure you're doing a great job with those eager beaver young pilots. A much-needed job, too.

'Babysitting!' scorned her brother. She heard the click of his cigarette case being flicked open. 'Oh, drat!'

There was a tinny clatter at the other end of the line.

'What's up?' asked Carrie.

'My fags are all over the floor. The hinge on my case has gone – I need a new one. Hint, hint.'

So Johnnie was down on Carrie's list for a new cigarette case, and her father for a new cap – the lining of his old one was in shreds. Uncle Charlie would be getting a new tie – she'd have fun choosing that – and for her mum . . .well, there were endless possibilities.

The money Norman gave Mary for housekeeping had always easily covered the cost of food, with a little left over for the odd treat for herself. But everything cost more now and Mary stinted herself so much to keep their meals appetising and to keep the house nice, the family rarely saw her with anything new.

'This'll do me another year,' she'd say as she darned the elbow of a cardigan or mended a laddered stocking. 'Who sees me, anyhow?'

Now she had another excuse. The war had put up prices

of the basics, but profits had dipped at the shop, so Norman hadn't been able to increase her housekeeping. And there was a blizzard of leaflets and posters encouraging house-wives to be thrifty, and not just with food.

There were still clothes in the shops, of course, but with so much wool and cotton going for uniforms, they were more and more expensive. Just this week, *Woman's Own* had run a feature on 'Five Ways to Freshen Up a Favourite Dress', suggesting a crisp white collar, a smart belt, a corsage, changing the buttons and, radically, inserting a contrast panel into the bodice and skirt. Mary had lapped it up.

All of which made Carrie all the more determined to spoil her mum this year. Bath salts and nice-smelling soap, a brooch, a necklace or a scarf, maybe even a shop-bought jumper instead of a home-knit, or a new blouse instead of a rummage-sale find. She'd have fun choosing for her too.

As for Carrie's friends . . . Eric wouldn't be there to make a fuss of his mum, so Bette deserved to be treated on her first Christmas without him. Now that Carrie knew Penny's back-ground, she'd be embarrassed to give her anything tawdry, so she was going to be a challenge. Ruby would be easier. She'd been a late addition to the list, but knowing her better now, Carrie had resolved to get her a little something too.

Of course, there was one name missing from her list. Had things been different, Carrie would have been buying a pres-ent for Mike. With every batch of books she unpacked, she mentally put aside one or two she thought he'd like – he'd have had a whole colony of Penguins by now. She'd have had to ask Johnnie to make him a bookcase. But wouldn't books have been the easy way out? If they'd had the chance to get to know each other better, she'd have been able to buy him something rather more personal. She touched the locket he'd bought her. A tiepin, cufflinks, a watch, a shirt, even?

The thought made her heart skip a beat. But she knew the memory of being held against him as he kissed her was fading, however much she tried to hang on to it.

'Well, are you going or not? I'm not stood here for the good of my health!'

'Sorry, Uncle Charlie,' Carrie apologised, coming back to the present. 'Just thinking, you know . . . about what I had to get.'

'I don't know why you women get so aerated about Christmas shopping,' her uncle marvelled. 'I just go on Christmas Eve, boom, boom, boom, I'm done inside an hour.'

'Typical man!' smiled Carrie, though you'd never have known it from the thoughtful presents Uncle Charlie always gave, like the bracelet she still wore almost every day because it matched Mike's locket. 'I like to take my time.'

Uncle Charlie took it in good heart.

'Off you go then,' he grinned. 'And don't go spending your money on me. I'll be happy with a card.'

'Well, I can assure you that's not going to happen!'

'Get away with you,' Uncle Charlie tutted. 'Now scoot!'

So as Uncle Charlie shooed her away, Carrie set off on her shopping trip in high spirits. She headed straight for Lovells, Brockington's smartest department store. She might not be able to afford to get everything there – in fact she very much doubted it – but she was certainly going to enjoy seeing what they'd got.

*

The uniformed commissionaire held open the door with a discreet inclination of his head and Carrie gave him a gracious smile as she passed, trying to look as if she got this sort of treatment every day. She certainly felt she looked the part. She'd polished her shoes to a mirror shine and had taken extra care with her makeup and the placement of her brown felt hat. She had to admit that sometimes her mother's thriftiness came in handy, because Mary had found a remnant of fake astrakhan fur on the market and had used it to trim Carrie's camel coat, disguising the worn collar and cuffs.

Once inside, Carrie literally stepped into a different world. Uncle Charlie, with his frequent trips 'up town', was always banging on about Selfridges and Marshall & Snelgrove, the smart department stores where he bought the odd phial of perfume for his lady friends or took them for tea. Lovells might not quite be in their league, but it certainly liked to think it was, and it was the epitome of luxury in suburban Brockington.

On either side of Carrie the perfume and cosmetics counters stretched away with their enticing scents, beautiful packaging and exquisitely groomed salesgirls. Further over, ladies' accessories were on display – handbags and hosiery and gloves. Plaster half-busts with cleverly draped or tied scarves were a rare splash of colour in what had become a drab world of khaki and camouflage enlivened by the odd dash of navy and air-force blue. Carrie breathed in the exotic scents and revelled in the soft lighting reflected in the mirrored pillars, which even signs saying 'In Case of Air Raid Assemble at Staircase A' couldn't totally disfigure.

Lovells had decked itself out with a huge Christmas tree at the bottom of the sweeping staircase and wide red-velvet ribbon studded with baubles and tiny gold bells was looped around the banisters. Carrie had seen the same decoration in their windows the year before and the year before that, but it was still a better effort than the paper chains and tired strips of lametta that were the best most shops could manage.

However, when Carrie started to look more closely, she could see that the war had made a subtle difference. The displays of gloves and trays of purses were a little sparse – leather was prioritised for army belts and the seats of Jeeps, not non-essentials – and the scarves were a shocking price. In Cosmetics, there were gaps on the shelves and Carrie remembered Ruby's devastation over the bombing of the Bourjois factory. Coty and Revlon were making foot powder, not face powder, and anti-gas ointment, not eyeshadow. *'Beauty is a Duty'* said the advertisements – but you were lucky if you could get your hands on the stuff. Her dad said it was the same with sweets. The manufacturers kept advertising, though, to keep their names in the public eye.

But even so, there was more than enough choice. Carrie decided not to get distracted – she could spend hours browsing for her mum and women friends. She decided to tick off the men on her list first, so she headed towards the escalators that would take her to the first floor, where she'd find Gentlemen's Outfitting for her dad's cap and Uncle Charlie's tie.

The escalators had been installed just before the war to great fanfare, and Carrie enjoyed the sensation as she glided gently upwards. Was this how it felt for Johnnie as the nose of his plane lifted off the runway – but about a thousand times faster? Maybe it was more how you felt when you . . . but that made her think about Mike again. She glanced down at the floor below. Mike . . . Mike . . . And suddenly – there he was!

He was standing with his back to her at one of the counters, paying for something – surely it was him? It certainly looked like him – the same thick, dark hair, the same parting, the same slim hand passing over a note. But it couldn't be! Here? In Brockington? It made no sense. If he was here, why hadn't he got in touch?

'Excuse me!' Carrie pushed past the couple ahead of her, past a woman holding the hand of a small child, past another with a large, jutting-out basket. She reached the top and swiftly turned to step onto the downward escalator, almost stumbling in her haste. Past another couple of shoppers, who tutted as she barged by, arriving at the bottom in a heap and almost turning her ankle. She rushed towards the counter where she'd seen him – but he was gone.

'That man – he was just here – paying—' she gabbled to the assistant, looking around wildly. 'Oh, no, never mind, there he is!'

And there he was, heading for the door! Carrie charged in the same direction, frustrated that the throng of Christmas shoppers, who'd have the management of Lovells rubbing their hands, were in her way.

'Sorry!' she called over her shoulder, bumping into a woman in furs deliberating over a pot of rouge.

'You might be advised to take two,' the salesgirl was

saying. 'I don't think we'll be seeing many more of this brand come in.'

Through the double doors without a glance, let alone a gracious smile to the commissionaire, out into the street – and there he was again, striding away through the crowds. Carrie started to run, but the pavement was wet and her feet went from under her. She almost sprawled.

'Aargh!'

A soldier in a corporal's uniform stepped smartly out of a bus queue. He caught her arm and began hauling her back onto her feet.

'Wotcha, sweetheart! Been on the sauce?'

'No, I have not!' snapped Carrie.

'All right, all right, no need to get shirty! If that's the thanks I get for being a gentleman—'

'Sorry, I'm in a hurry—' Carrie began, but the incident had lost her vital minutes. She craned over the heads of the crowd – there he was, near the turning to West Street! Carrie started to run. It had to be him – the same height, the same brisk walk, the same tilt of the head. But why hadn't he let her know he was back?

Unless . . . All her wildest fantasies about what had happened to Mike in the six long months since Dunkirk came flooding back. He'd had a bang on the head. He'd got back to England somehow, or been brought back, but had been lying in a coma ever since. He'd lost his memory as a result. Maybe he was just out of hospital. He was passing through Brockington on his way home to Leamington, like he had before – if he still knew where home was. Maybe the army medics had told him that much, but he hadn't seen anyone from his old unit, like Stan Thompson, who'd have reminded him about the girl he left behind. Maybe his full memory would come back in time, he just had to be patient. But for now, the bit that was still missing was the bit about her.

All these thoughts flew through Carrie's head as she ran. He was just about to turn the corner when she caught up with him, reached for him, caught his arm.

'Mike!' she said urgently. 'Mike! It's me, Carrie!'

He turned then, puzzled astonishment on his face – and Carrie let go of his arm as quickly as she'd grabbed it.

'I'm . . . sorry!' she stammered. 'I'm so sorry . . . I . . .'

It wasn't him. Height, walk, stature, they might have been the same, but the face was completely different – fuller cheeks, heavier brows and a weaker chin. The man said nothing, just shrugged and walked on. Humiliated as well as devastated, Carrie fumbled her way to the sill of a shop window and sat down. She put her head in her hands.

Of course it hadn't been Mike – how stupid of her! She'd heard about this kind of thing when you'd lost someone – thinking you saw them everywhere or heard their voice. It was all an illusion, born of wanting to believe it could be true, and she'd fallen victim to it.

There was nothing for it. Carrie went back to her shopping, but the fun had gone out of the day. She didn't go back to Lovells. She went to Littlewoods and British Home Stores and Montague Burton and looked at caps and ties. She looked at cigarette cases in the windows of the jeweller and the pawn shop. The jeweller's one was rather expensive, and the pawn shop one looked pretty new ... But was a second-hand case a miserable gift for Christmas? She couldn't see a scratch on it . . . Would Johnnie mind a second-hand case? If it did have the odd mark from use, would he notice? So thrown by the incident, Carrie felt she didn't even know her own twin now, and it disheartened her still further. She couldn't seem to make up her mind about anything.

Finally, the familiar surroundings of Boots, where she'd used to work, helped her to marshal her thoughts. She bought a little manicure set for Ruby and bath salts in a mock-crystal jar for Bette. Then things started to unravel. Penny remained a problem. It was no good getting her a photograph frame when she didn't seem to have anyone's photo to put in it. Cosmetics? Perfume? And as for her mother . . . the more she browsed, the more befuddled and despondent Carrie became. She couldn't shop for something special for her mum in this kind of mood. She'd have to come another day. Her heart simply wasn't in it any more.

Chapter Thirty

Carrie managed to cover her feeling of hopelessness when she returned to the stall. She had to, for Uncle Charlie.

'I hate to say "I told you so" . . .' he crowed when she returned pretty much empty-handed.

'But you're going to anyway.'

She stowed her almost-empty shopping bag in the little cubbyhole office as Uncle Charlie shrugged on his British Warm overcoat, getting ready to go.

'Never mind, love,' he soothed. 'There's still time.'

'Yes, I know, Christmas Eve, with all the other last-minute merchants,' Carrie replied flatly. 'See you there!'

She didn't tell Uncle Charlie the real reason for her unsuccessful trip and she couldn't ask him to step in and cover for her again, over and above his regular day. There were a lot of motors in for pre-Christmas rush jobs, he'd told her, and he and Des were taking their mechanics out for a slap-up Christmas dinner to say thank you for their hard work throughout the year, so the afternoon of Christmas Eve was the only option left to her. Carrie had had a notice up for weeks warning customers that she'd be shutting up shop at one o'clock that day. Between now and then, though, there were other plans to put in place.

'Have you decided what you're doing for Christmas yet?' she asked Bette the next day.

Bette had an offer to go to her brother's, and though she wasn't entirely keen, she confirmed that this was what she'd decided to do. Her sister-in-law had had an operation, and the good-hearted side of Bette had come to the fore.

'I'm not that close to him,' she confided. 'Never have been. And I can take or leave her' – she meant her sister-in-law – 'but family's family, and it is Christmas.'

Carrie couldn't disagree.

'It's not entirely a bad thing.' Bette winked. 'If she's off her legs, I can have charge of the kitchen, so I won't have to put up with her thin gravy and soggy roasties.' Then she said more soberly: 'At least it might stop me thinking about Eric, and what he's got to put up with.'

'They'll do their best to have a bit of a Christmas, even if the camp won't make any effort,' Carrie reassured her. 'I bet they've been hoarding stuff from their Red Cross parcels – and what about the mince pies and shortbread you sent? I'm sure they won't let Christmas pass unnoticed.'

Eric's letters often trailed way behind events: Bette's latest had told of a cold snap the camp had suffered in late October, freezing the standpipe where the prisoners washed. The camp censor had let that little nugget of information through; it wasn't as if it was a deliberate act of cruelty, and the fact that it was cold hardly gave away precise details of the camp's location. The Red Cross had told Bette, anyway: it was in Poland, one of the German-occupied countries.

Carrie was still writing to Eric every fortnight and sending him books she knew he'd like: pulp westerns and thrillers.

She also sent books he might not initially have chosen but which the other men might enjoy and persuade him to try – he had nothing else to do, after all. If he was going to be shut away for possibly years on end, he could only profit from something a bit more demanding than *The Shadow* and *The Phantom Detective* – the pulp magazines he'd read in his tea breaks when he'd worked at the station.

Ruby hadn't shown Carrie any more of Eric's letters, but she was still writing to him once a week, and going through several drafts before she produced a 'best' copy, judging by the amount of lined pads she bought from the bookstall. Bette had realised she couldn't stop Ruby writing, but from what Carrie could deduce from his letters, he still sensitively sent two to his mum for every one he wrote to Ruby or Carrie. Bette also got the majority of the four postcards a month he was allowed to send, so honour was satisfied.

'Sure it's still OK for me to come and stay for Christmas?' Penny asked, passing with a mop and bucket.

'Of course,' Carrie insisted. 'You are not spending it on your own!'

Penny's landlady was going away to relatives.

'Ha ha, you're funny!' Penny had said when Carrie asked if Penny had any plans to be reconciled with her own family. 'Why would I want to spend Christmas in a freezing pile in Norfolk with my equally Arctic father when I can have the full run of my lodgings in Brockington for once? I can spread out in the usually off-limits parlour, build a roaring fire and eat chocolate all day!'

When Carrie relayed this to her mother, Mary had been scandalised.

'We can't have her doing that!' she cried. 'She's to come and stay here from the minute the station shuts till the minute it reopens on Boxing Day. I don't care what she says. The very idea of Penny being on her own at Christmas!'

So it had been arranged. Penny would sleep on a camp bed in Carrie's room, as Johnnie would be in his own bed. He'd come good with promises of tinned ham and tongue from the NAAFI. There was even a rumour he might bring tinned peaches and butter, so teatime on Christmas Day would be something to look forward to.

Mary, Carrie and Norman had foregone meat for a couple of weeks to hoard the coupons for a piece of beef, and Carrie and her mum had made the Christmas cake and pudding on the traditional day, Stir-up Sunday.

'There's a lot of carrot in it,' Mary had warned her husband. 'It might be a bit wet.'

'Don't worry, love, I'll be heavy on the brandy when it comes to flaming it!' grinned Norman in reply.

So Christmas itself was sorted to everyone's satisfaction. There just remained the question of everyone's presents.

Christmas Eve morning at the station was extra hectic as travellers made a frantic dash to the West End for shows and shops, or away to relatives for the festive season. Soldiers, sailors and airmen, liberated on Christmas leave, were full of a different kind of Christmas spirit and sang, joshed and jostled their way between trains. Penny scurried to and fro with suitcases and parcels; Mr Bayliss scuttled about the platforms, consulting his watch, pointing passengers in the right direction or advising on the timetable. In between serving customers, Carrie could see streams of travellers going in and out of the tearoom. Busy, yes, but happy. The jolly atmosphere was infectious, and by the time she drew down the shutter at one o'clock, Carrie was full of the joys of Christmas herself.

Before she could leave for her second and final – well, it had to be – shopping trip, though, she had to give Bette and Ruby their gifts. The tearoom was busy. Bette was taking someone's order, so Carrie tapped her arm to indicate that she'd tucked her present under the counter. Bette signalled back that her own present to Carrie was under there too, and from the size, shape and powerful smell of lavender it was giving off, Carrie guessed that it was a box of soaps – they'd had almost the same thought!

She found Ruby out the back, cutting bread for sand-wiches.

'It's like feeding the five thousand!' she groaned. 'You'd think they weren't going to eat for days, instead of having their best feed of the year tomorrow!'

'Human nature,' grinned Carrie. 'And, um, look, I've got you a little something for Christmas, Ruby.'

'What? For me?' Ruby dropped the knife with a clatter. 'Oh, Carrie! I ain't got you nothing!'

'This is nothing,' Carrie insisted. 'Really, it's not much, but—'

'Oh no, I feel dreadful now!'

'Don't be silly,' said Carrie, and then, echoing Uncle Charlie, 'I don't want you spending your money on me.'

'I hadn't got none left by the time I'd bought for Mum and Dad and me brothers and sisters,' mourned Ruby. 'And there's little Ron as well. Now he's old enough to take notice, I had to get him summat.'

'Of course you did. Family comes first. Always!'

'But you've done so much for me.'

'Nonsense!'

'You have!' Ruby insisted. 'That horrible business with . . .' she cocked her head in the direction of Mr Bayliss's office '. . . *him*, and before that, squaring things with Mrs Saunders over Eric. You can think what you like, but I know you've done me good! You've helped me to feel different about meself.'

And it was true – there was something different about Ruby. Mr Bayliss had been successfully subdued, and since the fracas with Bette over the letter, Ruby and her boss seemed to have come to a new understanding. In a funny way, Carrie thought Bette almost respected Ruby for showing some initiative. Until then, she'd never thought the girl capable of it, let alone given her the chance to demonstrate it.

Now, however, Bette had begun to give Ruby a bit more responsibility. She let her do some basic ordering and trusted her to do some of the baking without Bette standing over her. True, attempts to explain double-entry bookkeeping had fallen at the first fence, but as Bette said, you couldn't expect miracles from a girl who'd likely addled her brain with her excessive use of peroxide. Carrie realised that Bette needed to retain some sense of superiority, and had probably guessed that even simple accounting would be beyond Ruby's capabilities. But, overall, the girl did seem to have gained a bit of confidence.

Carrie gave her a quick hug.

'If there's any change in you, Ruby, you've made it happen for yourself,' she smiled. 'And now, I must fly!'

She made her way up the crowded platform, finding Penny counting a handful of tips by the fire bucket.

'Wotcha,' Penny said, shovelling coppers into her pocket. 'See you later!'

'Yes, see you at home!' Carrie called as she dashed past.

The way Penny played up to her role as porter with her laconic shrugs and slang did amuse her. They were in for a gay old time with her added to the mix. And even if it was poignant for Carrie, she owed it to them to be as bright and cheerful as she could be on the day. And she'd do it, too!

Carrie even felt brave enough to go back to Lovells, where the atmosphere was, if anything, even more festive than before. As well as the decorations, the crowds of shoppers, the buzz of chatter and the exotic smells of the perfume hall, they'd somehow managed to rig up a gramophone to play carols over the Tannoy system. Carrie rose up the escalator this time to the strains of 'Hark! The Herald Angels Sing'.

She was on her way to Gentlemen's Outfitting again, though she'd already bought her dad's cap from Dunn's. On reflection, she'd felt Norman would have been embarrassed to take off his cap in the Rose and Crown and have his mates josh him about going up in the world when they saw a Lovells label. But Uncle Charlie would be happy to wear his tie inside out to show off a label from a smart store, so that was what Carrie was on her way to buy.

As she floated upwards, she couldn't help but glance down again to the counter where she'd seen the phantom

'Mike'. And he'd been just that – a phantom – a phantom in a fantasy.

With a deep breath, she stepped off the escalator at the top and made her way around the rope that was now in place to control the crowds. Looking about her, she spotted a display of ties fanned out on the back wall like the spokes of a wheel and headed determinedly towards them. This time, she was not going to be deflected!

She found the perfect tie – grey with a geometric pattern in gold and burgundy – and then – because hang it, she had the money and Uncle Charlie had been awfully good to her – a plain gold pocket square. With her purchases stowed safely in her bag, Carrie descended to the ground floor to shop for her mum and Penny.

Penny could adopt the blokeish attitudes and vocabulary that she imagined went with being a porter all she liked. But those camiknickers proved that underneath it all – literally – and contrary to what Penny had told Mr Bayliss when she first arrived, there beat the heart of a woman, not a man. So at one of the cosmetics counters, and bearing in mind what she'd overheard on her previous trip about such things getting scarce, Carrie bought Penny a pretty gilt compact of pressed powder. For her mum she chose a headsquare – only artificial silk – but a beautiful design in Mary's colours: pink and cream roses and peonies on a pale green background.

'It's a beauty, isn't it?' the salesgirl said as she folded it up. 'You can almost smell the flowers!'

There was only Johnnie left on her list now, and Carrie headed out of Lovells and straight for Cross Street. Her favourite brother – not that he had any competition – was not getting a cigarette case from a pawn shop, oh no! She'd buy him the pricey one she'd seen in the jeweller's.

As she passed the commissionaire, she made a point of thanking him and wishing him a Merry Christmas to make up for dashing past so rudely before. There'd be no chasing someone who wasn't Mike down the street this time. With much sorrow Carrie knew she had to accept she wasn't going to see the real Mike again. Last Christmas, they'd been at the very start of their romance. But it was *this* Christmas: life went on, they said, and so must she.

Chapter Thirty-one

So here it was – the second Christmas of the war. Mid-morning, and the Anderson family, with Penny, were sitting around the table, drinking final cups of tea after their breakfast of scrambled eggs and – as it was Christmas – a precious rasher of bacon each. The table was still piled with breakfast crocks and there were scraps of wrapping paper and string on the floor. Mary, instinctively, had collected the bigger pieces and smoothed them out for next year.

Carrie's presents had gone down well, and she was the happy recipient of a new purse from her parents, a slim clutch bag from Johnnie (showing off his RAF pay, but very gratefully received) and from Penny, a powder compact – exactly the same as the one Carrie had bought her, which made them both chuckle. The compact wasn't the only present Penny had received: Norman and Mary gave her a box of chocolates, and Johnnie a photograph frame, an idea Carrie had rejected. But in it he'd put a photo of the three of them, taken on his new camera when he'd been at home in the autumn. He was in the middle, with the girls either side of him, and they were all smiling widely.

'I don't expect you to keep that picture in there for ever,' he said. 'I'm sure there's others you'd rather have on show – but I thought it'd start you off.'

'I jolly well will keep it in there,' Penny replied. She seemed quite moved. 'Thank you!'

Now, Mary organised her smoothed-out paper into a neater pile and said: 'Well, I'd better get this table cleared. We'll soon have to be making a start on the dinner!'

Everyone groaned, as if the thought of more food was the last thing on their minds, when in fact everyone was hugely looking forward to it. Then came a determined knocking on the shop door.

'You have to be joking!' Norman exploded. 'Christmas Day? What can anyone possibly want from the shop? Well, they've had it! I am not going to answer it.'

'It can't be a neighbour wanting to borrow something,' reasoned Mary. 'They'd have come round the back.'

Johnnie held up his hands in surrender. 'It's not for me. I'm on official leave. I can show you my chit. And there's been no newsflash to say there's a flap on.'

It was true. In the background, Sandy MacPherson, a stalwart of the BBC Home Service, was still burbling away at the theatre organ.

Carrie and Penny looked at one another.

'Unless . . .' Penny began.

'Bette,' said Carrie.

'I thought she was going to her brother's?' asked Mary.

'She was,' Carrie replied. 'But what if there's been some problem and she couldn't get there? We can't leave her standing in the street!' She stood up. 'I'd better go and see.'

'Well, if it isn't her and it's some cheeky beggar run out of humbugs, tell them "Bah humbug" from me!' Norman called after her.

Carrie went through the little hall, parted the bead curtain and stepped into the darkened shop. She knew the way so well she didn't need to put the lights on or raise the blackout blind on the door to pull back the bolts and release the lock. Opening the door, she felt a rush of cold air on her skin. She was wearing a new dress: short-sleeved, sea-green crepe with a sweetheart neckline that showed off both Uncle Charlie's bracelet and Mike's locket.

As she opened the door wider, she almost fell backwards in astonishment. There in front of her, not a dream, not an illusion, not a fantasy, but really there, in the flesh – was Mike.

'Hello, Carrie,' he said. 'Happy Christmas.'

Then she was in his arms and he was kissing her, hard. All the emotion of six months of waiting, wondering, hoping, giving up, weeping, falling apart, putting herself together again, believing and not believing – Carrie put all that into kissing him back. Longing and desire, sorrow and regret, delight and disbelief, relief and . . . rightness. Rightness that they were together again.

Finally, they pulled apart. He held her face, studying her, drinking her in.

'Carrie,' he said softly. 'Still beautiful. You haven't changed.'

He had. His lovely face was thinner and his eyes were older. He'd felt thinner when they'd embraced. What had he been through?

'Oh, Mike. You're home! You're alive! Oh, thank God! Oh, I do love you,' she said.

323

The words were completely inadequate for what she was feeling, but they were all she had. He seemed to understand.

'I love you too. More than words can say.'

They clung together again, neither wanting to let the other go.

'They'll be wondering what's happened to me,' Carrie whispered finally.

'I know.'

She could hear the smile in his voice. That much hadn't changed.

'Well, you were always accusing me of turning up unannounced and taking you by surprise. Now we can both surprise them!'

Holding his hand, never wanting to let it go, Carrie led him through to the back room.

The table was cleared and Mary and Penny were spreading the best lace cloth for dinner. Norman and Johnnie were laughing and clattering in the kitchen. Mary looked up as she heard the bead curtain, and her mouth fell open, as did Penny's.

There was a moment's silence, as if both women were gasping for air.

'Norman! Norm! Johnnie!' Mary finally managed in a shaky voice.

Carrie's father and brother appeared in the kitchen doorway. Like his wife, Norman merely gaped.

'Oh my God!' exclaimed Johnnie, coming forward to shake Mike's hand, the one that wasn't clutched tight in Carrie's. 'It's you!'

Mike grinned.

'Hello, everyone – Penny,' he began. 'Look, I know this is a huge surprise for you, a shock, even. I'm sorry to barge in like this, though I know I've made a bit of a habit of it in the past.' He took a breath, sounding more serious. 'I also know you'll have a million questions to ask me, and you're quite entitled to, but I only got back yesterday. I'm still being debriefed and even when I have been, I – I shan't be able to tell you much. I hope you understand.'

Mary stood transfixed, while Penny pulled a serious face. Johnnie and Norman nodded gravely.

'You all deserve to know where I've been since I've put this one' – he looked at Carrie – 'through such torture. I'm sorrier than I can say about that, but please believe me when I say I couldn't help it. I really had no choice.'

Penny looked at Johnnie and Mary looked at her husband.

'We understand,' said Norman.

'Course we do,' echoed Johnnie.

'Thank you. I'm on my way to see my folks, but . . .' he gave Carrie that look again and the smile that made her feel weak at the knees '. . . I had to come here first.'

Carrie looked pleadingly at her father and Norman took charge.

'Of course, lad, of course,' he said simply. 'Let's just say it's very good to see you. But you and Carrie'll want some time together. Erm . . .'

'We'll go for a walk,' said Carrie quickly.

'We can do better than that,' smiled Mike. 'The army have lent me a car. If you like, Carrie, we could take a little run out.'

'I'd love that!'

Mike squeezed her hand.

'I'll bring her back in good time for lunch,' he assured Mary. 'I'm sorry to take her away from you on Christmas Day.'

'Don't be silly, of course you must!' Carrie's mother replied.

'And as for dinnertime,' Norman added, 'you'll join us, won't you? What time are your parents expecting you?'

'Well, I didn't really say. Not till late afternoon. They're saving Christmas dinner till this evening.'

'There you are, then,' Johnnie chipped in. 'As long as you can eat two – and frankly, you look as if you could do with it!'

'Thanks!' But Mike was grinning. He turned to Carrie. 'Do you want to get your coat?'

'Yes, sure,' Carrie nodded. But still she didn't move.

'Er . . . could I make a suggestion?' Penny put in. 'You'll have to let go of his hand!'

Carrie fetched her coat and they went out through the back, their progress slowed by the fact that they had to keep stopping to give each other little kisses and hugs. When they got into the street, there was a regulation, khaki-painted—

'A car, you said!' exclaimed Carrie. 'This is a Jeep!'

'More fun, don't you think?' grinned Mike.

'Yes! I've never been in one. Never thought I would.'

'Now's your chance. Hop in.'

He unlocked the door.

Excitedly, Carrie clambered in. Mike got in the driver's side, gave her another kiss, and they set off.

Mostly, they drove in silence, Carrie just loving to look at him: his firm profile, his lovely hands on the wheel and his eyes when he glanced at her. He was thinner, definitely, his tunic jacket a little big on the shoulders and his belt surely a notch tighter. When he wasn't changing gear, he rested his hand lightly on her thigh and Carrie closed her eyes in bliss.

She knew where they were going as soon as he negotiated his way through the empty streets – Petts Wood, their favourite place. Mike parked the Jeep and they got out.

Carrie made to walk on Mike's right-hand side, but he stopped her.

'I'd better come clean,' he said. 'My right shoulder's still a bit dodgy.'

'Oh, I'm sorry,' Carrie said quickly, realising. 'Is that . . .'

'It's where I was hit.'

Carrie had told him briefly on the way about Stan's visit and what he – or they – had concluded must have happened on the jetty. Mike hadn't contradicted any of it, but he hadn't added any details – yet.

'It's OK,' he smiled. 'Just come the other side. The other shoulder's still A1, I promise.'

Carrie swapped sides, pillowing her head on his shoulder as he put his arm around her.

'All right?'

'Very much all right,' she confirmed.

'Not too cold?'

'Not with how warm I feel inside.'

Mike pulled her closer against him.

'Me too.' As they walked, their feet automatically followed the path that led to the clearing with the fallen log.

'You will tell me, won't you?' Carrie said. 'I need to hear all of it. Please. And if you really can't do that, even with me, then please tell me what you can.'

The log was still there in the clearing, so they sat down. And he told her.

'OK, here it is.' Mike took a breath. 'The evacuation effort was brilliant, of course it was – amazing that it happened at all – and I know that's what you were told over here. But at the time, when we were there, it felt like chaos. It was chaos. There was this long jetty thing, and when our turn came, we were all crammed on it, trying to embark with German planes bombing ships, machine-gunning from all sides.' He sighed, his mouth twisting. 'And just after I'd seen Stan and the others on board, I got hit. Bullet, shrapnel – I didn't know what it was. There was just searing pain and I went flying. I dropped into the water. I went under, and that's all I remember. I must have got carried out to sea in the wash of a boat or by the current, because I fetched up somewhere else, much further along the beach.'

Carrie nodded, silently urging him on.

'So when I came round,' Mike went on, 'I managed to drag myself up on the sand. It was dark by then. My right arm was pretty useless, and I lay on my other side, hoping for . . . I don't know what. That any of our chaps still there might come and find me? There seemed to be no one around. It was all quiet and I was pretty out of it. And then I heard voices. Speaking in German.'

A little noise escaped from Carrie's throat; she couldn't help it. She could only imagine the terror.

'They were coming up and down the beaches, looking for what they could take – equipment, of course, but personal things too, watches and whatever.' Seeing Carrie's face, he said, 'You needn't look so shocked. It happens. Like the looting that goes on after a bombing raid here.'

'I suppose so.' But somehow it seemed worse – the thought of a Nazi soldier going through Mike's pockets as he lay semi-conscious was horrible to her. 'Go on.'

'The voices came nearer and I knew what'd come next. I lay as still as I could, playing dead. This soldier came up to me, shone his torch, flipped me over onto my back with his boot. I managed not to cry out, but I must have winced or made some movement, I don't know. Anyway, he crouched down, shone his torch in my face. And I opened my eyes. I wanted to see who it was who was going to rob me – or shoot me.'

'Oh, Mike!' Again, Carrie couldn't help herself.

'Sorry, but that's also standard practice. There's a limit to how many wounded prisoners they want to deal with. And frankly, if you think that someone's badly injured, it can be a kindness.' He paused, as if he was weighing up whether to say more. Then he added: 'I've done it myself.'

Carrie closed her eyes. During the Battle of Britain and at the start of the Blitz, they'd said on the wireless that the home front was now the front line, and it had felt like that; it still did when a raid was on. But Carrie realised now that this could never be true – not to anyone who'd had to look the enemy in the eye.

'He didn't say anything,' Mike went on, 'but when another voice shouted, "*Lebendig?*", meaning "Alive?", he called back, "*Nein.*"'

'He said "No." He spared you,' Carrie said softly.

'I'll never know who he was.' Mike sounded choked. 'Or why he did it, but he did. Maybe, like I say, they didn't want the bother and expense of patching me up – or perhaps he thought I was for it anyway, and he wasn't going to waste a bullet.' He shook his head. 'Or maybe he was just a good guy, caught up in a fight he never asked to be part of. I know it's not what the army teaches you, but there must be some, you know, on the other side – well, there's some on both sides, let's be honest. Anyway, he took my revolver off me and moved on.'

Chapter Thirty-two

Carrie heard voices in the distance – people out for a bracing Christmas Day walk, she supposed. She wondered for a moment who they were, and if the war had touched their lives in anything like this way. Tracing the intricate pattern of the bark on the fallen tree they were sitting on, she wondered what other confessions it had heard over its long life. It must have heard many things, happy and sad, and shocking, too.

She could tell Mike was trying to tell her as plainly and as kindly as possible, but she was finding it hard to hear what he'd been through – and he hadn't got off the beach yet.

Carrie swallowed hard.

'Then what happened?' she faltered.

'I must have blacked out again. I came to with someone else bending over me, patting my pockets to see what they could find.'

'Not another German?' said Carrie, horrified.

'French.'

'French!'

'Yes. The local partisans, come to see what the Nazis had missed. I was parched, so I asked him for some water. He whistled to his mates and they carried me off.'

He stopped. He could see Carrie's anguish.

'Cheer up, this is when things get better.'

'I hope so!' Carrie exclaimed. She wasn't sure how much more she could take of Mike lying in pain on the damp sand, kicked by a Nazi jackboot and having to beg for water.

'Well, maybe not at first,' Mike backtracked. 'Because my shoulder was a bit of a mess – still is, I'm afraid. I'll spare you the details, but I had the local vet operate on me in a bicycle workshop.'

'What?' A little squeak escaped from Carrie's throat.

'They took me there under sacks in a wagon of cabbages.' Mike shook his head at the memory. 'The vet gave me some knockout stuff for that, so I was lucky—'

Carrie was getting bolder now.

'Lucky? What was it, the kind of stuff he'd use to put down a cat?'

Mike grinned. 'A horse, more likely! Best not to ask. Anyhow, my recovery wasn't too straightforward. He did the best he could, but the wound wasn't exactly clean to start with and I had to keep being moved from one barn or cellar or outhouse to another and back again.' He grimaced. 'I got through a lot of bootleg brandy.'

'Oh, Mike. When do we get to the cheery part?'

He gave her a quick kiss.

'The cheery part is how amazing those people were – are, I mean. I hope they're all still alive.' He paused for a moment, thinking. 'Jean-Paul, who found me, and Yves, who first took me in, and Gaston the vet – and the others and their families – they risked such a lot for me. I hope one day when all this is over, I might be able to go back and thank them properly.'

Carrie squeezed his hand.

'Anyway, it was the end of August before I was in any fit state to think about moving on. My French was pretty fluent by then – the curses, anyway! So we decided they'd get me some false papers and I'd pass myself off as French. And try to get away.'

'But how?'

'There's this huge network of the French Resistance. The idea was to get me from one group to another right down the country to Free France – the bit in the south that's not occupied – and across the border to Spain. There's a route across the Pyrenees they call the Chemin de la Liberté – the Path to Freedom.'

Carrie was stunned. 'You travelled all that way?'

Mike grinned again, and there was a hint of pride in it.

'A lot of it on a bike. My shoulder may be shot to pieces, but my legs are fit for the Tour de France.'

'I should think so. It's miles!'

'Kilometres,' Mike corrected her. 'I had to think in French, remember.'

'But so dangerous . . .'

'There was no choice, Carrie.' He gave her a quick grin. 'Anyway, didn't you want me back?'

Carrie looked at him in loving exasperation. 'You think you have to ask?'

Mike smiled. 'Just testing.' Then he sobered. 'Anyway, the danger to me was nothing compared to the danger to the people who hid me and helped me. If I'd been caught, I'd have been taken prisoner. They'd have been shot.'

They both fell silent, thinking about it. Then Carrie said:

'You must have had some scares.'

'Plenty,' Mike agreed. 'Hiding in a hayloft with a troop of Germans having a cigarette down below – and once in a cupboard with a false back . . .'

'Oh, Mike, it's like something out of a film.'

'Some close shaves,' he agreed. 'But I always thought I'd make it. Get back home. Get back to you.' He leaned his forehead against hers for a moment. 'I'm so sorry for what I put you through. It must have been so hard, not hearing a word.'

Carrie made a dismissive little gesture with her hand. It had been beyond hard; it had tested her to the limit, but it was nothing compared to what he'd endured.

'I couldn't write,' he explained, answering her question before she'd asked it. 'The Nazis had guards outside every post office. I could hardly bowl in with a letter addressed to England, nor could any of the French people helping me. Far too much of a risk.'

Carrie nodded her understanding.

'We walked over those mountains for hours and hours, in the dark. And when I finally got over the border, it was more of the same – I was still in hiding.'

'But Spain's neutral – isn't it?'

Mike grimaced. 'In theory, yes, but their General Franco's not too keen to be seen as collaborating with Hitler's enemies. They round up anyone who they reckon is anti-Nazi.' He sighed. 'But look . . .' He glanced at his watch. 'I think that bit of the story will have to wait for another day.'

'Must it?'

'We've been gone long enough. It's not fair on your family.'

He was right, of course. Time was getting on.

'All right,' Carrie conceded. 'And thank you for telling me. I needed to know. But I won't breathe a word.'

'No, you mustn't. You really mustn't. Not to anyone – not to Johnnie, or Penny, or anyone, because I know they'll ask.'

'I won't. I promise. You can trust me.'

He smiled, and his eyes crinkled at the corners in the way she loved.

'I know I can. Always. You waited for me all this time, after all.'

Carrie said impulsively: 'Can I tell you something? It'll sound mad . . .'

'Go on.'

'I saw you,' she said simply.

'What?'

'In Lovells. I was Christmas shopping. I'd spent so long just . . . just willing you to be alive, and it seemed impossible, but I was so sure it was you that I followed you out of the store. But when I caught up with you – well, it wasn't you, of course, so . . .'

'Oh, Carrie!' Mike's voice cracked. 'I'm sorry, I'm so sorry, sweetheart.' His eyes held hers, honest and true, and she felt a huge swell of love for him, the love she'd carried for so long. 'I'd like to say I'll never leave you again. But you know I can't do that.'

It was hard to hear, but she knew it had to be that way.

'It's not all bad,' he went on. 'The MO thinks there's more they can do for my shoulder, so I'm likely to be in England for a while. Does that help?'

'Oh, yes! I can't tell you how much!'

Mike took her face in his hands and kissed her softly.

'I should be here for a good few months. We've got a lot of time to make up for, you and me, in the next few months and beyond. And we will, we will, Carrie, I promise.'

Back they went then, buoyed by love, to join Carrie's family, and Penny, for lunch. The back living room, with its fire in the grate, sprigs of holly among the cards on the mantelpiece, faded paper chains pinned to the picture rail and lights twinkling (in the daytime!) on the small spruce tree in the corner, had never looked more welcoming or more festive. Mary was in the kitchen, naturally, but everyone else was there – and very merry, in both senses of the word.

'If you two could see yourselves!' chortled Johnnie, pouring Mike a beer at the dresser. 'You're the very picture of people who've had all their birthdays and Christmases come at once!'

'And what's wrong with that?' challenged Penny, pressing a glass of something ruby-red into Carrie's hand. 'What do you think?' she asked, before Carrie had even tried it. 'It's special Christmas punch.'

Carrie took a cautious sip and blinked.

'It certainly packs one! What's in it?'

'Secret recipe,' said Penny, with a wink. 'You'd be amazed how much hooch your brother's got stashed in his kitbag. We had fun concocting it – and trying it out along the way!'

'I'd never have guessed,' said Carrie drily. Penny's eyes were bright. She'd come down to breakfast in her usual slacks and jumper, but had changed into a smart dark blue dress with a bold red and white print, sheer stockings and navy court shoes that looked like glacé kid. She obviously hadn't left *all* the trappings of her old life behind! 'It looks like you've been trying out that powder compact too – and are you wearing lipstick?'

'Well, you've always wanted me to be a bit more feminine, haven't you?' Penny retorted, but she blushed. 'And it's a special occasion. The conquering hero returning and all that.'

'Talking about me again?' grinned Johnnie as he came over, draping an arm round each of them. Both girls rolled their eyes.

'You'd like to think so, wouldn't you?' teased Penny, taking the words out of Carrie's mouth.

Carrie let them get on with it: she still couldn't take her eyes off Mike, who was talking to her dad about Norman's ARP work. It seemed unreal: when she'd woken up that morning, he'd been as far away as ever – now they were in the same room. He glanced over and caught her eye, just as Mary called from the kitchen for 'an extra pair of hands, please!'

Bit by bit, the feast was brought to the table. A piece of beef, Yorkshire puddings, roast and mashed potatoes, sprouts, carrots and cabbage. Carrie brought the gravy boat and Penny carried the plates. Everyone took their places, but Norman remained standing at the head of the table, theatrically sharpening the carving knife against the steel. Thanks to his contacts in the trade, he'd managed to get hold of a box of crackers – pre-war, of course, because they certainly weren't making them any more. The snaps were a bit feeble, but at least they had the regulation hat, gift and joke or motto. Carrie's hat was green, like her dress, and Mike put it on for her as Penny and Johnnie read out the jokes.

'Why can't penguins play football?' Johnnie began.

'No idea,' chorused the others obediently.

'Because there's *snow*ball! Geddit?'

Everyone groaned, which, as Mike said, was the whole point of Christmas-cracker jokes.

'OK, OK, what about this one?' Penny volunteered. 'What do you call an alligator in a vest?'

'Go on, tell us!' they chorused again.

'An investigator!'

Cue more groans.

'Who writes these things?' asked Carrie.

'Another sideline of your uncle Charlie's, probably,' said Mary. She'd had an unaccustomed glass of sherry and was already fanning herself with a napkin. Mind you, the half-pound of tea and two of sugar that Charlie had suddenly turned up with a couple of months back had come in very handy. She'd been torn about accepting them, but Charlie had said, 'Ask me no questions and I'll tell you no lies,' so she hadn't. She'd invited him for Christmas, of course, but he was going away for the holiday, to Torquay. Mary suspected there might be a woman involved, but with Charlie, as with the extra rations, you didn't ask.

One by one the plates were passed round.

'Help yourself, Mike, please.'

Mary offered him the potatoes.

'Thanks, Mrs Anderson.'

But he stopped, serving spoon poised, as Norman tapped his knife on his glass.

'Oh no, here we go,' teased Johnnie. 'Dad's Christmas broadcast!' Turning to Penny, he explained: 'I should have warned you. It happens every Christmas. He gets all sentimental.'

'Me? Sentimental? What rot!' Norman protested.

'Shush, Johnnie, let him speak,' smiled Carrie.

She hadn't been sure whether to sit next to Mike so they could hook their ankles together, or opposite, so she could look at him all the time. She'd decided to go opposite, and it had been the right decision; his foot had already found hers and their ankles were entwined anyway.

'Thank you, Carrie,' said Norman with an air of assumed dignity. 'All I want to say is what a joy it is for us all to be together, and with not one but two extra guests. Penny, you're very welcome – and as for you, Mike . . . We couldn't be more pleased to see you back – though by the look of Carrie, she could teach us all a thing or two about what being pleased looks like!'

'Hear! Hear!' said Penny and Johnnie together, as Carrie blushed and Mike raised his glass.

'I think we need a toast,' he said. 'Thank you so much for letting me join you. And my toast is to all of you: the very best of the home front and' – he looked at Johnnie – 'the forces.' Then he looked at Carrie and reached for her hand across the table. 'When Carrie and I were walking in the woods, and now, here, with all of you – well, this is what we're all fighting for in our different ways. Our country and our countryside, our towns and cities, but also our way of life. Family, friends and the freedom to say what we think, to do as we please and to love who we choose.' He pressed

Carrie's fingers. 'And however long it takes, however hard it is on all of us personally, we're going to do it. We're going to win this war and come out the other side! So . . .' He raised his glass, and his eyes held Carrie's as he said: 'The future!'

'The future!' they all replied.

'Hooray to all that!' said Johnnie. 'And now let's eat!'

THE END

How It All Began . . .

Devon, 1934

Allen Lane, of The Bodley Head publishers, patted the brief-case beside him as the little local train bore him towards his connection to London. Inside were signed contracts for further translation rights on Agatha Christie's first five novels, and two special editions for book clubs. Yes, all in all, a successful weekend. Max and Agatha were generous hosts at Ashfield, Agatha's childhood home, with its wonderful views over the sweeping bay of Torquay. And Agatha was still, as the papers called her, the Queen of Crime.

The train banged into the buffers at Exeter. The passengers gathered their belongings and, as he waited to get off, it was second nature for Allen Lane to observe his fellow travellers' reading matter. There were plenty of newspapers and magazines, of course. Novels from Boots' lending library by Kate O'Brien and Dorothy Whipple, two popular women writers, peeked from shopping baskets. A young chap in a corduroy jacket shuffled forwards in the queue to get off, still deep in his copy of *Brave New World* – well, good for him! Another man was stuffing his book in his pocket: a Sexton Blake-type potboiler from the look of it, but you couldn't win 'em all . . .

Ticket produced, Lane changed platforms. A chance to check out the bookstall, to see if any of his own titles were in stock. Doubtful, as The Bodley Head dealt in weighty hardbacks – only the most dedicated reader would lug one of those around!

Sure enough, the bookstall carried a few cheap hardback editions – trusty classics, mostly. But as for the rest . . . there was nothing much above the picture-magazines – poorly-produced penny dreadfuls, thrillers or Westerns – and, for the woman reader, a slushy romance.

As Lane watched, a well-turned-out young woman and an older, military gent arrived. They looked over the books on display: in the end the young woman reluctantly turned away, choosing a copy of *The Listener* and a women's magazine. The man settled for a copy of the *Shooting Times*.

The train was delayed; for the next half hour Allen Lane watched in silent fascination and mounting horror. A captive audience, with no decent paperback to read on their journey? It wouldn't do, it simply wouldn't do! But more than that – it was an opportunity!

Back at the office, he set to work. The Bodley Head wasn't exactly awash with funds, and setting up a paperback arm was a gamble – a huge one. Perhaps, then, he could start with just ten titles? There were some on the Bodley Head's own list that would do – Agatha's first book, *The Mysterious Affair at Styles*, for instance. That would go like a rocket in paperback! He could buy the rights to other titles from other publishers. But they wouldn't all be crime and they needn't all be fiction. There could be a mix: memoir, history, biography . . . something worthwhile!

By the time he presented his idea to his co-directors, who happened to be his brothers, he had it all worked out. A classic typeface for the print: Times New Roman, perhaps, and the covers – ah, the covers. Not the lurid hotch-potch he'd seen on the bookstall. They needed to stand out: two colours only would be striking. And the price? Just sixpence – the same as a pack of cigarettes.

His brothers were incredulous. They made all the arguments he'd expected. The Bodley Head was in choppy waters financially: not the best moment to launch a new and risky venture! Not at all, Allen replied – this was the idea that could stop them from sinking! Finally, very reluctantly, they gave in.

All they needed now was a name. There was already a paperback imprint called Albatross, and Allen Lane fancied using a name from the animal world, too. But something more cheerful, more chirpy. Panda Books? Giraffe? The debate wound back to birds. Parrot books? Parakeet?

'If you're going through all the "P"s, what about Penguins?'

It was Allen's secretary, Joan, listening in as she typed behind her plywood partition.

Allen Lane sat back. Penguin Books. It was perfect.

As Jeremy Lewis notes in his brilliant biography Penguin Special: The Life and Times of Allen Lane, *the idea for Penguins being born on Exeter station is perhaps a myth, but, keeping the legend going, there's now a special Penguin Books vending machine on one of Exeter's platforms.*

Joan's inspired suggestion, though, was remembered by a Penguin employee as how it happened – not the first time a woman's had the best idea!

Acknowledgements

I have so many people to thank for the fact that you're reading this. Apart from my own love of books and obsession with the film *Brief Encounter*, the book emerged from a discussion with my inspiring editor Katie Loughnane, her assistant Jess Muscio and my brilliant agent Broo Doherty. I'm so lucky to have the enthusiastic support of a fantastic team at Century, from Lucy Thorne who designed the beautiful cover, through to the skill and huge attention to detail in the copy-edit, proofread, marketing, publicity and sales. And of course, from my husband John, the best plot-wrangler not in the business!

We moved house twice during the writing of this book, so a huge thank you to everyone who's made us so welcome in our new life in Somerset. We moved to be nearer to family, so Livi, Ashley, Clara and Cressie – it's all down to you!

I read scores of books, but Patrick Bishop's *Fighter Boys: Saving Britain 1940* was especially illuminating, as were all the Mass Observation diaries of the time. I had huge fun researching on the Gloucestershire Warwickshire Steam Railway (GWSR) and the Avon Valley Railway – thanks to Gay Carter and Claire MacRorie for extra photos.

Most of all, though, I'd like to thank you for reading it – what would be the point otherwise? If you've enjoyed it, please find me on Facebook, Instagram or X and let me know. And if you have time to post a review on Amazon or Goodreads you'll be helping other readers to meet Carrie, Bette, Penny and the station crew too.

I do hope you'll want to read more about them in the next book: *A New Chapter at The Little Penguin Bookshop*!

Jo x

Facebook: /joannatoyewriter
Instagram: @joannatoyewriter
X: @joannatoye